Faults

Book Four • Island Series

Tudor Robins

Tudor Robins
www.tudorrobins.ca

Faults / Tudor Robins. -- 1st ed.
ISBN 978-0-9958887-0-8

Other Books by Tudor Robins:

Island Series:

Six-Month Horse (Prequel)

Appaloosa Summer (Book One)

Wednesday Riders (Book Two)

Join Up (Book Three)

Stonegate Series:

Objects in Mirror (Book One)

After Lucas (Book Two)

Throw Your Heart Over (Book Three)

Chris & Tilly Series:

Meant to Be

• AUSTEN •

Prologue

We're on our way home from the island – sand in our underwear and under our nails, lots of fresh air and too-much-sun making even my usually pale sister look like a healthy Canadian kid – when my mom springs it.

"Wouldn't it be nice if we didn't have to go back to school and work tomorrow?"

I assume she's talking to my dad – it's the kind of thing they say to each other on the way home from weekends when our down-the-street neighbours rent their underused cottage to us.

Of course, once we're home for an hour, with the washing machine running, and my dad mowing our overgrown city lawn, and me trying to get my homework done while ignoring my little brother's whining, and my big sister's sulking, it always feels like we've never left.

It is nice while we're there, though ...

"Wouldn't that be nice? Kids?"

My mom is turned around in her seat; hand on Shaw's swinging four-year-old foot, eyes on my sister and me.

Eliot's plugged into her music, and Shaw's concentrating on kicking my mom's hand right off his foot, so it's down to me to answer. As usual.

"Um, sure. Yeah." I mean, of course it would be, in the way that it would be nice – but completely impossible – to live entirely off ice cream. It seems like a harmless answer to give.

My mom beams. "I was hoping you'd feel that way." Her "you" is bigger than me – her smile encompasses all her offspring in the backseat – I'm their spokesperson, even if none of us are going to end up being happy with that arrangement.

"Mrs. Traherne told me she and Jack are taking an extended holiday in Europe this summer. They've offered us the cottage for the entire school break."

Oh, wait now ...

She's on a roll. "I actually spoke to Meg, Austen, because I wanted to find out if she'd have a horse to lease us for the summer."

It's one of the things I like about the cottage. There's a snug paddock right behind it and Meg, the Trahernes' daughter, runs a barn just up the road from the cottage.

Whenever we've stayed for more than a few days, we've leased a horse from her so I can ride right from our back door.

As I've gotten older, and had to leave friends and activities behind to go away with my family, I've known the horse was a bit of a bribe. Now I have the feeling I'm going to pay for my past willingness to be bribed.

With my summer.

"Um ..." I say, but before I can continue, my mom steamrollers on.

"As it turns out," she says. "Meg is running day camps this summer and she said Jared's cousin, who normally works for her is away for most of the summer, so she could use some help. You could have a job, Austen. With horses."

"I already have a job, Mom."

"Oh, not like this one. Why would you want to scoop frozen yogurt inside, when you could be outside with horses all day?"

Because my boyfriend has a job across the street? Because we were going to take every lunch break together?

Totally not arguments to use on my "we-don't-turn-our-lives-inside-out-for-boys" mother.

"And, I have a horse to ride this summer, Mom."

Her eyebrows fly up. "That's arranged?"

"Well. Nearly." I cross my fingers. Something I've been doing a lot of lately. It's true I did a great job on my pitch to Ace's owner; a former-A-circuit rider recently returned to riding who's part of the Monday night lesson I share with my best friend Manda.

"Don't sell him now," I'd said of the OTTB who'd tempted her back into riding, but was proving to be too strong for her. "He doesn't have any showing under his belt and you can't ask much for him. Let me take him on a show lease this summer – I'll cover a chunk of your expenses, and if he does even half as well as I think he will, you can sell him for much more in the fall."

She's "thinking about it." I'll see her tomorrow. I'm sure she'll say yes – why wouldn't she?

"Absolutely, almost." I nod to emphasize the likelihood of it to my mom.

She sighs. "The truth is, Austen, it's not really optional."

"What do you mean?" I look to my left and right for support from my siblings, but one's four years old, and the other one has turned up the volume on her player and is staring out the window as though there's a blockbuster movie playing outside.

My mom gestures for me to lean forward. "Eliot," she whispers.

My head starts to turn to my left, and my mom hisses, "No, don't look."

"What about her?" I ask.

Keeping her voice low, my mom says, "Her doctor thinks it could be a good change of scenery for her. And, there's a new doctor on staff at the hospital in Kingston who's had promising results – we can get in to see her over the summer."

"So, it's for Eliot."

My mom nods.

"Does she know about this?"

Before my mom can answer, my sister pulls her right earbud out, bumping me in the process, and says, "Yes, she does." Then she looks straight at my mom. "I'm not deaf, you know."

If only. Some days I wish my sister's sickness was something we could pin down. Something fixed, that doesn't keep changing forms and playing new tricks.

I shift toward her as best I can in the crowded backseat. "So, what do you think about it?"

She shrugs. "As if I care. The island's fine. I like running there." Then she pops her earbud back in.

"See?" My mom says. "She's looking forward to it. Which I have to think is a good sign."

Yeah, mom. She's looking forward to going to a place with endless kilometres of flat, straight running roads. Sounds like the exercise addiction's already under control.

How can I say no to something for Eliot, though? If there's a new wonder doctor who'll help, if being out of the city is good for her ... How can I worry about my quality of life, when it's my sister's entire life that hangs in the balance?

• RAND •

Prologue

For the few seconds before I open my eyes, I'm supremely comfortable.

I'm talking the kind of temperature-just-right, no-pressure-points, no-cares-in-the-world, one-warm-sunbeam-hitting-in-just-the-right-spot comfort I'm lucky to feel once a week, if that, when I wake up in my bed at home.

Except I'm not in my bed at home.

I know that, deep down, even before I lift my lids, but it hits me in the face – quite literally – when I do finally look around.

There are intricate, intersecting spider-webs of shattered glass splintering my vision. They're part of a car windshield; one whose shielding days are now over.

My feeling of comfort was from being cradled in the burgundy velour driver's seat of this piece of crap car –

the running joke of our street, next to all the BMWs, and Audis – but the only one available to me, with my driving privileges suspended from our family car.

Also, it was kind of nice to drive.

Was nice to drive. The body-hugging seats were part of that.

I'm warm and wet. Blood?

I don't smell that tinny odour, though – the one I associate with the gushing nosebleeds that hit me in dry midwinter. And nothing hurts.

It hits me then, and my only pain is the complete mortification of realizing I. Have. Wet. Myself.

Oh wow. Not for – what? – fifteen years, give or take, but, yes, now I've pissed my pants.

The view out the unbroken side windows of the car is familiar, but not. Familiar because, framed in the driver's side window, is my own house. *Not,* because I've never looked at my house from this angle.

This angle being my neighbour's front porch. My neighbour's brand-new front porch, hand-crafted by a solitary, meticulous, heritage woodworker over the last two months – nearly done, but not before half the neighbourhood had a dig at Joe about letting the carpenter move in with him, or the Sistine Chapel being painted quicker.

Joe's brand-new front porch is now being supported, not by the corner post carpenter-man meticulously sunk three feet below the frost line, way back in May, but by the hood of Joe's ancient-but-comfortable Ford Tempo.

Driven by me.

Without Joe's permission.

Double-shit.

It shouldn't be this quiet, should it? I mean, when you crash a car – especially when you crash a car into someone's house – there should be commotion. Reaction. Emergency services of some kind.

But Joe and his wife are at their cottage – I should know because I wouldn't have "borrowed" their car if they were in town. And, it's early. As in, that one ray of sun tickling my cheek was the first one of the morning – *that* early. And, in a neighbourhood where every house has central air, and every household plugs in the minute the temperature clears twenty degrees, I guess it might be possible to sleep through the sound of a seventeen-year-old screw-up plowing a not-quite-stolen jalopy into a post.

"Joe?" The voice contains equal measures of worry and incredulity. Then it says, "Margaret! Come here!" and I know it belongs to our neighbour on the other side of our house, Keith.

I can't count how many times my sister and I have made fun of Keith and Margaret for walking their Shih-Poo four times a day, starting at the crack of dawn. My mom, when she tells us not to be mean, has to bite back her own smile.

Now that Keith, and Margaret, and little Hamlet (Keith is a retired high school English teacher) are advancing toward me on their first walk of the day, I don't know what to feel. Relief, worry, hope, and dread juggle with each other.

In the end, I guess it doesn't matter. In a few seconds the first people will know what I've done. Then the consequences will start.

• AUSTEN •

Chapter One

I don't expect to see Tyler before school – he has rugby practice Monday, Wednesday, and Friday, so he walks up before me.

It is a bit weird not to see him at lunch, but Manda falls against my locker in dramatic fashion, telling me she's actually, literally, and completely in caffeine withdrawal, and if I don't go to the Fine Grind with her my death will be on her hands.

The last few years of living with my sister have worn me down to emotional blackmail involving the health of others, so I go with Manda and listen to her complain about her half-leaser.

"She never rides on her nights – even though those were the nights *she chose* – so Bandit is a complete hyper-case on my nights."

- "She re-arranges my tack and takes stuff off, then doesn't put it back again, so I get to shows missing – oh, say – the running martingale attachment for the breastplate."
- "After not riding on her nights, she tries to ride on my nights – and she doesn't even *ask*. She emailed me this morning to say since she couldn't ride on Friday, she'll come tonight instead."

"What did you tell her?" I ask.

"I told her it's my lesson night with my best friend," she gives me a big wink, "so she should go screw herself."

"You didn't say that!"

She sighs. "I should have said that. Since Bandit wasn't ridden last Wednesday or Friday – *her* days – and since I didn't have my running martingale, she was a nutbar at the show yesterday and, not only did we not win anything, she kicked the whipper-in."

"But you are riding tonight?" I clarify.

"Yup," she says. "Tonight's the night Clarice gives you her answer about Ace, right? I wouldn't miss it for anything."

I wrinkle my nose, "Yeah, well, a complication's come up." I look at my watch. "We'd better get back to school. I'll tell you on the way."

***

I stay after school to watch Tyler's rugby game, so I can walk home with him after.

"Hey, you," I say, as he comes off the field mucky, sweaty, and with the requisite two or three fresh bleeding scratches. "Nice game."

"Thanks," he says. "We really wanted to beat them."

"How was the weekend?" I ask as we start walking home, and wait for the usual barrage of details about which extreme sports he did with which of his friends. Who ruled, who puked, and what they ate afterwards. Tyler is my boyfriend, not because we do things in common, but because we give each other the space to do the things we like doing apart. And, I've known him since kindergarten, and he's magazine good-looking, and he makes me feel sweet and pretty when he hoists me over his shoulder to celebrate a rugby win. Not that he's done that so often lately ...

In a strange twist, he doesn't give me any information about his weekend, but just turns it back on me. "How was yours?"

"I ... uh ..." I'm totally unprepared for this question. I don't mind listening to all his stories, but he's actually fallen asleep listening to me talk about riding. Telling him about the round-up I went to on the island is not going to fly. "Well, my mom has this weird new idea that we can cure Eliot by spending the summer on the island."

He stops in front of Alanna Currie's house, where we both attended a birthday party in grade two, and he threw up foamy pink icing after four slices of cake. "What?"

I try to keep walking, but he's stuck in place. "I know. I mean, there are so many things there. Like, as if one thing's ever going to fix Eliot. And the island, for the whole summer ..."

"Are you supposed to go?"

"Um ..." I take a step, tug on his arm, and he slowly starts moving again. "My mom definitely wants me to. I mean, I could make a big deal about it, and stay here, but if she's taking Eliot over to the mainland for appointments, I know she'll need help with Shaw. And, I'm always afraid if I don't spend time with my sister now ..." I don't finish the sentence, but he knows how it goes. I wait for him to acknowledge it. *It'll be too late.*

"Geez, Austen, when will this end?"

Now I'm the one stopping. What I think is, *Probably when Eliot dies.* What I say is, "What do you mean?"

"What about your job?" he asks. "What about us learning to kayak this summer?" He points to his chest. "What about me?"

I reach out for his arm but he yanks it away, and I have to scramble to catch up to him as he continues his march toward home.

"I don't *have* to go. This wasn't me telling you I'm leaving for sure. You asked how my weekend was, and this was part of it, so I'm telling you. You know, sharing information."

We're at the corner now – where we go two opposite directions to get home. "You know, Austen, go. I think you should go. I know things are complicated with Eliot, so do what you have to."

"Listen," I say. "We can make it work. It might even be more fun. You can come to the island. You can try parasailing – you'd love that – and there are always good rugby games at the university ..."

"No." He shakes his head, and doesn't quite meet my eyes again. "I'm saying you do what you need to, because now I have to do what I need to. I'm sorry – I know it probably sounds selfish – it probably is selfish, but the Eliot thing has just come between us too many times. I need a girlfriend who's mine."

"What do you mean?" I know, though.

We're both thinking of the last time Eliot had a crisis – when in an unprecedented miracle, Tyler's parents and mine were both supposed to be out of town the same weekend. "I'll get champagne," he'd told me. "Or at least a bottle of wine."

I screwed up my courage to go into an actual lingerie shop and buy pretty underwear.

His parents went. Mine packed the car, buckled Shaw in and, when my mom went for her final bathroom trip before they hit the road to visit my aunt and uncle in Peterborough, she walked in on Eliot bent over the toilet with her fingers down her throat.

Tyler was less-than-understanding when I called to tell him there was a change of plans. "Since when is your goddamn sister bulimic?" he asked.

Which, I admit, was kind of what I was thinking.

Since then, Eliot's never tried making herself puke again – not that any of us know about – but that's not the only thing that hasn't happened again. Tyler's stopped trying to slip his hand up my shirt, or to ease my pants undone when we're kissing, and there's been no more talk of parents going away and having houses to ourselves.

And now, this.

"Austen," he says, "I'm sick of watching you do everything in the world to avoid upsetting your family. You gave up your pony ..."

"I grew out of her!" I interrupt.

"Hmm ... yeah, at exactly the same time as they needed to pay for Eliot to go to rehab the first time. You're on notice twenty-four-seven to watch Shaw if they need to run off somewhere with Eliot. And now, this."

"What am I supposed to do?" I ask.

"Beats me, Austen. I get it. It's not that you're a bad person – if anything you're too good – but the fact is if you always put them first, somebody else has to come second."

"Like you," I say.

He shrugs. "Or maybe, like *you*."

***

Me: **Come pick me up. Now. Please. Now.**

Manda: **Where are you?**

Me: **Home, but hiding. Snuck in with nobody seeing me. Changed for riding. Will leave a note for my mom, sneak out and meet you out front.**

Manda: **Be there in five.**

I dive into Manda's car and she pulls away from the curb as quickly as I could want her to.

"What's up?" she asks.

I lift my sunglasses and she claps a hand over her mouth. "Oh my God! What happened? Did you have an allergic reaction?"

"I've been crying for an hour."

"Over what? Did your second guinea pig die?"

"Oh, Mo-o-olly ..." My already-tender nerves can't handle the reminder of how devastated I was when our first guinea pig died six months ago. Fresh tears brim. "She was *such* a great pet ..."

We're driving by the school and Manda pulls into the now-empty parking lot. From here I can see the rugby pitch where I watched Tyler play just a couple of hours ago. I press my hand against my chest. "It hurts …" I moan.

"Seriously, Austen. What happened?"

I look at her and don't even bother to wipe at the tear dripping off my chin. "Tyler broke up with me."

"Oh." She straightens and I swear a micro-smile flashes across her face before she says. "You must feel terrible."

"I know you don't like him."

"No, I don't. But I love you, and you gave him a lot of your time and energy, and I'm here for you."

"Manda?"

"Yes."

"You haven't even asked why. Don't you want to know?"

She puts her hand on my shoulder. "Oh, babe, I heard about him and Cleo Thornton in Geography this afternoon. I was going to tell you on the way out to riding, but I guess, for once, Tyler used those balls he supposedly has and actually owned up to something."

I'm staring at her. The tears have stopped. So has my breathing. So has my heart.

"Cleo?" The lack of oxygen makes it come out of me in a squeak.

She tilts her head and gets an *Oh Shit* look on her face. "Ye-e-s. Cleo. They hooked up at Alanna Currie's party."

"Alanna Currie?" My heart's going again. Fast. Too fast. It hurts.

"Austen, are you telling me you didn't know about this? Why on earth did he tell you he was breaking up with you?"

"He ..." my voice trails off, then I recite *Cleo Thornton, Alanna Currie,* to myself and stoke my anger so my next words are strong and clear. "That asshole stood on the curb in front of Alanna Currie's house two hours ago and told me I give too much time to Eliot and my family, and I neglect him, and he needs a girlfriend who has time for him."

"Oh God," Manda says. "I am so phoning him."

***

She does it on the way to riding, driving full-speed on the highway with the windows down and her phone coming through the car speakers.

The first time he answers she says, "Hey you lying scumbag. What's it like to be the only male rugby player without a set of balls?"

He hangs up.

She calls back, and he answers. "Why is he answering?" I mutter.

"Because he's an idiot," she tells me, and him at the same time, due to speaker phone. "You never realized this, because you're a nice person, Austen, but your ex-boyfriend is dumb. Everybody knows he's dumb, and he's just proven he's dumb by messing around with some equally dumb chick at a public party, then lying to you about why he's breaking up with you, and thinking you wouldn't find out. Super-duper-dumb."

He hangs up again, and Manda calls back again, and my obviously dumber-than-I-thought ex-boyfriend answers *again*.

"Seriously, Tyler!" I yell. "Have some pride! She's not going to say anything nice to you."

Manda giggles. "Actually, Tyler, I called to tell you that while you guys were going out, I kissed Austen, and she liked it. So there."

This time she's the one who hangs up on him.

He immediately calls back, but neither of us answers.

"Manda!" I say.

"What?"

"The kissing thing!"

"Well, I did kiss you. Remember? My mom had that mistletoe hanging up at Christmas and I kissed you. And you laughed, which told me you liked it."

"But you made it sound ..."

"I didn't make it sound anything. I just gave him something to think about."

The phone's ringing again. She selects bluetooth, turns it to "off" and says, "OK, now let's talk about horses."

***

We pull into the driveway, park across from the sand ring, and while Manda talks to Ingrid about the fall-out from the kicked whipper-in fiasco of the weekend, I walk inside to where petite Bandit lives next-door to big Ace – the OTTB I've been hoping to lease.

Except his stall is empty.

Not happy-horse-frolicking-in the paddock empty, but bedding-stripped, rubber-mats-swept-clean-and-left-to-dry-out-before-a-new-horse-moves-in empty.

"Manda!" I call. "Manda!"

Manda comes fast and Ingrid comes with her.

"What the ...?" Manda stares at the vacant stall.

Ingrid furrows her brow. "Oh, yes. His new owner came and picked him up today." She turns to me. "Didn't Clarice tell you?"

I just stare back at her, and she says. "Ah. I see she didn't. I'm so sorry, Austen."

***

And that's my day.

"What's the third thing that's going to happen?" I ask Manda.

"Since Helen's out of town, and Clarice better be smart enough not to show up, I'm going to bow out of our lesson and you're going to ride my mare and have a private lesson on her and teach her why we don't kick whippers-in."

"The third thing's supposed to be something bad," I say.

"Oh, she's been very badly behaved lately. She'll probably break your neck."

"In that case, fine. How can I refuse?"

Manda legs me up. I take the lightest possible hold of my reins, and Bandit steps forward in that bold big-horse walk of hers that I really do love, and I rub her withers and say, "No kicking horses, people, or anything on the ground."

She arches her neck and gives a long, loud snort and, by doing everything I ask when and how I ask it, protests *I would never, ever, try to kick anybody who didn't deserve it very much*.

I adore her, and I love riding her, but still and all, it's been a shit of a day.

On the way home I turn to Manda. "I guess I'm leaving."

She sighs, "I guess you don't have much to stay for."

"Well, there is you."

"And I'm a great kisser," she points out.

"That you are."

"But I know you were mostly being a good sport – you didn't like the kiss that much. I think you should go, and be surrounded by horses all summer, and maybe I'll come visit you."

"You're a very good best friend," I tell her.

"Don't forget it," she says.

• RAND •

Chapter Two

"So, you've pissed a lot of people off."

I don't hate Marv as much as I thought I would.

I definitely like him a lot more than when I was first told I'd be seeing "Dr. Pulvermacher" as part of my court-mandated counselling.

Ugh.

His office building just one block shy of some of the city's dodgiest addresses, and his tiny cinder-block walled office, decorated with high-gloss, once-white paint, cooled by an extremely noisy window-unit air conditioner which every few minutes sends a fat drop of condensation plummeting to the garish linoleum floor, didn't improve my first impression.

But he introduced himself as Marvin – "Call me Marv; I hate all this 'Dr. Pulvermacher' stuff" – opened a mini-fridge built into his desk and asked me if I wanted Sprite, Ginger Ale, Coke, or Root Beer, then said, "Listen, I'm retiring at Christmas. I'm old school. I do care about you – I'd like to help if I can – but you can imagine that if you're obstructive, or a complete asshole to me, I'm pretty happy to just put in the time and tick off your hours."

Quite a bit of what we've done would probably be considered "ticking off hours" by other people, but I've enjoyed talking basketball with him – I used to love playing myself before my mom started sleeping with my basketball coach – and because their affair was part of what propelled me into the perma-angry state I'm in these days, it could be argued that basketball is very relevant to my counselling.

This is our last session. All my punishment is coming to an end. I have one more volunteer shift before my community hours are done. Tomorrow is my last day of school; bringing a close to my period of perfect attendance required in my conditional sentencing agreement. My mom's shunting me out of the city, her house ... her life, the day after tomorrow. So this is the last hour I'll spend with Marv.

With the basketball play-offs over, I guess it's officially time to talk shop.

I point to a Coke when Marv opens the fridge, I stretch back on his vinyl couch and let the too-cold AC wash over my skin – still clammy from the close humidity of late-June in this heaving city – and, finally, I answer. "Yup. You got that right."

"How do you feel about that?"

I take a slug of the Coke before looking at him. "Honestly? I don't feel much at all."

"What do you mean?"

I set the drink on the floor, and spread my hands wide. "It's just been a really, really long time since I've respected anyone enough to even care about what they're feeling."

Marv nods. Slowly. Takes a sip of his own drink – a Sprite – he always has Sprite. "You know, kid, I get where you're coming from. The thing is, though, I've had fifty-nine years to get to this point. You're only seventeen. I feel like you might be in trouble if you're despairing of humanity this early in life."

"So what should I do about it?"

"Well," he says. "It's pretty obvious."

I lean forward. Great. Awesome. Final session and all will become clear. "Yes?"

"Find people you respect. Spend time with them. Then you'll start caring."

Oh. Great. Perfect. Easy.

"Well, that is million-dollar advice, Marv."

He winks. "I think we can agree the advice is worth the price you paid for it."

"This was free ..." I stop. "Yeah. OK. Got it."

***

We stop and start through ridiculous Toronto traffic - where are all these people going in their cars on a Saturday? Don't they have better things to be doing?

It's made even worse by our car having a manual transmission and my mom not being the world's best stick driver.

Lurch, stop, hop-hop, lurch.

Do you want me to drive?

I'd ask, but my mom and I aren't speaking these days – or weeks, or months – so I fix my gaze on a stationary object in the distance and try to stave off the threatening nausea.

It gets better after we drop my sister off at the airport. She's off to Libya, or Liberia, or Lagos, or some other place where people need help and bright, pretty, privileged white girls like my sister go to give it. My mom sniffles a couple of times and murmurs, "So proud" and "Send pictures" and I say "Safe travels sis. Guess I'll see you on Facebook."

And at least after that the highway's clear and our trip is mostly smooth.

We pull into line for the ferry, and my mom cuts the engine, and in the sudden quiet I give in and ask, "Why am I coming here, again?" I also want to ask, 'What am I supposed to do here?' and 'How am I supposed to get around some backwoods island with no driver's licence?' but five words in a row is the most I've said to my mother in a while, so I'm not about to push it.

"Because your school won't take you as a boarder until September, every summer Bootcamp we looked into cost the equivalent of your first year's university tuition, and your uncle said he'd have you."

"And, because you don't want to see my face anymore." I've become skilled at pushing my mom's buttons.

The scary thing is she's gotten good at pushing back. "You said it, Rand, not me."

My brain knows I'm in a full-on war with my mom, but this tiny, hidden part of something inside me still expects her to say, 'Don't be silly, Rand,' 'You're my son,' 'I'll always want to have you around.'

Then again, maybe something deep inside her wants to hear me say, 'I love you, Mom,' and that isn't happening either.

The ferry docks in a little cluster of buildings. "This is the village," my mom says.

"Good thing you told me." I let sarcasm flood my voice. Still I manage to note the General Store contains a Beer Store, there's a place that calls itself a Pub & Pizzeria, and a ramshackle house that looks original – complete with peeling paint – houses a bakery. Semi-civilization, I guess.

Except we then drive, and drive, and drive away from that hub of development. The highway isn't the widest, and the centre line wobbles, like it was painted by a drunk guy, or in the dark, or maybe both, but when we turn off it onto a gravel road, I want the blacktop back.

We then turn onto a narrow, twisting, rutted drive with trees touching overhead the entire way, and I want to go back to the luxury of the gravel road.

I've met my uncle before. Once – at a funeral parlour in the posh suburb of Toronto where my mom's parents had retired and, one after the other, both died. It was a few years ago, but even much younger, and much less aware of social conventions, I knew he was out of place with his sun-crisped hair, his ruddy complexion, his bolo tie, and the beer he was necking at eleven a.m.

Now it's our fuel-efficient bright blue bubble of a car, my mom's swishy floral skirt and pedicured feet, and my white, soft skin that are strange.

Two dogs appear first – one black, thin, whippy; running to us in a submissive, sideways fashion, like his front and back legs are on two different tracks. The second is yellow, chunky, and drops to a walk about halfway to the car.

Both have wagging tails and that expression so many Labradors sport, that makes them look like they're smiling.

A man steps forward next, out of the weathered barn the dogs came from. He's wiping his hands on a rag. His appearance is somewhere between the two dogs; lean and athletic like the first one, but not hurrying – taking his time – like the second one.

"Hey Liv," he says, and I look around for who Liv could be. I vaguely remember my dad calling my mom that, a long time ago. These days she's at least "Olivia" to everybody. More often – like when she answers her phone, or when I see her quoted in work documents on her screen or printed out in the house – she's "Olivia Nicklesen." No abbreviations, no nicknames.

My uncle doesn't know that, though. Or maybe he doesn't care. He certainly doesn't seem to care when he reaches his tanned arms coated with bits of sawdust out toward her.

"Oh!" she says. "I'm a mess from the drive."

What she really means is, 'You're a mess – please don't touch me.' I smile when he puts his arms around her anyway.

He steps back and holds his hand out to me and I know what to do here – I'm not stupid – take the hand, make eye contact, nod. He might hate me eventually, but at least I'll pass the first impression test.

I almost say, 'Nice to meet you,' which would be wrong because, of course, I've met him. It just seemed like another lifetime, another Rand.

Fortunately he says, "Nice to see you again," and I can nod and say, "Yes."

So far, so good.

"I'm afraid I'm not much of a housekeeper," my uncle says. "There isn't much food in the place – but I could make us some tea or coffee, or we could go into the village for a bite to eat."

"No, thank you," my mom says. "I want to get on the next boat. I need to be back in the city to prep for a big meeting tomorrow. There are just a few things ..."

She stares at me, and I know she wants me to leave so she can talk about me.

I consider lurking around, just to frustrate her but at this point I want her to go, too, so I wander down to the dock and walk right out to the end.

It says something, I guess, about the state of my relationship with my mom, that I'd rather she go and leave me with this person I really don't know at all, than stay with me, or take me back with her.

I look back at them talking. My uncle makes my mom look small. There's something reassuring about that. In the city nobody can diminish my mom's presence.

And there are the dogs. I like them. I trust them. They're lying just a few feet away from him. If the dogs love him, he's gotta be OK.

And, really, what are my choices? Nobody likes me much right now. Nobody who knows me. My uncle doesn't really know me, but he said, "Nice to see you," which would suggest I'm starting with a positive, or at least clean slate with him. It's better than any other alternative I have.

I turn back to the river. There's a wide bay opening around me and, unlike my friends' cottages in Muskoka, hardly any other buildings around. To my right my uncle's land curves out to a point which I can't see past, and to my left the shore scoops in a half-circle through a stand of cattails, under a truly enormous weeping willow, along a stretch of what looks like pasture, then to one other building – a cottage, I guess – probably about five hundred metres from here as the crow flies.

At first I think it's really quiet, then a bird cries way out in the bay, a frog nearby begins banjoing, and the breeze lifts ruffles in the water and slaps them against the dock.

I kick my feet out of my shoes and find the wood warm and smooth under the soles of my feet. There's something about the weathered, grey grain of the planks I find more soothing than the water, or the huge expanse of sky above.

It takes me back years to when my dad was around more and we'd work together on projects to keep our century house in decent repair. Replacing a step here, fixing a railing there. Him showing me how to sand with the grain, reminding me to measure twice, very occasionally letting me cut the wood we needed.

"Rand!" With the wind behind it, my mom's voice carries easily.

I walk back, still barefoot, and the yellow lab heaves himself up and brushes his cold nose against my hand. He sits by my side as my mom says, "There are a few things your uncle and I have discussed that I need to make sure are clear to you."

"Shoot," I say.

My mom's nose wrinkles in the way it does every time I open my mouth these days, but my Uncle Kurt speaks up. "I should be better at grocery shopping, but I'm not. I should be better at keeping the house, but I'm not. If something bugs you, and you're thinking of complaining, I suggest you just go ahead and fix it yourself." He pauses. "Got it?"

I nod. "Yeah."

"There won't be any drinking around here. I also don't have cable, or satellite, and my internet connection is dog slow. I don't have a cell phone, but most people tell me the service here is terrible."

I shrug. *Whatever*. My phone got wrecked in the accident and my mom refused to replace it. Part of my punishment. The phone thing kind of freaked me out, actually; no bones broken, but my phone, in the cargo pocket of my shorts, splintered into pieces. A couple of centimetres and that would have been my leg. I suppress a shiver now, just thinking about it.

"OK," I say.

"I'm pretty busy. I keep a hunting and fishing lodge for a group from New York. They often fly in at the last minute; sometimes they stay for less than twenty-four hours, sometimes for days at a time. When they're here I need to be available, so you'll be on your own," Kurt says. "Things could get pretty boring if you don't find a way to fill your time. I know your mom wants you to make some money ..."

We both look at her. She pushes her lips together. "Yes, well, Rand has a car and a porch to pay for."

My uncle continues. "Most of the jobs around here involve long hours and hard work. I can't give you full-time work, but I can pass off a couple of my smaller side jobs to you. If you look for work on your own, I'll help you."

Yeah, I'll get right on that, I think. Long hours and hard work sound awesome. "Fine," I say.

My mom looks at her watch. "Listen, I have to go if I'm going to get on the next ferry." She fixes her eyes on me. "That thing I said about Bootcamp? We'll pay for it if we have to. You're not to cause any trouble for Kurt, and I'd recommend you try to figure out how to make some money."

I wonder if she'll hug me. Will I get a kiss on the cheek?

Instead she turns to Kurt. "Anything – the smallest thing – you call me. He knows he's not allowed to drive, so if you have a bike or something ..." Her voice trails off and I wonder if she's maybe realizing it might have been a good idea to at least bring my bike with us. To even attempt to set me up in some small way for being able to function out here, in the middle of nowhere, not knowing anybody, and with no transportation.

Apparently not, though, because she gives her head a quick shake, and turns to me.

"Oh, and ..." She puts her head down and digs around in her purse, "... before I forget. Here." She holds out an envelope. I recognize the insignia of the private school I've attended as a day student for the last five years. "It's the boarding questionnaire. I can't answer it for you – they want you to fill it out."

"But ..." I start.

"It's only going to take a few minutes of your time, and there's a self-addressed, stamped envelope inside." The look she gives me dares me to complain.

Fine then, I will. "But, I don't want ..." I try again.

She cuts me off. "Rand, we went past what you wanted the night you destroyed our eighteen-year relationship with our next-door neighbour. Maybe one day I'll be ready to listen to what you want, but that day is not here yet. Fill out the form, send it in on time, don't miss the deadline."

As my mom drives away Kurt whistles. "So, she's not exactly your biggest fan right now."

I think of the family down the street who fired me from my job as their thirteen-year-old son's math tutor after two years of working with him. I liked that kid, I liked the job, but they were unbending. "You can hardly blame us Rand; your actions were a terrible example to Trevor."

I remember Ms. Pike, taking me aside to tell me I wouldn't be going on the debating team trip to Ottawa. "But I founded the team," I said. "But you missed all the practices for the last month," she said. "But ..." that's when I stopped, because I was about to tell her the practices were scheduled for the times I had to do my community service. Kind of the point, I guess.

"Nobody's my fan right now," I tell Kurt. "You might as well just start hating me now."

"Humph," he says. "I usually make up my own mind."

Which is fine, except I haven't been that successful at making people like me lately.

***

Once my bag's in my room, I find out pretty quickly my uncle was right. It's boring around here.

My stomach rumbles so I head down to the kitchen, open the fridge door wide, and stare at the illuminated white expanse inside.

"Told ya ..."

I turn to face him.

"... no food, no beer. I get by OK on my own, and I'm not that used to company."

"But," I say. "In Toronto. At the funeral."

He nods. "Yup. I used to drink. A lot. So did my fiancée – I don't know if you ever met her. She was driving over to stay with me after a girl's night out and she never got here. Hit a tree out on the highway. So now I don't have a fiancée, and I don't drink much anymore."

Wow. That's crazy. Hitting a tree and dying. That's extreme.

That's what I did, just about.

"Shit. I'm sorry. I feel stupid for not knowing about that."

He shrugs. "You might have noticed your mom and I aren't exactly on 'talk every day' terms. By the time I got around to telling her, a while had passed. You were younger – she probably thought it would upset you to know about it. The point is, I can't undo it. I can just try to make sure it doesn't happen again on my watch." He grabs a ballcap from a hook by the door. "Come on. Let's go into the village and get a pizza for dinner."

I close the fridge door. "OK. Sure."

I wonder if we'll drive by the tree on our way into the village.

For the second time today I damp down a shiver.

• AUSTEN •

Chapter Three

"What do you think?" Meg asks. "Could you work with him?"

"Are you kidding?"

We have our feet up on the fence rail watching the massive horse rip and tear, rip and tear at the lush island grass.

His gleaming bay coat stretches tight over lines of muscle and a hint of ribs. "He's ..."

"What?" Meg asks.

"He's just like this horse I was trying to lease this summer. Except a bit bigger. Flashier, too. And better-looking." I turn to her. "He's perfect. Are you seriously going to let me work with him? He looks really valuable."

"Well, he could be. My friend, Angie, has been eventing him. He was going well – lots of promise, good results, moving up levels – and then he just flatlined. Bad jumping form, refusals, the whole bit. They've had him checked out every way imaginable – teeth, feet, chiro, massage; you name it – and nobody can find anything wrong with him. Linda figures maybe he's just sour. Because he was so capable, and did so well, she brought him on fast, and now she thinks maybe it was too fast, and he's just had enough."

"So ..." I prompt.

"So, she sent him here and paid for outdoor board and said she wants him to just be a horse for a while."

"Just be a horse," I say.

"The only thing is, I kind of promised her I'd keep him within sightlines of the barn – you know, in case of emergency – so he can't stay down at the cottage, but he's yours to hack, swim, just goof around with – whatever. You can still treat him like a backyard pony."

"Like the scruffy backyard pony I expected you to cough up for me."

She bows. "I aim to exceed expectations."

"Ha! You've been successful."

Meg claps her hands together. "OK then, that's settled. Mac is your project for now." She steps back from the fence and heads for the barn. "Now let me show you everything so you're ready for the onslaught when the campers show up on Monday ..."

I hang back for a second, snap a quick picture of Mac, and text it to Manda. **My horse for the next little while. Can you believe it? Talk about landing on my feet.**

Later, when I check her reply I laugh out loud. **He's better-looking than Tyler! Moving up in the world Austen!**

• RAND •

Chapter Four

Kurt's gone on a supply run to the mainland and left me alone.

And he was right – I'm bored.

I prowl around, exploring the property which, frankly, looks terrible.

I squint my eyes against the morning sun and evaluate the property. The house is fine. White, clapboard, farmhouse. Some people would call it quaint, and calling it that would make the peeling paint part of the charm.

The house and century barn – used for storage – are nicely framed by mature trees. The ever-present island breeze ruffles their leaves. Very pretty. Very soothing.

I feel like if I had the tools, and maybe a bit more expertise, there are things I could do to straighten some of the sagging parts of the porch. And some of the wood stacked in the barn is full of amazing character – it would make beautiful furniture.

Those are all longer term projects, though. For now it's the lawn that's the biggest problem. It looks like complete crap. Ragged, uneven, made up of half-a-dozen kinds of vegetation.

Messy lawns drive me crazy. Mowing and raking are the only chores I've ever done unasked. I might not be diagnosable, but I'm pretty sure I possess elements of OCD. A tidy lawn soothes me.

What doesn't soothe me is the fresh email from my mom with the subject line **Questionnaire?** I read and delete all the other emails around it, carefully avoiding opening it, and leave it nice and bold underneath the **Questionnaire?** message she sent yesterday.

I look at the self-addressed, stamped questionnaire sitting on the edge of my uncle's kitchen counter and head outside to look for a lawn mower.

I find one in the barn, with gas in it, which roars to life when I pull the cord. I start mowing the lawn.

It's only halfway through that I wonder if I've screwed up. His sagging jeans, and the lawn chairs in the living room tell me my uncle's not hung up on appearances, but I heard him on the phone yesterday telling somebody,

"No, whatever you do, do *not* change the oil in that boat – I had to drain it and start again last time."

In other words, he has a way he likes things done. Me, mowing his lawn, might not fit with how things should be done.

It's partway done now, though, and the same part of my brain that likes woodworking – that enjoys refining coarse things – would never rest if I left the grass half golf-course-smooth, half hayfield, so I'm just going to have to finish and take my chances.

My uncle rolls his truck to a stop in front of the barn as I'm finishing. He steps out, looks around, and grunts. "You do that?"

If it was my mom asking I'd say, 'You see anyone else with a lawn-mower around here?' For my uncle I muster a bit more respect. "I thought the grass needed it, and the mower was gassed up, so I went ahead."

I wait to hear how I've messed up. How he likes it a different length, or I haven't taken proper care of the mower. Instead he snorts. "Hmm ... thought I'd have to do it this afternoon."

I choose to hear a "thanks" there. "My pleasure." I say. It's something my favourite English teacher taught me. Never say "no problem" because then you're making people think it actually was. Tell them it was "your pleasure" and they'll believe you.

It seems to work on Kurt because he says, "The lawn over around the lodge could use mowing. Want to drive back there with me now and do it?"

If I'm meant to stay out of trouble, and maybe even be a little helpful, mowing lawns is a relatively appealing way to do that.

I nod. "Yeah, sure."

Kurt looks me up and down, the longest time he's ever spent scrutinizing me. "Alright then. Hop in."

***

We're cruising down a driveway toward the cottage I spotted across the bay yesterday. It's one of those picture-perfect country lanes – the kind that are just two narrow tracks between long, waving wildflowers, with shorter, low-growing flowers in between.

Small stones are pinging the underside of the truck, and every now and then a taller, encroaching clump of grass brushes the body, and my uncle's humming.

Nice that he's happy.

That makes one of us, because ever since ten minutes ago when he whistled me awake, and said, "Since you turned out to be so good at it, I've got another lawn for you to mow," my stomach's been churning.

"I'm, uh, not sure," I said, and he laughed, and pushed a travel mug of coffee into my hands. "Come on – the truck leaves in three minutes."

I don't drink coffee and, even if I did, I couldn't right now because of the flutter in my gut.

It's stupid to be nervous over something as simple as mowing a client's lawn, but I *am* nervous, so I *do* feel stupid, and I'll mask both those feelings by being rude. It's my MO.

We roll to a stop and Kurt asks, "Good?"

I grunt. That's what I do when I'm not good. Grunt. So people think I'm a sullen asshole. I know how it comes across and I've resolved to change it more than once, but it never works for me.

I have this cousin who everybody loves. Adults especially. It's not that he's better-looking than me, or smarter – we're pretty even in every way, but when we were twelve, at a big amusement park together, staring up at the hulking roller coaster, he opened his eyes wide and said, "I'm really nervous," and everyone melted and said, "There, there," and he got to choose his seat, and after everybody congratulated him on overcoming his fear.

A year or so later, when our parents showed us ET, he wiped his eyes and said, "I'm really sensitive – this movie makes me cry," and there was a murmur and a sigh rippled through the room, and he got offered an extra bowl of popcorn, and my mom said, "So sweet ..."

Meanwhile I grunted through both experiences – and many others like them – and when my mom talks about me, she says things like, "Oh Rand can sit anywhere – nothing bothers him," or "Rand won't want to watch this movie with us – he has a heart of stone."

Right now I should tell my uncle, "No, I'm not good. I'm nervous. I don't know the people at this place, and I've never mowed a lawn bigger than a football field, and I don't know how careful I have to be, and I'm afraid they'll get mad at me, and you'll get mad at me," but I don't. I follow him to the shed at the side of the property where he opens the double doors to reveal a ride-on lawn mower that jumps sweat to my palms, and armpits, and the back of my neck.

"You used one of these before?" Kurt asks.

Of course I haven't. Our lawn at home is less than twenty by twenty, and the neighbours would shun us if we used anything other than a reel mower "I ... no. Never."

"Well, have you driven manual?"

Joe's car was manual. An expression I'm not aware of must cross my face when I think that, because Kurt steps toward me. "Are you sure you're OK?"

I clear my throat. "I'm, uh, not supposed to drive."

The furrow lifts from his brow. "Oh, *now* you want to follow the rules?" He laughs. "I think your suspension applies to cars, on streets." He claps me on the shoulder. "Don't worry – you can use a ride-on mower."

It's so stupid to be feeling my pulse fluttering, then pounding as I look at this small tractor that's going to carry me at less than ten kilometres per hour.

"... mow away from the flower beds ..." my uncle's saying. "... watch for shallow tree roots over there ..." "... careful on incline to water ..."

It would be logical to listen as carefully as I can – to conquer my fear with knowledge – but, instead, all I can think is *I'll figure it out when I get to it.*

If I have to do this, I just want to get going.

I'm about to climb on board when a small body comes hurtling past me and leaps into the seat. "I'm mowing Kurt! OK? Can I mow?"

Kurt grins and lifts the boy off the tractor and high into the air. "You can fly – how about that instead?"

A woman's voice calls, "I'm so sorry, Kurt. He saw you and was out the door before I could grab him."

A red flush joins the smile on my uncle's face. *Aaahhh,* so *this* is the source of my uncle's humming and whistling. She looks pretty – for a mom – I'll give him that.

She starts down the stairs in bare feet, until my uncle calls over. "Don't worry about him. I'm just getting my nephew started here, then I'll bring him back."

She waves. "OK. I'll pour you a cup of coffee if you like."

"That's Mrs. Delaney," Kurt tells me. So formal. I wonder if the "Mrs." is just for me, or if he calls her that over coffee as well.

"That's my mom," the little boy breaks in.

"Yes, that is your mom," Kurt says and lifts him high again; earning a squeal and a giggle. "Shaw's family is renting the cottage for the summer and he's staying here with his mom and his sisters."

Shaw – funny name for a little kid – is squirming now. "I wanna go back inside!"

"Go ahead," I say. "I'll get started on this." Truth is, I'd rather tackle it without an audience.

"You sure?"

"Positive."

"I'm heading onto work after. You good to walk home from here?"

I glance across the bay to my uncle's dock. It's about half-a-kilometre over water – probably three or four times that by driveways and gravel roads. "Yes, sure." If I actually finish this job without disfiguring the lawn, or myself, walking home will be a breeze.

I settle onto the wide tractor seat, and the springs give beneath me.

"All OK?" Kurt asks.

The lawn in front of me is huge. I should have listened to my uncle's explanation of how he breaks it into sections. I should have asked for more help. He's still standing here. I still could.

Instead, I grunt.

"Alright, then," he says, and I'm left alone.

***

It goes surprisingly OK at first.

I mean, it's amazing how fast ten kilometres an hour feels when you take a corner too sharply, and my uncle wasn't kidding about those tree roots being shallow, but I'm mostly following straight(ish) lines; leaving nice even grass behind me, and I haven't destroyed anything on the lawn, killed myself, or broken the mower.

My stomach, pulse, and breathing have settled, and the only sweating I'm doing is from the heat of the sun, and under the gigantic (and ugly) bright yellow ear muffs Kurt told me I have to wear.

So ... good.

There's lots of evidence of kids around. There are small swim trunks and bright beach towels on the clothesline. The sandy beach area that faces my uncle's dock is strewn with buckets and spades and it sports a lopsided castle-like sand structure. I wonder if Shaw's two sisters are as quick as the little boy. I hope they all stay inside until I'm done since I could really, really do without running over a small child.

I still have the sticky incline bit of the lawn to do – need to try to remember what Kurt said about tackling that – and there are a few spots where weeds have popped up and are waving in the breeze that I'll go back over, but the end is in sight and I've conquered my first bout of nervousness about driving again, and trying something new, when the tractor stops.

Sput, put, dead.

I look over to the empty spot where my uncle's truck was before, as though I hadn't watched him drive away at least half-an-hour ago. Of course he hasn't miraculously returned, so I've got no back up at all.

Crap.

Problem number one: I can't finish this job – which will probably make Shaw's mom and my uncle angry. Problem number two: I've broken the mower and I don't even know who it belongs to – the owner of the cottage maybe? – which makes another potential person to be pissed off at me.

Bottom line is, I've screwed up. Again.

Shit.

I step onto the ground, and walk around the tractor, and the only thing I know for sure is nothing's hissing, or smoking, or steaming. It looks fine. Just not moving.

I guess the next step is to go knock on the cottage door and explain that the lawn's going to remain not-quite-cut, and there may be a broken-down tractor as a lawn ornament for a while.

"Hey!"

My head snaps up.

A figure's walking toward me with the early-morning sun rays slanting behind her. It's hard to see her properly, but I can tell she's not the tall, willowy woman who pinked my uncle's cheeks. Nor is she a little kid like the boy I already met.

So who is she?

She gets up close, and the answer is, she's perfectly perfect.

Her body's the ideal balance of sporty and curvy. Lean, but with muscles that shape her small shoulders, tanned arms, and slender legs.

Licks of sandy brownish-blond hair flick around her face, framing the most perfectly almond-shaped eyes I've ever seen, a snub nose, and a mouth smiling not in a wide-open-showing-teeth way, but rather in a way that suggests she's finding amusement with life – maybe with me?

I'm too busy staring at the freckles smattered just below her collarbone to notice she's holding out a hand. By the time I clue in, it's too late – she's withdrawn it again, and she's shrugging, and she raps the tractor with her knuckles.

"What's up with this thing?" There's a lift running through her voice that makes me want to keep listening to it.

Which would require me saying something, so we can have an actual conversation.

"Uh. I'm not sure." *Great start, Rand.* "I don't know anything about engines," I add.

She bites her lip. "Hmm ... me neither. But ..." She flips up the whole front cover of the tractor – grabbing a handle I didn't know was there, and lifting – and exposes the engine underneath. She unscrews the cap from a bright yellow plastic tank and bends over to peer in. "Yup. That's it."

"That's what?" I ask. How can this pretty teenage girl who said herself she doesn't know anything about engines, have diagnosed the problem so quickly?

She winks at me. "Empty gas tank." She flutters her hand against those freckles on her chest. "That'll do it every time."

I. Am. An. Idiot.

I feel it. Acutely. And she's standing there, not even knowing my name, but already knowing how useless I am.

"Come with me," she says.

Wrong-footed + overheated + embarrassed + hungry. It's a killer combination for me.

"No." I say.

Having already taken a couple of steps, she stops. "Pardon me?"

"I'm done."

She shrugs. Starts walking again, tossing words over her shoulder. "Sure. Fine. Whatever. Go ahead and quit. I'll sort it out."

• AUSTEN •

Chapter Five

The shed smells like the hot sun that beats down on it every day, and the skunk that sprayed it our first weekend here, and – faintly – like gas. It's the last smell that has me rooting around behind beach umbrellas and soccer balls until I can put my hand on the rough-surfaced red plastic of the gas container.

"Ah-ha!" I knew it was in here – knew I could find it. If Mr. Sulks-a-lot doesn't want to finish mowing the lawn, I can do it. No problem.

I back out of the shed, keeping my head low as a defense against concussion. When the outdoor breeze hits my skin, I turn toward the mower, only to be pulled completely off-balance.

"Hey!" I say. The guy's grabbed the handle of the gas can.

"No," he says. "It's my job. I'll do it."

"You didn't want to come with me. I'll finish it."

He yanks. "No. I will."

I yank back. Grit my teeth. "I will."

When he yanks again, there's an almighty slosh. Whoever last used the can didn't screw the lid down tightly enough, and liquid sprays out onto his neat, city shirt and shorts.

I clap my hand over my mouth. "*Shoot* ..." I breathe the word long and slow.

I brace for anger – glaring eyes, raised voice – but instead, when he flicks his gaze to mine, his eyes are wide, pupils dilated. His nostrils flare and his breathing is quick and audible.

I can't count how many times I've been on the end of a lead shank staring down a horse in just this state. Enough times that instinct kicks in. "Shhh ..." I say. I bend at the knees to lower the gas can to the ground; never dropping eye contact with him. "It's OK. It's fine. No big deal. It's just gas – just a bit. They're just clothes."

He takes one deeper, longer breath – we're getting somewhere – then the screen door slams, and my mom's voice carries across the lawn. "What on earth is going on out there? Breakfast has been on the table for five minutes."

He glances at her, then back at me. "Shit!" The word, when he says it, is sharp and panic-backed.

I take a decisive step toward him, still like I would with a horse, and circle my hand around his wrist. I squeeze. "Listen. It's fine. Let go of the gas can and come with me. I'll take care of it."

I try not to let him know I'm waiting for another "No!" I channel confidence. And, just like at the barn, the minute he takes his first step beside me, I know we're good.

"Hey Mom!" I call. "We have a bit of an issue here. But I know you can help ..."

• RAND •

Chapter Six

OK, I'm calmer.

The plate of bacon, eggs, baked beans, and toast separating me from the girl is helping.

Grease and carbs – what could be more soothing?

The girl's mother is placing ketchup, and jam, and maple syrup – not the supermarket maple syrup lurking in the door of my uncle's ancient avocado fridge, but local stuff with a screw top crystallized with maple sugar and a crooked stuck-on label saying **Honey Suckle Farms** on it – on the table between us.

With that done, the mom turns her hands backward against her waist, leans back, and says, "I think that's everything. Now, would you like to do the introductions, Austen?"

The girl looks at me, reaches her hand across the table and says. "Hi. I'm Austen."

"Huh?" I say.

"Pardon me," her mom corrects me.

I turn to the mother. "Huh?"

She shakes her head. "No, not 'huh?' – you never say 'huh?' when you don't understand someone; you say 'Pardon me?'"

"Mom!" Austen's cheeks flood with pink. "You cannot just start in on people like that. People you barely know."

"I can if I'm feeding him breakfast. Plus, I'm trying to get to know him."

"Mom, it's so not cool."

"Austen, I've just had to find a t-shirt and shorts of your father's to sort of fit this young man, his clothes are hanging on my clothesline, and I'm feeding him. I think we're past 'not cool,' here."

"Oh, Mom ..." The girl leans forward and juts her chin at her mother. I jump in.

"Pardon me?" I look right at the girl named Austen when I say it. It's the first time I've been able to find my voice since she knocked on the bathroom door while I was changing and asked, "Would you like some breakfast?" I meant to say, 'Yes, please," but just then my stomach rumbled so long and deep she gave a small giggle and her voice, slightly muffled by the door, said, "I'll take that as a yes."

"Huh?" she says now. Then her eyes flick to her mom before returning to me. "Pardon me?"

"Your name," I say. "Did you say 'Austin' – like the city in Texas? South by Southwest?"

She relaxes back in her seat. "Isn't that one with an 'i?' No, mine's A-U-S-T-E-N as in *Pride and Prejudice*."

I lift my eyebrows.

She lifts hers back. "*Emma*? *Sense and Sensibility*?"

I shrug. "Pardon me?"

She laughs. "Jane Austen? The early nineteenth-century novelist? Famous?" When I don't respond, she shakes her head. "What can I say? My mother's obsessed. She's an English Lit university prof."

For the briefest of seconds my mind flashes to my retired-high-school-English-teacher neighbour and his dog named Hamlet, pulling me out of the wreck of that car, calling 9-1-1.

Austen just keeps on talking. "My sister's named 'Eliot,' as in 'George,' as in another famous nineteenth-century novelist – a woman, though – despite being named 'George.'" Austen pauses, then continues. "*Middlemarch*? Ringing any bells?"

"Not a single one."

"Ha! Well my brother's named 'Shaw' for George Bernard. Eliot and I were quite relieved for him. We were terrified he'd be named 'Shakespeare.'"

That explains the weird name. Sort of, anyway.

I look at the small boy boosted to table height by a bright plastic chair, dipping pancake chunks into a lake of maple syrup and smushing them into his mouth. "Shaw is my name!" he mumbles through chewed-up pancake.

"Yep." Austen leans over to squeeze his chubby arm. "Shaw certainly is your name."

"An-y-way ..." She offers her hand across the table again. "I'm Austen. Nice to meet you ..."

It takes me a second to realize there's a blank there for me to fill in. "Oh, Rand."

"As in, Ayn?" While Austen was running through her sibling's names, her mother was fetching a wet facecloth. She hovers over Shaw with it now, eyes wide. Wow, Austen's mother is pretty when she smiles. No wonder she makes my uncle Kurt lose his cool. No wonder her daughter is knock-out adorable. This whole family's out of my league.

"Um, no. As in 'Randall.'"

"Oh." Austen's mom sighs and sets to scrubbing maple syrup from her sticky child.

I catch Austen's eye and mouth, 'Who is Ayn Rand?'

She winks. "Don't worry about it. Just eat your breakfast."

• AUSTEN •

Chapter Seven

While I slot the dishes into the dishwasher, I glance out the window to see that Rand seems to have mastered the gas can, and the mower's tank, and is ready to finish the lawn.

Dishwasher loaded, I step outside. Rand looks up and I walk over.

"So, good to go?"

"Yeah. Thanks." I choose to interpret the last word as "Thanks" but it's really more of a grunt.

His eyes slide past me and I turn to see my mom approaching. It's unusual for her to leave Shaw unsupervised, the dishes unwashed, and Eliot unpestered in her bed, to seek me out.

"You'd better get going," I say.

Rand doesn't need telling twice. With another half-grunt, that could – maybe – be another "thanks" he starts the engine and eases the tractor forward.

"What was that?" my mom asks.

"Oh, I just said, 'Happy mowing.'"

"He's cute," my mom says, shading her eyes to track Rand's progress as he mows the last uncut area up on the flat part of the lawn.

"I won't tell Dad you said so."

"Seriously, Austen. I can see he's charming, but he's here because of something that happened in the city. I don't know the details, but Kurt told me he was in trouble."

Her disapproval brings out the devil in me. I tsk. "He's got bad manners too: he didn't even help clear the dishes after breakfast."

"Joke all you want. There's something about him I don't like."

"So maybe Dad doesn't have anything to worry about after all? You're not that into him?"

"Austen, I've got one daughter willing to push every button I have. I don't need you starting."

I turn to face her. "Mom, from where I stand, I haven't done one single thing to push any of your buttons. I'm sorry if you think I have."

She presses her lips together until they pale. "You'd better get going to work."

She's right. Especially if I want to fit in a quick ride on Mac first.

Still, even though I should leave right now, I give in to a sudden impulse that makes me run toward Rand. He brakes, and puts the tractor in neutral, and I should probably be pleased he at least knows how to do that. "I guess you're going to mow the slope down to the water on the diagonal like your uncle usually does – right?"

He blinks twice, then gives his head a small shake. "Yeah, right. Of course I am." This time it's not a grunt, or my imagination. This time he says it: "Thanks."

As I run over to pick up my bike, I catch a glimpse of my mom watching me through the screen door. I don't pause to look too carefully – if I do, I'm afraid I'll see a woman who has just had one very big button pushed.

***

Mac dances sideways, but the lift in his ribcage, and the set of his ears tell me it's a shimmy, instead of a shy. *I-feel-fantastic*, rather than *I'm-scared-and-want-to-be-somewhere else.*

I rub his withers – "Good boy" – and he flexes a deeper arch into his shiny bay neck, confirming this is a horse so full of himself it just has to spill out.

I know how he feels. In fact, I have a hunch Mac and I are ping-ponging joy back and forth between us. A kind of "I feel great," "No, I feel great," dance.

Mac's joy, exuberance – just his general horsiness – have helped me forget everything my mom said. Except the bit about Rand being cute. And charming. The more I think about it, the more I think both are very, very true.

When we turn back into the driveway from our extra-quick before-work hack, Meg looks up from raking gravel into a couple of rain-eroded potholes. "How is he?"

"Happy, prancy, amazing."

She squints against the morning sun. "He looks it." She folds her hands over the handle of her rake. "And you sound it."

I grin. "Yeah, well, you know ..."

A familiar blue van creeps respectfully around the turn into the drive and Meg and I both watch as the side door glides open. The first of our gaggle of pony-obsessed day campers spills out and waves her sparkly pink-and-purple crop in our direction.

Meg turns back to me. "No, I don't know, exactly. You'll have to tell me later."

"Will do." I cluck Mac forward again. "I'll just turn this guy out, and be right back to start work."

***

Thank goodness Meg wants me to start the morning by cleaning the barn.

I love making what was messy, neat. I love setting myself the challenge of being as careful with my mucking as I can; sifting the clean bedding from the soiled, with the personal challenge of dumping as little as possible on the manure pile.

There wouldn't normally be stalls to muck smack dab in the middle of the glorious island summer. These days, with their high daytime temperatures and blazing sun tempered by the never-still island winds, are the perfect days for horses to live outside, stretch their muscles, kick up their heels ... not poop in stalls to make work for people like me.

Unless you're a short, chunky pony prone to laminitis. "That grey will founder if he even looks at grass," Meg had warned me about the heaviest of the four we have on inside board.

Short, and fat he may be, but also apparently highly successful in pony divisions at the big hunter shows around Toronto, along with the other three ponies who've all come with their owners to "have fun" and "run wild" on the island – except not during the day lest their dark glossy coats bleach out and endanger their ribbon-winning streak when they all go back to their regular show barns.

I catch a glimpse of Mac outside with sun washing over the smooth nap of his thoroughbred coat and nobody worrying whether he goes a shade, or four, lighter. He's beautiful now, and he will be no matter what colour his coat ends up. He's the equine equivalent of a teenage boy, but no teenage boy I've ever met is that good-looking while not possessing an ounce of arrogance. Not Tyler, for sure. Rand, on the other hand ...

The pitchfork starts to slip out of my relaxed grip. *Get a move on, Austen*. I'm not being paid to stand around and daydream about horses and boys all day. *Remember, no time for guys*.

It's time to sweep and Meg's left the watering can full – it's little things like that that make it easy to work for her.

I stride up and down the barn, sprinkling figure-eight patterns on the floor. Next, I make a brisk back-and-forth pass with the broom down the centre, then whisk the left-over bedding and good old barn dirt into the stalls, and it's done. The place looks perfect.

I step out into the searing sun to give Meg some back-up on helping the posse of girls learning how to pull their ponies' manes.

***

Meg's got her head in the fridge at Jared's house where she's living while we rent her cottage and while Jared's mom is away nursing his sick grandmother. She's handing me cold drinks, the sandwich I stashed in there this morning, a big container full of pasta salad, a jar of pickles ...

I tap her back. "Hey, hold up. I'm going to drop this stuff."

She straightens, grins. "You're right. Most of it's for Jared, anyway. If he wants more once he comes in for lunch, he can dig it out himself. Let's eat."

We sit side-by-side on the sun-warmed planks of the porch steps and watch the girls building a "horse" out of a bunch of hay bales – they're putting a bareback pad on top, taking turns "riding."

"They're so funny, aren't they?" Meg asks. "They're spending the whole day with horses – there are ponies right there ..." She points to the sand ring where each corner holds a haynet with a pony working his way through the flake of hay inside, "... but they can't even take a break for half-an-hour to eat lunch."

"One-track minds," I say.

She smiles. "I know. I was the same way before I discovered boys." Jared's pick-up truck rolls into the yard. He parks, gets out, and waves over at us, holding up a "one-minute" finger and pointing at the barn. Meg waves back. "Well, one boy, anyway."

On his way into the barn Jared pauses in front of the camp girls and says something to them.

Once he's disappeared through the doors, one girl thumps her hand over her heart and gives an exaggerated knee buckle, and the rest giggle.

There they are, all horse-crazy, with boys just a hint on their radar, and next to me is Meg who's been dating the same guy for years – happily it would seem – and I guess I'm somewhere in the middle.

Recently dumped, but since the sight of Mac pretty much wiped out my heartache, I guess not by the love of my life. OK with looking forward to Friday nights spent detangling Mac's tail, or using a bot knife to remove eggs from his legs, or just sitting in the hammock at the cottage watching the big horse graze.

Meg elbows me. "Hey, I almost forgot; what had you smiling this morning?"

"Oh ..." It's true there was something light and fun about having Rand in our kitchen for breakfast, but I doubt I'll see him again – his uncle will probably pull him off lawn-mowing duty if he finds out Rand couldn't even diagnose an empty gas tank.

I answer Meg with a question. "You know Kurt Nicklesen?"

She swallows a mouthful of her cold drink. "Kurt across the bay from the cottage? With the ever-barking dogs? "

The reminder of my mom, just last night, yelling, "Oh! Shut Up!" across the water makes me giggle. "Yeah. That's him."

She shakes her head. "Not really, other than once our floating dock broke free and washed up over at his place. And, of course, my parents pay him to keep an eye on the cottage when we're not around. He's mowing the lawns there this summer, isn't he?"

I nod. "Yeah. Well, sort of."

"What do you mean, sort of?"

"He brought his nephew to do the mowing this morning. Which would have been fine, except ..."

"Except what?"

I giggle. "Except the mower ran out of gas and he had no clue. I found him standing there, scratching his head, staring at the thing."

Meg laughs. "Where's he from? No, wait, don't tell me ..."

"Toronto!" We both say it at the same time.

Then she straightens, tilts her head and looks at me. "That's funny, but that's not the kind of smiling you were doing this morning. Is he cute?"

Deflect, deflect, deflect. My cheeks are warming and I have to find a way to distract her. "Oh, God, it's not like that. My mom says he was in trouble back in the city."

Guilt instantly seizes me – *nice job of throwing the poor guy under the bus to save your pride, Austen.*

Meg lays her hand on my arm. "Look. Here comes Jared. He'll either know about this problem nephew from Toronto, or he'll find out."

"Maybe I shouldn't have said that. It was probably just third-hand gossip my mom got wind of."

Meg cuts me off. "Don't you want to know more about him?"

"I ... uh ..." I smile. "Yeah, I guess. I mean, now that he knows how to gas up a mower it's conceivable he could come back; maybe I should know a bit about him."

"Cool," Meg says. "Hey, Jared, c'mere. We have something to ask you ..."

• RAND •

Chapter Eight

Turns out I don't have to walk home from my mowing job after all.

I'm halfway up that long country driveway when my uncle's truck turns onto it. Seeing me, he backs out again and waits on the road.

When I'm level with the mailbox he calls out of his open window, "Change of plans. Hop in."

"OK, where ..." While I'm fumbling for my seatbelt, he's already accelerating, and the air through the open windows, combined with an assault of thunderous classical music, puts an end to my question.

Finally I point at the radio on the dashboard and yell, "What *is* this?"

"Huh?" he asks. Then lifts his eyebrows. "Oh. Rachmaninov."

"Of course it is." I keep my muttering too quiet for him to hear, though, because the opus is better than the country music I expected.

We drive, and drive, and drive. This island is so unexpectedly big.

We cruise through the village, and my stomach rumbles as I remember the near-empty fridge at my uncle's house. Stocking up wouldn't be a bad idea.

We're not going to do it now, though. We keep driving to the half of the island I haven't seen yet – west of the village. The highway hugs the shoreline here, with the land dropping away sharply to my right. Looking straight out my window I have sweeping views of the lake and of Kingston on the other side of it.

There's a flotilla of sailboats bobbing about halfway between us and the mainland, and I'm trying to count the sails when the truck slows and we turn left.

Up a rise that looks slight, but the truck engine's labouring, and the gears are switching, and we keep climbing until we hit a flat spot already occupied by multiple pick-up trucks.

Now I can see what I couldn't from the road; the outline of a large building – a foundation I guess – and all around it men wearing tool belts.

My uncle cuts the engine and the music dies with it.

It's not quiet, though, because now I can hear hammering, sawing, shouting, laughter.

"What ...?" I try again.

"A barn-raising." My uncle climbs out of the truck.

"Huh?" I hop to the ground and close the truck door behind me.

"This is the Clancy farm."

"OK." I saw the name on the mailbox.

"The barn was struck by lightning a couple of weeks ago. Burnt to the ground ... well, to the foundation anyway."

We're walking toward the foundation now – my uncle buckling on a tool belt he pulled out of the back of the truck – and the boards I originally thought were randomly sprinkled on the ground, now come into focus as structures, with shapes.

"We were meant to do this last weekend," my uncle continues. "But it poured rain and there were more thunderstorms. Turns out a bunch of guys are available today, so today it is."

"Today it is for what?" I ask.

"For building the barn."

"In one day?"

He nods. "The foundation's fine. Ian Clancy and his sons have all the materials. The walls are even framed up.

We'll get the whole exterior done – including the roof – before we leave today."

I have dozens more questions to ask, but I can't figure out which one to ask first, and there's a guy walking over, holding his hand out, saying, "Hey, Kurt, great to see you."

"Brought my nephew, Rand," Kurt says.

The man reaches for my hand. "Ian Clancy. Thanks for coming. We can use all the help we can get."

I think of me not even knowing when a lawn tractor was out of gas. I'm not likely to be much help. I look at my uncle, waiting for him to point that out, but he just says, "Point us in the right direction."

It turns out I was wrong about helping. It's not glamorous, for sure, but I'm busy from the moment we get close to the build. The men never stop moving and their labour leads to all sorts of small jobs that need to be done.

I fetch nails, screws, and other equipment. Instead of a tool belt, I carry a garbage bag with me everywhere and scoop up anything that won't burn – broken nails, offcuts of metal sheeting, and more.

If it will burn – sawdust, splinters of wood, no-longer-needed shims – I sweep it up and dump it in an ever-growing bonfire pile.

I meet Mrs. Clancy when she beckons me to the house to carry Thermoses of coffee and tea, and a huge plate of muffins, to the construction site.

I'm surprised this isn't bothering me – doing grunt work, being a gofer – I'm amazed my fists aren't clenched around the broom handle and I don't grunt at Ian's wife when she hands me the tray to carry.

The fact is, I like being here. The smell of fresh-cut wood, and the fluffiness of sawdust soothes me. The progress of the barn is fast, and fascinating, and I have a front-row seat. And nobody else acts like what I'm doing is silly, or embarrassing.

So, if I worked myself into an attitude, I'd be the sole source of it and, for once, I don't have the will, or energy to do that.

Turns out my earlier worries about food were ridiculous. At lunch there are huge vats of steaming chili, and baskets of corn bread, and ice-filled buckets of drinks. The biggest pan of brownies I've ever seen tops the whole meal off.

I'm squinting up at the nearly covered roof, watching one of the Clancy boys, who's about twelve years old, handle himself, and a hammer, and nails, when my uncle taps my shoulder. "Hey, time to go."

"Huh?" It takes me a minute to focus on him. "How old is that kid?"

He looks up at him and answers my real question. "He's grown up doing this stuff. You did good today."

No I didn't ... Who are you kidding? ... Oh yeah, I'm the maestro of sweeping. I think them all, but I say. "Thanks."

Then I add, "Really? It's time to go?"

My uncle shrugs. "It's up. It's weathertight."

It's amazing.

"Anyway," he continues. "The guys from the fishing lodge are going to be on the next boat. Since I'd planned to do a day's worth of stuff before they arrived, I guess I'd better at least make sure I beat them there so I can have food cooking when they show up. I'll drop you home on the way over there."

"Home," he said.

Home.

I'm still not sure if it sounds right, but it definitely doesn't sound wrong.

• AUSTEN •

Chapter Nine

Maybe it's because there was an extra body here at breakfast – an extra broad-shouldered, tall body who ate a lot, and smelled like gasoline in a weirdly OK way – but with just Shaw, my mom, and me at the dinner table, it feels really quiet.

"Eliot not coming down at all?" I ask my mom.

She shakes her head, only meeting my gaze on the final pass. Her eyes hold equal parts frustration and fear.

I shouldn't have asked.

"I feel like it's getting worse again," I say. Knowing better still doesn't make me able to shut up.

"We have an appointment over in Kingston tomorrow," my mom says.

"That's good." I believe it is, but not for the reasons my mom might think. I believe it's good because letting a professional deal with my sister's anorexia for an hour means that's an hour my mom's not shouldering it. "Do you need me to watch Shaw? Meg probably wouldn't mind if I brought him to work."

"I think he'd kill me if I didn't take him with us. There's a Lego set he has his eye on in the toy store on Princess Street." She pauses, reaches across the table to lay her hand on my arm, and squeezes. "It was really sweet of you to offer, though."

I freeze at the contact of her smooth, cool palm on my skin. My dad's the toucher in our family – full of hugs, and kisses, and tickles, and pats on shoulders, and arms, and bums. It's fine that my mom doesn't initiate physical touch. It's just her. She shows her love in healthy meals cooked, and routines carefully implemented and strictly observed, and weird, literary names bestowed upon her children.

Here, now, her touching me right after we've talked about my sister seeing the latest in a long parade of eating disorder specialists – it sends a shiver up my spine.

Don't show her. Keep it light.

I take a deep breath, meet her eyes, and smile. "Speaking of sweet, do we have any dessert around here?"

"Dessert! Dessert! Dessert!" Shaw bangs his fork on the table in time to his chanting.

My mom lifts her eyebrows. "Hmm ... thanks for that Austen. Tell you what – you hang up Shaw's wet stuff from our swimming today, and I'll see what I can come up with to satisfy my two little sweet tooths here."

***

"How many towels can one four-year-old use?" I say it even though there's nobody to hear me.

I know it wasn't just one four-year-old – Shaw spent the day splashing with the twins who live in the bungalow that sits where our gravel road intersects with the highway – and I actually quite like hanging the brightly striped towels to flutter dry in the evening breeze, but the pile does seem to be bottomless.

I snap the wrinkles out of them, and peg them tight against the gusts of wind that have been known to whip across the bay. From right over there ... I squint into the distance, my eyes finding the point where Rand's uncle lives.

What's that on the porch? Movement. A hand? Rand's hand? I shake my head. More likely one of the dogs whose barks carry clearly across the water on windless days, drawing sighs from my mom, and mutters of "Barking dogs in the city, barking dogs in the country – can't get away from them."

I keep looking. Why? It's not like he was nice to me. It's not like he was easy to spend time with.

But ...

There was something about him. Something that felt familiar. Something *wounded*. Something I feel somehow compelled to fix – or at least investigate.

It can't hurt to investigate ... right?

I drop my eyes to the surface of the water. It's still. As happens fairly often here, in these low-lit hours after dinner and before the moon takes over from the sun, the wind has died off. It'll be back; starting with a breath here and a flurry there, and building to a steady blow, but for now it's in abeyance.

I secure the last corner of the final towel and run inside. "Forget dessert, Mom! Water's flat. Doing a dock swim!"

"Right now?"

I'm wrestling the straps of my sleek training suit over my shoulders. "Yup!" I yell through my open bedroom door.

"It'll be dark soon. The wind'll come back up."

I'm in the hall now, shoving stray strands of hair under my swim cap. "That's why I'm going right now."

"They said there was a chance of a thunderstorm."

"You know those always stay over the mainland."

"Take your swim safe float!"

I wave the inflated neon orange bag in front of her face. "Got it. Going."

"OK ... have fun ..."

"I will ..."

As I slip into the water I tell myself the hammering of my heart is from my run down to the shore. That's it. Nothing else. I'm not even looking across the bay at the far shore, and the dock, and the flutter of movement that was, or wasn't there, a few minutes ago.

***

I play the inches game. If I get an extra inch out of this stroke, and one more out of this one, and then another inch *now,* and *now,* and *now,* I'll take multiple strokes off my trip.

Get there that much faster.

I want to get there while Rand's still outside.

Urgency is the enemy of good form: good swimming. Urgency tightens my chest, constricts my lungs, tenses and shortens my muscles.

Inches, inches, inches. Losing all those inches I fought so hard to gain.

Chill, Austen.

The quickest way to get there is to relax, glide, slide, ease through the water.

I take my deepest exhale yet – bubbling the water all around my face – and refocus on the length of my strokes.

Imagine the dock's straight ahead. Imagine I'm reaching for it now.

Stroke, glide, stroke, glide, and my rhythm's recaptured.

Stroke, glide, stroke, glide ...

A two-hand touch and I'm done. There. Arrived.

"Ha!" I pull my goggles off. A surge of triumph always hits me when I'm done my assigned set. It could be just a short two-hundred metre freestyle in the pool, or a much longer stretch than this one, but something about yanking off my goggles trips a sweet sense of completion in me.

Rand's here. I didn't want to count on him being here, but I would have been deflated if he wasn't.

"What on earth are you doing?" he asks. His question sparks a fizzle of pride in my chest. I think he's impressed.

A grin stretches my cheeks. "I do it all the time. Best thing in the world to have after dinner is a long swim."

He's crouching low, and he loses his balance a bit. He throws his hands in front of him, and one comes down on the dock incredibly close to where my own hand's gripping the boards. I could reach my pinky finger out and touch him. I almost do, but then he talks. "Funny, I always think a big bowl of ice cream is the best thing to have after dinner."

Mmm ... ice cream. It's become a loaded topic in our household. One of the many things Eliot hates finding in the kitchen. So, even though I love it, and so does Shaw, we rarely-almost-never have it. Thinking of it now, the munchies I always get from swimming intensify. "You just made me want ice cream!"

"There's that place in the village – is their ice cream any good?"

My heart double-thumps. Is that a quest for information, or an invitation?

But, remember, I don't have time for dates with guys.

I could have time for ice cream, though ...

I should just be direct – 'Why are you asking?' That would be the simple, smart, straightforward thing to do. I take a deep breath, and open my mouth, and I'm cut off by a blinding flash followed almost instantly, by a resounding boom, and Rand's yelling, "Holy crap! Get out of there!" and I'm not thinking about ice cream anymore.

• RAND •

Chapter Ten

Whoa, OK, this super-pretty girl is standing in a bathing suit, in my uncle's kitchen dripping river water all over the door mat. With her wet hair slicked back, her eyes look huge, and her skin's all rosy from the exertion of her swim and the dash into the house.

My eyes are drawn to the goosebumps on her arms, then across her chest to where her nipples are poking up under her bathing suit and ... *I should not be looking at those.*

Her eyes. Look at her eyes. I yank my gaze up, and ask, "Are you cold?" and dig my left thumbnail into the soft skin of my right palm because I'm positive she knows exactly what prompted my question.

She crosses her arms across her chest – yup, I'm busted – but all she says is "Freezing," then nods.

"Do you want some tea or something?" I am so lame. I don't even know if there are teabags in the house.

"A towel would be awesome."

"Oh, shit, yeah. A towel. Sorry."

There's this kind of utility-slash-laundry-slash-junk-slash-mud room off the kitchen and I turn there to look for a towel. I'm halfway across the room when the yellow dog who, as it turns out, is named Dole – as in pineapple-coloured – noses right up to Austen and starts licking water drops off her leg.

"Oh God," I say. "I'm sorry. He's so disgusting." I back-track and reach for a collar, but the stupid dog must have slipped it off. Again. Trouble this dog is. Always trouble.

I grab at the ruff of his neck but it's too fat for me to get a grip.

"You're so bad," I'm telling Dole. "Really terrible." Finally – desperately – I stick my hand between his tongue and Austen's skin.

"Whoa!" she yells. "It's really fine. I can take care of him. Just get me a towel. Please."

Note to self – do not touch bare legs of girls I hardly know.

The towel I find is deeply worn in the middle. I normally don't notice the state of linens – much to my mom's chagrin – which shows how bad it is; almost see-through.

I watch while Austen finds enough terry left on the edges to dry herself with – maybe it's a good thing both dogs are now licking water drops off her skin.

My attention flicks to outside. It's gone nighttime dark, just like that. The lightning keeps illuminating the roiling clouds, and the thunder is so close I can feel it in my chest. It's raining now, too, so hard that during the lightning flashes the drops are visible bouncing off the deck, dock, surface of the bay – everywhere.

I gaze back at Austen bent over, drying her feet, and she looks up. "Could you stop staring? It's kind of freaking me out."

Back in the city, back not so long ago, I'd say something like, "Don't flatter yourself. I have better things to stare at than you."

And she'd know I was lying because I'd be blushing furiously.

Today, though, I'm mellow from my long day of tiring, but interesting work.

For the first time in a long time I can't feel the huge, lumpy knot right under my breastbone. The crazy thing? I didn't even know that knot was there. Until now. Because it's gone.

And, yeah, I am staring. We both know I'm staring.

So, instead of denying it, I ask, "Did you just wipe between each individual toe?"

Her already-huge eyes widen even more. Wow. She's adorable even as we discuss foot-drying techniques. "Of course I did. You should always do that."

"Seriously?"

"Unless you want athlete's foot."

"Wow, I guess I've been living dangerously all these years." Although, actually, I have had a couple of cases of athlete's foot ...

She straightens and her look intensifies to a glare. "I am not having this conversation with you. It's completely rude to stare me down while I dry myself ... listen, do you at least have some clothes I can put on?"

"What clothes would I have that you could wear?"

"My dad's clothes. The ones we loaned you this morning ... you know, those ones?"

Crap. Where are those clothes? Not neatly washed-and-folded ready to return to her. Oh yeah, they're in a ball on a lawn chair in the corner of the room where my uncle chucks all the bills, and flyers, and free newspapers he brings in from the mailbox.

I start for the chair at the exact same time as the phone rings. I fumble the receiver from the base, wedging it between my chin and shoulder and saying "Hello? Can you just wait a sec?" then I grab the wadded-up t-shirt and shorts, hand them to Austen and wave in the direction of a doorway.

'You can change over there,' I mouth, then turn my focus back to the phone. "Yeah, sorry. Hi."

"Rand?" the voice on the line says. "Is that you?"

All the mellow, all the chill, and the amusement of bugging Austen about her toe-drying meticulousness evaporate.

The voice on the phone is my mom's.

I take a deep breath and, yup, there it is. Sharp and pointy. My good friend the anxiety knot poking at me from the inside out.

"Hi Mom," I say.

• AUSTEN •

Chapter Eleven

I find a powder room, struggle out of my wet suit, use the least-damp bits of the sad towel to dry the skin that was under my suit, and pull my dad's way-too-roomy t-shirt over my head, then roll the far-too-big waistband of his shorts over several times.

The cotton's wrinkled from Rand's throw-in-a-corner clothing storage solution, but it's soft and dry and I've rarely felt anything nicer against my skin.

I throw my shoulders back; ready for commentary from Rand, only to find he's still on the phone.

"Yeah, I know Mom."

His voice is different. Less laid back. Younger. More tense.

"I saw your messages. I'll fill it out tomorrow."

He reminds me of the guy I met this morning. Which, true, was not that long ago, but he's seemed completely different tonight. Until now.

"No, I'm not drinking." Which is true, although he does take a mighty swig from his can of root beer.

"Yes, fine, go ahead and ask Kurt. No trouble."

"No, he's not here now, but if he was, he'd tell you."

"A couple of small jobs for Kurt." He pauses. "Well, it's not exactly easy to get a job in the middle of the country with no car."

"No!" He bangs his can on the counter and rubs his hand across his forehead. "Listen, I'll find something. You don't have to call that place."

"Yes. OK. I hear you ... Yes, I'll mail it tomorrow."

It's only when he turns and faces me that I realize I've been standing, listening pretty much the same way he stood and stared at me drying myself off. He pauses for one second, then sticks his tongue out at me.

Nobody's done that to me since I was Shaw's age.

Shock. Anger. Laughter.

They hit me one after the other.

Closely followed by a feeling of *Oh Yeah?* that makes me wrinkle my nose and cross my eyes right back at him.

Then, since I'm no longer frozen in one spot listening to him, I pad across the floor – my bare feet sticking to something suspicious on the linoleum – and fill the kettle, turn it on, and start opening and closing cupboards evaluating the hot drink selection.

Rand watches me the whole time. I've found packets of the horribly unhealthy hot chocolate my mom will never buy for us – "It's all sugar and God knows what else," – pulled them out, and am about to close the cupboard when he steps behind me and jams his hand in the way.

I feel the warmth of his body behind me. I hear a woman's voice rising and falling in the phone receiver he still has pressed to his ear. I smell root beer on his breath. His hand, right in front of my face, points into the cupboard and I stand on tiptoes and look deeper and see a bag of marshmallows. *Cool.*

When I let myself down from my toes, my heel lowers onto his foot.

He whips it out from under my foot and, faster than I can blink, slaps his foot on top of mine.

A video clip flashes into my head of Bandit, resting her muzzle on Manda's right shoulder. When Manda reaches back to tickle her muzzle, Bandit whips her nose over to Manda's left shoulder.

Responding to that memory, wanting to bring back the version of Rand from before the phone call, I whip my foot out and smack it right back on top of his.

'Hey!' he mouths, and gets me back.

'No way!' I answer wordlessly, then go for him again, trip, and grab at the counter.

I'm gasping for breath, and so is he. He barks out a short, sharp laugh. "What? No, I'm not laughing at you Mom. One of the dogs just got in my way."

The kettle's boiled and I'm pouring our hot chocolates by the time he hangs up the phone.

"Aggressive," he says.

"Me, aggressive? You're the aggressive one."

"No, you definitely started it."

I point to the phone. "Did your mother not teach you anything? The guest is always right." I wave the spoon I'm using to stir our drinks. "And, before you ask – yes, I'm your guest."

"Hmm, yeah, well, as you might have heard, my mom's not really into spending time with me these days. Hence, me being here. Hence, her plans to send me to boarding school."

The marshmallows are stiff and stale, but I figure the hot drink will soften them. Marshmallows don't really have a best before date, do they?

"Speaking of moms, mine is probably freaking out right now. Any chance you can drive me home?"

He pops a hardened marshmallow straight into his mouth. "No chance at all since a) look outside – do you see a vehicle? And b) my license is suspended."

I'm carrying the mugs to the table, and the jerk of my hand sends a slosh of hot chocolate down the side of the both cups. "Suspended?"

He nods. Looks me straight in the eye. "I drove to a party. I drank when I was there. I kind of forgot there wouldn't be anybody else to drive the car home, and I really had to take the car back because I'd borrowed it from my neighbour without asking. It would have been fine, except I fell asleep right before I got to my house. I woke up crashed into my neighbour's porch. And, before you ask, yes the same neighbour whose car I borrowed."

Stole, I think. "Did you hurt anyone?" It's my biggest fear. I'm a drunk driving activist's wet dream. I can look at a perfectly good car, and a perfectly whole person, and imagine both twisted and bloodied. At a party earlier this year I sat on the hood of a car so the guy who brought it couldn't drive away. When he did anyway – rolling me off the hood as he turned out of the driveway – I went inside, repeating his license plate under my breath, and called the police.

Rand is talking calmly, evenly, about something that gives me heart palpitations just to think about.

"Nobody hurt," he says. "Not even myself."

"You were so, *so* lucky."

He tilts his head, furrows his brow. "I ... *really* ... lucky? I lost my job, lost what friends I had, my parents won't talk to me, I'm in exile at my uncle's bachelor pad, and I'm headed to boarding school. That's your definition of lucky?"

Is he joking? He must be joking. "But those things are all your fault. They're natural consequences of what you did. You can get past all those things. You could never get past killing somebody."

"Wow, tell me what you really think."

Move on, Austen. I don't have this guy pegged as someone who responds well to preaching.

"I really think I'd better call my mom before she has kittens."

"Why?"

"Why what?"

"Why would your mom be freaking out? Why do you have to call her right now? I mean, you're how old?"

I dither between answering 'Sixteen' and 'None of your business.' I settle on, "It's not about me. She's got my brother and sister to deal with. I help."

"So your sister's young? Like your brother?"

There's no way I can tell him Eliot's eighteen. "It's complicated," I say.

He shakes his head. "Whatever. You're old enough to look after yourself, and you're on a frigging island, and it's not even late. You can at least drink your hot chocolate in peace before checking in."

I lift the receiver from the table between us and punch in the numbers silently – purposefully – staring at him as the phone rings.

My mom answers and, for the second time tonight, a mom phone call becomes a spectator sport.

"Austen! Oh my God, where are you? I've been calling your phone ..."

"My phone's at home Mom. I was swimming. You knew that."

"Yes, I knew you were swimming and then a thunderstorm came up! Austen, you could have been killed."

My mom's voice is shrill with emotion and from the lift of Rand's eyebrows, I'm pretty sure he's hearing everything.

"I'm not dead, Mom. I'm fine. I'm at Rand's – Kurt's – across the bay. He made me hot chocolate. But, he doesn't have a car, and it's pretty dark and still raining, so I was wondering if you could come and get me."

The news that I'm not dead seems to have shifted my mom from worried to annoyed. "Well, I do have two other children to take care of here, Austen."

"I know that, Mom. I'll just finish my drink and start walking."

"No! No. Don't be silly. But I need to get Shaw into bed. That storm riled him up. As soon as he's down, I'll come get you."

"OK, Mom. Thanks." For a second I picture my family in the snug cottage. Eliot upstairs, plugged into headphones, Shaw peeling off his pyjamas as fast as my mom can put them on, and my mom, worrying about the dangers threatening Eliot from within, and the risks endangering me from the outside world, all while trying to cope with the over-exuberance of an over tired four-year-old. "Sorry," I add.

"It's OK baby. I love you."

"I love you, too."

I hang up and slide into my own chair behind my hot chocolate. Pick it up and sip to find I was right about the marshmallows – they've formed a sweet gooey sludge – and, for once, I won't be burning my tongue on a still-boiling drink.

"*I* made *you* hot chocolate?" Rand asks.

I shrug. "It was a feeble attempt to make her like you more."

"Why do you care if she likes me?"

"Good point," I say. "Note to self. Save lies to mother for truly important things."

Rand's brought the marshmallow bag to the table with him. He helps himself to another stale one.

"So, how long do you have?"

"What?"

"Before your mom gets over here. I mean, if you're right that she was wound up before, she must be losing it to think of her hot young daughter alone with an undesirable guy like me."

I look down at my dad's baggy Ottawa Race Weekend shirt – fifteen years old, from before they gave out slick, high performance running gear. I look back up at Rand. "I'm not actually that hot. I think it's mostly the outfit."

He laughs. That bark again. Except this time it goes on for longer. Finally he says. "You're so right. Thanks for pointing that out."

Then he stops and there's this quiet moment where my joke hasn't quite taken away the fact that he called me "hot."

Nobody's ever called me that before. Which, considering I had a boyfriend, is probably a bit weird. I'm not sure how to react.

There's a whine at the door and I almost knock my mug to the floor jumping up to run over. After the earlier lick-fest, Rand must have banished the yellow dog to the great outdoors. Now he's back, completely soaked, and I can smell his wet-dog odour through the screen. Wet and smelly, he's still a welcome distraction.

"Hey bud," I open the screen door and slip through. "Poor guy," I say to Rand. "He's drenched."

"Don't be too sympathetic. That dog is the most accident-prone animal you'll ever meet. He's been skunked so many times my uncle has a tomato-juice cellar instead of a wine cellar, and my uncle got him from a family who had to give him up because they had a porcupine family on their farm, and he got barbed three times in six months."

I scratch his ear. "That makes me love him even more."

"Hmm ..." Rand says. "You're one of those then? A sucker for a sad story?"

I'm about to defend my tendency to root for the underdog – I'm thinking of pointing out I actually saved Rand's butt earlier today – when the clouds part and the moon washes the river. "Whoa ..."

There's an old porch swing right perfectly aligned with the path of silver beaming out from the big moon and I drop into it – the dog doesn't even miss a beat; just comes along with me and shoves his head in my lap.

"This," I say. "Is perfect."

"What's perfect?" Rand's standing, staring at me.

I tap the wooden seat beside me. "Everything. That huge moon, and the gorgeous river, and a porch swing – who even has porch swings anymore? And even this wood ..." I run my hand over what feels like well-worn barnboard just as Rand settles onto the seat, and have to yank my fingers back to avoid making contact with him.

"Yeah," he says. "It's probably the nicest part of this wreck of a porch."

It's true the porch slants a bit, and could use a lick – or a complete coat – of paint, but I like it.

For the first time that I can remember, I'm totally relaxed. Feet swinging, body swayed by the swing. Rand and I both staring at the moon – no need to make eye contact, or conversation. I could stay here forever.

Except I called my mom.

Maybe Rand was right about that – maybe I should have just held off a while.

Moon. River. Swing. Porch. Rand's story drifts back into my head. About crashing the car into his neighbour's porch.

"Were you scared?" I ask.

"Huh?" The jump in his body travels through the swing to me.

"When you crashed the car? I mean, it's good you weren't hurt, but it sounds scary anyway."

"I ..." He looks at me for a second, then back to the river for a much longer time. I wonder if he's going to ignore my question. "I guess, yeah, I was," he finally answers.

He turns back to me. "Nobody's ever asked me that before."

I don't have time to say, 'Really? Never? Nobody?' because twin headlights appear from between the trees that line the driveway.

My mom.

When I step to the porch my legs stop moving, but the rest of my body holds the motion of the swing. I sway, and throw a hand out.

Rand catches it and our fingers twine. "I'm OK," it's my automatic reply, but his hand is warm, and his grip is strong, and, while it's true I was OK before, I'm better after he steadies me for a moment.

Fortunately my mom's now parallel to the porch, headlights beaming across the lawn to the shore; not highlighting hand-holding between Rand and me – even if it's not *that* kind of hand-holding.

I open my fingers, drop the contact, clear my throat. "Thanks for the hot chocolate."

The moon illuminates his grin. "Yeah, I did a great job making it."

"Well, thanks for not letting me get electrocuted in the river."

He shrugs, "I hate burying bodies."

"Really? It's not that bad. I'll give you some tips the next time I see you. For example, always dig your grave six inches deeper than you think you need."

I'm developing a weird fondness for his barking laugh that follows me down the stairs.

***

The raindrops start again as my mom and I bump along the driveway toward the road, and by the time we get to Kurt's mailbox, the windshield wipers are sluicing rain across the glass and still not keeping up.

My mom's already asked me how I ended up in Kurt's house.

"It seemed preferable to being hit by lightning," I said.

Now she makes a sniffing noise. "Why do you enjoy that boy's company?" She takes her eyes off the downpour for one second to shoot me a quick glare. "I hope you don't have some kind of saviour complex about him. You can't rescue everybody, you know."

I don't know if it's being tired, or the strange high I'm still on from the freedom of those moments on the porch, or what, but I blurt out, "What about Eliot?"

My mom stamps on the brakes and the car lurches. "Seriously?" She shakes her head, then accelerates again. "That's just such a stupid thing to say, Austen. Of course we *all* want to save Eliot."

I sigh. "Yeah. I know. You're right ... because he's funny."

"Pardon me?" Polite, even when irritated – that's my mom.

"You asked why I enjoy Rand's company. He's fun. That's why."

Before my mom can say anything, an almighty jagged fork of lightning splits the night sky, and the biggest crack of thunder yet booms out.

"Whoa!" I say. "That hit somewhere close."

My mom flexes her fingers, then tightens them around the steering wheel. "Let's hope it didn't wake Shaw up," she says.

Shaw's sleep – or lack thereof – and Eliot's eating – or serious lack thereof – can always be counted on to distract from my less immediate problems.

Which, right now, I'm fairly grateful for.

• RAND •

Chapter Twelve

With Austen gone, and the thunderstorm blown past, the house is quiet.

I'm not, though. I pace. The dogs follow me, nails clicking on the floor, until I tumble kibble into their bowl.

I was relaxed before, or maybe just exhausted, by the long day of hard, interesting work. I let my guard down with Austen and we had fun. At least I did. I think she did, too.

But now, I'm thinking again. Overthinking. Maybe overtired. Becoming overwrought.

I clear the hot chocolate mugs off the table. My hands want to be doing something.

Austen's words scroll through my head.

"Were you scared?"

Was I scared ... only when I was alone. Only when I'd been asleep for a few blissful minutes, just to jerk awake, breathing hard; once sweating so much I thought I'd done it again: wet myself. Black smudges developed under my eyes, and I fell asleep twice in class.

The school called my mom in the second time. She was embarrassed, defensive to the principal. "I'm doing my best. I don't know what to do." She was furious to me. "Why can't you just pull it together, Rand?"

She became obsessed, convinced, I was drinking – she ransacked my room; searched the house for bottles.

I could have told her I didn't want to drink anymore. Didn't want to drive. Didn't want to do anything. Even though I was lucky – just like Austen said – to still be in one piece, the spot where my broken phone pushed against my skin was like an invisible scar; my hand could find it instantly, at any time.

I could have told my mom, but I didn't. Could have told Marv but, nice as he was, he didn't care that much. Could have told my dad – maybe would have – if he'd been in the country.

I *was* scared, but I told nobody and, over time, the fear began to lose its sharpest edges and then, when I came here, I slept.

In the quiet bedroom upstairs, in this peaceful house, on this island nothing like my home, I put my head down on the flat pillow and only lifted it up nine hours later.

And then I met a girl who finally asked me if I was scared.

Maybe I'm starting not to be.

I hear her other words, too. "A porch swing – who even has porch swings anymore?" And her hands tracing the grain of the wood.

There's wood like that in the barn – stacks of it. I wonder ...

I go to the door, press my nose against the screen and a fresh, new, blazing bolt of lightning pulses through the sky, followed by a clap of thunder that almost defibrillates me.

Dole whines and when I crack the door he noses his chunky body out to the porch, followed closely by his much sleeker, better-behaved, and darker brother, Coal.

Rain hammers the tin roof of the porch and runs off in a near-continuous sheet.

OK, the barn's not going anywhere – I guess I'll have a look around it tomorrow.

In the meantime, my dad.

I'm thinking of him now.

He's been so busy chasing conflicts around the world, I've hardly spoken to him since the accident – no doubt a minor conflict in his eyes. When he was in a country with a cell network, my dad used to text me fairly often. Usually photographs, with brief captions like **Stunning landscape** or **Interesting culture**. Once a picture came through of a bloodied piece of rag proclaiming **T-shirt ripped off 17YO boy**, followed immediately by, **Sorry, Rand, not meant for you. Pls. delete.**

Texts are quick and immediate and no-effort. They were the perfect vehicle for our no-effort relationship and, cut off from them, neither of us has bothered to find another way to communicate.

There are ways, though. Of course there are. In the olden days people didn't have texts, but they still kept in touch.

I'm going to email my dad.

Kurt's painfully slow laptop lives in what would be the dining room if he had a dining room set. It sits on what would be the sideboard, if my uncle had china. I press the power button and have time to wash, not only the hot chocolate cups, but every other dirty dish in the kitchen, while it boots up.

I log into my webmail account, delete the Viagra / new watch / military flashlight spam that's accumulated since my last login, and select my dad from my contact list.

Hey Dad,

I hope you're OK.

I thought I should let you know I'm here.

It's funny Mom would leave me here because this house is a dump. No, wait, that should have a capital "D" – it's a Dump. I'm surprised she didn't start renovating the kitchen when she dropped me off. Then again, I guess it shows what she thinks of me these days that she *has* left me here.

This place – well, let's just say, remember that day you told me from the back, or at a distance farther than fifty feet, you couldn't distinguish me from any of the other guys at my school? Well, yeah, not the case here. No-body dresses like me. I can see why. I've already found out boat shoes aren't really the most practical footwear for mowing lawns, and even on an island people who go on boats don't wear them.

Uncle Kurt told me I'd be bored when I first came here. No phone, no booze, no TV – not satellite or streaming – and an internet connection that's pretty early two-thousands. I believed him but, weird thing, I'm way less bored here than home.

And less lonely.

I spent the night – well, not the *night* – the early evening, with a girl. She's ... well, I want to first say she's hot – because she totally is – but God, she's funny. And smart. And nice. She's really nice, Dad.

Unfortunately she's also from this really A–type family and the mom already doesn't like me, and the daughter, Austen (See? Who names their kid "Austen?" – like I said: A-type) definitely has some uptight elements to her.

So, combine her smoking body and face, and her high-expectations background, and this girl is leagues out of my league.

Ha! Come to think about it, you're probably not the right person to be talking about relationship issues with, right? I mean, considering Mom and Dan are banging like bunnies while you're away. Don't worry, I don't necessarily think they do it in your bed, but it was a shock the time I skipped World Issues and walked in on them in the kitchen. I still can't eat at the breakfast bar.

Anyway, I don't have a job yet, and still haven't paid one cent of the insurance deductible I owe. I guess I need to do something about that since Mom made it pretty clear she wants me to show her the money – I guess she wants it to help pay for my boarding at school next year.

I might not be ready to say I love it here, but I'd hate boarding at school much more.

You know, Dad, it's not like I feel you could fix everything by being here, but I do think you could try.

I'm pretty sure you're busy, so that's all I'll say for now.

Take care,

Rand

P.S. That girl? The perfect one I told you about? She asked if I was scared after the accident. I can see why nobody really cared about me, and if I was afraid. But I was. Just for the record. If you were wondering.

I re-read the message, make a few edits, then look it over again.

Hey Dad,

I hope you're OK.

I thought I should let you know I'm here.

I'm pretty sure you're busy, so that's all I'll say for now.

Take care,

Rand

That sounds about right. I press send, and shut the computer down.

Lying in bed I think of what those few words from Austen unlocked in me. Wonder how things might change if I could be brave enough to actually say some of the things I think to my dad, my mom, the people around me.

But I don't think about it for long because, like every night so far in this bed on this island, sleep steals over me, sure and deep, in the matter of a few blinks.

• AUSTEN •

Chapter Thirteen

I walk into the cottage ahead of my mom, so I'm the first one to see Eliot, standing at the kitchen sink, holding a container of ice cream, running water so hot steam billows around her.

I'd like to think it's the warm air reddening her face, but I can also see tear tracks down her cheeks, so no such luck.

Shit. Crap. Why couldn't we have walked into the disaster my mom feared – Shaw, awakened by the thunderstorm? That would have been straightforward, simple, a walk in the park, compared to this.

My mom steps close behind me and I want to fling my arms wide, block her way and her view, and say, "Nothing to see here – thanks for coming to get me – why don't you go straight to bed?"

"Eliot? What are you doing?" My mom asks.

So much for conflict avoidance.

And so it begins.

"How could you?" Eliot screams. "How could you go out and buy my favourite ice cream in the world and bring it back here?"

"I bought ice cream for Shaw. I promised him a treat."

"Peanut butter and chocolate isn't Shaw's favourite! He likes Neapolitan much better!"

"Eliot, you're being totally unreasonable. There was lots there. It wasn't just for Shaw. If you wanted some, you could have it."

Oh, Mom. Oh my Lord. Really? And the first point of the evening for taking-it-up-a-notch goes to Pamela Delaney.

Sure enough, Eliot's face contorts. She switches from yelling to hissing. "Oh, don't I know it. Do you think I'm stupid, Mom? Do you think I can't see through your ridiculous plans? You would just *love* it if I ate some of this ice cream."

First point for direct-hit-on-the-undeniable-truth goes to my sister. She is one-hundred-per-cent right. My mom would die of happiness if Eliot sat down and ate a bowl of ice cream.

Because of that my mom can't answer, and Eliot plows ahead. "You're sick! Do you know that? Completely sick.

If I was an alcoholic, would you go out and buy bottles of whiskey and leave them sitting around the house?"

Although the argument's just started – I know from long experience Eliot and my mom have a good hour of weepy irrational accusations ahead of them – Eliot's already won. Because, in Eliot's food-starved mind, the illogical is completely logical. In her head ice cream is to an anorexic what whiskey is to an alcoholic. To her it's rational, factual, right. Therefore my mom is wrong. And Eliot, despite functioning on no calories at all, will drive that point home tirelessly for the rest of the night.

Shaw will sleep through it. I'll slink away to my bed. I'll wonder if I should call my dad, then I'll reason, What's the point? He can't change anything, and he might as well get a good night's sleep so when he comes on the weekend he's in good shape to spell my mom off.

Since I came home barefoot, it's easy for me to pad near-silently up the stairs while my mom shuts off the hot water flushing the last of the ice cream down the drain and says, "Eliot ... Eliot ... Listen to me, Eliot ..."

These are the worst times for me. I know my sister has to eat. I know she's thoroughly screwing up everybody's life – especially her own. I know she can't go on like this.

But I also do, totally, understand how a bucket of peanut butter swirled chocolate ice cream looks exactly like a bottle of Jack Daniels to my sister.

Unfortunately, seeing both sides with absolute clarity doesn't make it any easier for me to know how to build a bridge between the two.

***

There are fewer sharp outbursts below – they've settled into the covering-ground-we've-gone-over-a-million-times-before phase of the argument. Both will be crying.

My dad's clothes are folded on the chair beside me, I'm in the stretchy tank-top I sleep in, and having hot chocolate at Rand's seems like a strange long-ago dream.

Tonight I have an internet connection. Faint, slow, and so delicate I have to turn my tablet toward the dormer window, but it's there.

This is something I've learned quickly – that on bright sunny days, there's no hope of connecting to the WiFi trickling out of the nearest neighbours' house – I guess the signal soars off into the endless blue sky – but on overcast, dim days, the signals stay below the clouds and I can piggyback onto Betsy and Carl's connection.

I spent my first week here going up to Betsy and Carl's house most days after work at Meg's, first cleaning their henhouse, or doing some weeding in the garden to "pay" for my internet use, then sitting on their breezy deck and connecting at my leisure. This week they're away visiting their grandchildren so I'm mostly logging in on the faint connection I get down here.

Between the just-plain-spam, and the more personal spam – sixteen photos of my cousin's new kitten, new posts from one of the seventeen riding blogs I follow, updates from my high school principal reminding us all that school starts in just eight weeks, and he hopes we're all pumped – is a name that makes my cheeks stretch into a grin.

Your Best Friend

One day when I was in the bathroom, or getting us a drink, or distracted in some other way, Manda went into my email contacts and changed her display name to **Your Best Friend.**

I'm going to kill her, is the subject line.

She hogged Bandit's mane.

I'm not kidding – full-on Mohawk. Then she said it was my fault because this weekend is her show weekend and Bandit's mane was too long to braid.

I was *this* close to taking the scissors she used to chop Bandit's mane and cutting off that long fishtail braid she always wears.

My fingers fly over the keys:

OK a) I'm sorry. You have the worst half-leaser in the history of leasing horses, b) check my Facebook timeline – I shared an article a couple of weeks ago about how you can use thinning scissors on a horse's mane – maybe you can at least get Bandit's to lie halfway flat.

I press send, and even before I can delete the rest of the fresh messages in my inbox, there's the chime of a new message from Manda.

She's online. I can picture her sitting in her room, probably waving her feet in the air as she waits for the latest crazy shade of nail polish to dry on her toes. It's weirdly immediate.

You're there! her message says. **Wanna phone?**

Would love to but a) Mom and Eliot are brawling downstairs b) phone is downstairs.

Do not go downstairs! I've only felt the deeply tense aftermath of a Pam-Eliot battle – can't imagine the ferocity of an in-progress fight. Stay safe!

The bottom stair squeaks. Battle over; Eliot's on her way up.

Gotta go! Sister mounting stairs. Must play dead.

I disconnect, put my tablet to sleep, and stow it under my bed in record time.

Head on pillow, back turned to my sister's bed, I close my eyes and regulate my breathing to a rhythm that feels forced at first, but soon comes with ease.

I'm on the edge of sleep – slipping – just barely aware of the night symphony of frogs and bugs in the fields outside, and of the breeze from the open window licking over the thin sheet covering me.

So nice ...

Then *pad, pad, pad* – barefoot feet scuff the wide-planked floorboards. My mattress dips, with an accompanying protest of springs, and my sister slips under my sheet.

She doesn't say anything, but every half-minute or so she hiccups – a soft hitch of leftover emotion when there are no tears left to spill.

I don't turn. Don't speak. But I do snake my hand back, across my waist and toward her, where I find her hand coming forward to meet mine. We lace fingers and I give hers a squeeze and that's the last thing I remember before sweet, sucking sleep takes me away.

• RAND •

Chapter Fourteen

Sunlight floods my room very, very early in the morning.

That'll happen when you don't close your curtains.

Which I didn't last night.

I lie in bed with my eyes still closed and let the early rays wash my face. I've always been able to see colours on the back of my lids when my eyes are shut, and this morning's no exception. I spend a few seconds watching the kaleidoscope of warm, happy hues.

I know my uncle thinks left to my own devices I'd be a stay-in-bed-till-noon teenager.

Which, to be fair, is all he's ever seen of me. All anyone's seen of me for a long, long time.

I can't remember the last time I didn't need three alarms to get me out of bed. For Christmas my sister got me this alarm clock that jumps down off my bedside table and rolls around my room emitting random beeps until I hunt it down. Some mornings I don't even bother – just put my pillow over my head and curse.

It's been hard to want to get up, when for so long the only quality shut-eye I've gotten has started somewhere around four or five in the morning. That's when the snap awakenings seemed to trail off and I could sleep solidly. So an alarm going off two or three hours later hasn't exactly been welcome. And sleep, when I could get it, was a great anaesthetic. I wasn't bored, angry, frustrated, or anything when I was sleeping. I was just not present … not anywhere.

I used to like to get up to run with my dad in the morning before work. Or to sit at the breakfast table with my mom and take the sports section while she read business. Or, even, to fight with my sister over who got the last bowl of mini-wheats.

But, hey, life moves on. Sisters go to university. Dads who are war correspondents for major news networks, and win prizes for their work, start covering scarier and more remote wars. And moms, well, should I really be mad at my mom for finding someone else to spend time with when my dad's so far away? It's maybe a bit unfortunate for me that the person she's hanging out with is my former basketball coach – when basketball was another thing that made me like getting out of bed in the morning – but, hey, I'm not supposed to be selfish, so I should be glad for Dan and my mom. Right?

Would things have been different if my dad had been home for a while and my mom had taken off?

Maybe. Maybe I wouldn't have felt such awesome satisfaction – such "screw-you" delight – in going out that night in direct opposition to my mom's prohibition.

Then I wouldn't have crashed Joe's car. Wouldn't entered the world of trouble I've been in.

I wouldn't have ended up here. Wouldn't have met Austen.

Austen. What is up with that girl?

She's all proper: talking about drying between every toe and natural consequences, but she's tough, too: taking everything I throw at her and giving back better than she gets.

I don't quite *get* her, but I do think today might be more interesting if I ran into her again.

I open my eyes, kick the covers off, and head downstairs of my own volition to start my day with breakfast instead of lunch.

***

If this is going to be my official return to rise-and-shine, and morning-meal-eating, I deserve to have a proper meal. Right?

Which is awkward, because – except for root beer – the fridge is empty.

As is the driveway. No truck, no Kurt, no ride into the village.

I stand in the barn and stare at the rusty ten-speed leaning against a pile of the exact barnboard I was thinking of last night.

The barnboard is a stack of potential. The bike is a death trap.

Forget it. That thing's older than me.

But ... bacon. And cold orange juice. Red River bread – toasted. Oh, and a fried egg. And I'll wear a backpack and bring back all kinds of stuff from the bakery.

Once I get going the bike ride won't seem so bad.

What would Austen do?

Who cares what Austen would do?

An image of her laughing after powering her way across the bay – head down, swimming hard – jumps into my head. She'd go.

I'm as tough as her. At least.

The bike gears stick, then give, under the weight of my body on the pedals. I should probably test the brakes before I actually need them, but I don't have the heart to brake when I'm having this much trouble just moving forward at all.

I can do better than this.

I throw a burst of effort into my pedaling, and my lungs balloon to support the extra work. Blood pumps. Core temperature rises.

I fly out of the driveway, onto the road and nearly hit Austen rounding the corner on her own bike.

"Oh my God!" She swerves, and in the seconds it takes for her bike to skid out on the loose surface, and her body to hit the gravel, my mind fast-forwards terrible thoughts. It's like having a nightmare while I'm awake.

She could have a broken bone, the gravel could imprint road rash on every inch of her smooth, tanned skin, she could whack her head and bounce her brain, earning one of the things we feared most back when I played basketball: a concussion.

Her voice comes to me, "you were so, so lucky." I didn't hurt anyone that night, but I might have hurt Austen today.

My heart hammers, and my knees are weak. The fear I've been living with – that I almost killed myself – expands until, for the first time, I am truly deeply horrified that I could have killed somebody just like Austen.

She's tough, though, and mostly fine. She stumbles to her feet with blood gushing from her knee but that seems to be it.

"What the ...?!?" She turns on me. "You didn't kill anybody when you drove drunk, so you thought you'd see if you could kill me on my way to work?"

The fear part of my adrenaline response is gone, and now I'm just giddy. Reckless. Flippant. "If I wanted to kill you, you'd be dead."

"Wow! Now *that* is sympathy. Not to mention a really nice morning greeting. 'If I wanted to kill you, you'd be dead.'"

"Hey, whoa, pipe down. I didn't say I wanted to kill you – in fact I said the total opposite – and here ..." I reach into my back pocket and pull out a bandanna. They were on the table in place of napkins at the barn-raising lunch yesterday. I didn't end up using mine. I hold it out to her.

"Is this clean?"

I clap my hand over my chest. "I'm hurt that you'd ask me that. Would I offer you a dirty dressing for your cut?"

"Fine. OK." She ties it around her oozing knee, then pulls her bike upright. Takes a tentative step. "I've got to get to work."

I walk my bike beside her.

She gives me a sideways glance. "What are you doing out so early? I didn't have you pegged as Mr.-Rise-and-Shine."

I shrug. "Who says I went to bed?"

She nods. "That makes more sense. Once I left, you switched from root beer to real beer. You're out now, so you're going into the village to get some more. Hate to tell you, I don't think the beer store opens for another couple of hours."

"Maybe I'll find some bacon and eggs while I'm in there."

"Oh yeah?" she asks. "No greasy breakfast at your place this morning?"

I wrinkle my nose. "No nothing. The only thing I liked about living with my mom is she always grocery shopped."

Austen stops walking and swings her leg over the cross bar. Lifts her foot to the pedal.

"You're going to cycle?" I ask.

"I'm going to try."

Pain flits across her face on the first stroke, but she keeps pedaling and, as I pedal alongside, her features relax.

Once we're in a steady rhythm, she looks at me. "So, was all that for real? That stuff you said last night? That you got sent away – that your mom wants to send you to boarding school?"

I swerve my bike left, then right – enjoying the swooping sensation as it loops across the road – "Let's just say, if I was going to lie to impress you, that's probably not the kind of lie I'd tell. I'm fully aware there's nothing very attractive about a dad who's never home, a mom who's sleeping with my basketball coach, a sister who rises above it all by doing good in dusty, disease-ridden places all over the world, and a kid who lashes out in every stereotypical way possible: lying, cheating, drinking, stealing, and then, bringing them all together in my grand finale act which earned me a youth record and a hundred hours of community service."

"So, booze and breaking the law," she says. "That's pretty lightweight, really."

"What?" I veer my bike too sharply and nearly go down. *Who is this girl?*

"Well, the old standard is sex, drugs, and rock and roll," she says. "I think we can both agree rock and roll is out of date, but you haven't even hit the other two – I mean, not unless there's stuff you're not telling me."

I shake my head. "No drugs, and sex would involve someone wanting to spend at least five minutes with me."

"Which makes me, what?"

"What do you mean?"

She looks at her watch. "We've spent at least seven minutes together. Three times now."

"But did you want to?" I ask. "Was it voluntary?"

I expect a "No way!" delivered quickly and without hesitation. But she does hesitate. I can almost see the gears turning in her head. I decide to cut her off while I'm ahead.

"Whatever," I say. "I've had three times seven minutes to charm the pants off you, and your pants are very firmly on so, no, sex has not been one of my huge vices."

"It's not a vice anyway."

We're slowing now, approaching the intersection of our narrow country road with the blacktopped highway. "Excuse me Miss Manners. Miss Dry-Between-Each-Individual-Toe. Miss Natural-Consequences. Sex is not a vice?"

She shakes her head. "It's natural. Horses do it."

I laugh. "Birds do it."

She grins. "Bees do it."

"I don't do it."

"See?" she says. "Total lightweight ..."

I want to protest it was her turn to say 'I do,' or 'I don't' do it too, but she's already stopping, bending over her injured leg.

She unties the bandanna carefully, and we both stare for a couple of seconds but no fresh deluge gushes out of the cut. The cloth is fairly bloody, though. "How about I wash this before I give it back to you?" she says. "I hope it wasn't too important."

"Nah. I got it yesterday at this barn-raising I went to."

"A barn-raising – cool. I've always wanted to see one."

"It was pretty cool, actually."

"So you were doing construction?"

I contemplate lying, then figure at least that's one vice I don't have. Stick with the truth. "Well, I was using a broom, not a power tool."

"Probably still important," she says.

"So, is that hot?" I ask.

"Is what hot?"

"The almost-doing-construction thing?"

"Three times seven minutes ..." she reminds me.

"Yeah, OK."

"It could be hot if it was another guy." She winks.

That wink undoes me. That wink pulls me in and, for the first time I can remember in ages, includes me. That wink says 'we have inside jokes,' and 'we can communicate without speaking.' It says – at least to me it says – 'I like you.'

I'm not about to show her, though. Instead I say, "For a well-behaved girl with nice manners you can be really bitchy."

She looks at her watch. "My boss won't think much of my behaviour or my manners if I don't head up to work now."

"OK, well, uh, have a good day working."

"Have a good day eating and drinking."

She cycles across the highway, and I advance a few metres along it, before turning around and calling, "Hey!"

"What?"

"Just for the record, I did go to sleep last night. And wake up this morning. I didn't drink all night."

"Noted," she says.

Why did I tell her that? I have no idea. It just seemed important.

I felt like I wanted to earn at least a tiny bit of her respect.

• AUSTEN •

Chapter Fifteen

When we turn into the yard, Meg's lining buckets up in the grass along the barn wall.

"Ah, they get to learn how to scrub water buckets today?"

"A very important skill," she says.

"I've got another one we can teach them." I thrust out my leg and grin. "They can bandage on me."

"Whoa! Nice gash. What happened?"

"Oh ..." I wave my hand in the air. "Gravel skidded bike, knee met gravel. What's up with you? You look distracted."

She sighs. "Oh, I'm trying to organize this surprise fiftieth birthday party for Jared's mom when she gets back, but the woman who was going to cater had a huge tree branch fall through her roof last night. So, now, far from asking her to cater our party, we should probably be hosting a fundraising party for her ..."

"Oh my gosh! Was anybody hurt?" I'm pulling the hose out so it's easily accessible for the girls, right next to the scrub brushes.

"Fortunately, no. But the impact, then the rain after, did quite a bit of damage. Apparently one of those lightning strikes last night was a direct hit on an old oak tree growing right beside their house."

"Was it the last one? I was leaving Rand's house last night and I heard it. It sounded unbelievably close."

"Rand?" she asks. "Gas tank guy?"

"Uh-huh. The very same." Why am I blushing? There's nothing to blush about. Then I think of our chat about sex. Him saying, *I don't do it;* me, performing an artful and, yes, cowardly dodge to avoid saying anything. Maybe reason to blush after all. Fortunately Meg is so preoccupied she doesn't seem to notice the colour of my cheeks.

Meg's brow furrows. "I think Jared found out some stuff about him, although it'll be a miracle if he remembers what. He's in the village now picking up a load of lumber coming off the boat. He's supposed to start building a lean-to onto the barn today and – wouldn't you know it – the husband of our caterer is the one who was going to help him, so he's got his own barn to re-build.

Now Jared has a heap of materials and none of the help he needs."

"Hmmm ..."

"Hmmm, what?" Meg asks.

"Hmmm, I might have a solution for Jared's work shortage problem. Depending, of course, what exactly his opinion is of Rand ..."

***

I stand in the kitchen at Jared's house, listening to Rand's uncle's phone ring when, in my back pocket, my cell phone vibrates.

I swipe it to life. Manda. **Whatcha' doin'?**

Working.

No you're not, or you wouldn't be answering my text.

OK, OK. Long story. Tell you later.

Long story involving adventure and romance?

Rand's uncle's phone has been ringing so long, I'm taken by surprise when an answering machine kicks on. The unfamiliar deep voice on the recording throws me off-kilter.

"Um, hi. This message is for Rand. It's Austen. From across the bay." I wince. As if he knows more than one Austen. "Anyway, I'm at work – I work up at Jared Strickland's place. Where you saw me going this morning? Jared needs someone who can help with a construction project and I, uh, thought you might be interested and available." *Crap,* "Interested and available" makes it sound like a singles ad. "So, if you are, you can phone me. Here's my cell number ... Bye!"

Well, that was an awesome message. Talk about giving Rand more fuel to make fun of me.

I text back to Manda: **Definitely neither. Duty.**

Boring then. You can tell me a different long story another day.

***

When the girls show up, my oozing knee does lead to a discussion about leg afflictions – in horses. About poultices and bandaging and boots. About prevention and cures and also, how sometimes a bright set of polos just looks really, really pretty.

On the grounds that being fussed over by little girls falls under the category of "just being a horse" – as well as because he has nice long legs for bandaging – I pull Mac in, along with Jared's cousin's mare Salem, for the girls to practice bandaging.

I watch Mac like a hawk, but he shows no signs of his racetrack or eventing side while the campers work on him. One girl wraps his front legs in pink polos, while another twines purple around his back legs, and he lets his head and lower lip droop low, and hitches his off-hind. I scratch behind his ear. "You're a good sport, aren't you?"

While Mac presses his face against me, I take a long minute to watch the girls, listen to them chatter, notice how much more even, and less lumpy, their wraps are compared to when we started. Meg has an agenda – there are chores that have to be done every day, and there are topics she wants to cover with the girls – but she's also flexible enough to go with it when they're enjoying something. This bandaging lesson is one they'll always carry with them.

However, speaking of chores that have to be done, I catch Meg's eye as she straightens from checking one of the polos. "The barn?" I ask her.

It's heating up, and a few strands of hair are stuck across her forehead. She brushes them out of the way. "Yeah. I guess it's time. The girls can get the ponies out for a quick ride before it gets too much hotter. That way you can do the stalls while they're empty."

The spot where we were practicing wrapping was shaded by the barn so I didn't notice how hot it was getting.

Now, though, closing in on noon, with the sun nearly directly overhead and – strangely for the island – no breeze at all, it's roasting. The air in the barn is muggy and close, and the path to the manure pile is exposed to the blazing sun.

There's no good way to stay cool around a barn. If you wear breeches, well, they're long and hot. If you wear shorts – like I am now – hay, grass, bedding, and dirt will stick to your bare skin. Like is happening to me right now.

Stalls picked, but still needing bedding, and the aisle to sweep, and my blood feels like it's simmering in my veins; cooking me from the inside out.

I step to the barn door, hoping to catch at least a puff of moving air, and Meg calls over from the sand ring. "Your sister!"

"Huh?" I call back. Rand's face rushes into my brain; eyes wide as my mom corrected him. Rand's voice, repeating, "Pardon me?" I shift from one foot to the other and revise my reply to Meg. "Pardon me?"

She takes a step toward me, cups her mouth, and calls "Your. Sister." Then points toward the road.

Oh no.

I wave to Meg, and turn to face the road, using my hand to shade my eyes from the sun.

She is not.

Her slight figure looks very solitary in the middle of the exposed gravel road; leaning forward into the slight rise. Not even wearing a cap or visor against the noon sun.

So, *yes,* she is.

"Oh God!" I don't know who I'm saying it to, but something about hearing my words out loud helps me jump into action. Water. Definitely water. And maybe an orange? Did I bring one for lunch? My bag's still hanging on the hook just inside the barn door where I left it when I arrived this morning. Which means the unrefrigerated cheese in my sandwich will be limp, oily, and disgusting.

Oh well; least of my concerns.

I fish around in the bag and pull up an orange. Awesome. Grab my water bottle out of the side pocket, and start running along the driveway.

Chill, Austen. Don't make it look like a big deal.

I scale back to a jog. Which to a normal person wouldn't be particularly convincing because who on earth would be out for a low-key, easy jog at noon in thirty-degree heat?

Eliot isn't normal though, and when I jog onto the road right beside her, she nods, then drops to a fast walk.

"Hey!" I say. Bright. Fake smiling.

I don't say 'Holy crap. Why are you doing this? Why do you have to abuse your poor, starved body? Why do you have to scare us all half to death?'

"Hey," she answers.

She doesn't say, 'Back off Austen. Leave me alone. Being out here, running, is the only thing that's keeping me sane today.'

All today's unsaid things have been said so many times before in our family, with so little impact, that I guess Eliot and I have just given up.

I, for one, am at the point of striving to reduce harm, rather than trying to eliminate it. Maybe that's because I no longer believe it can be undone. Maybe that makes me a terrible sister. Lying in our big loft bedroom at night, listening to Eliot's slight weight creaking the time-stiffened springs of her ancient bed, wondering if one night her heart and lungs are just going to give up struggling to do their jobs with zero nutrition to fuel them, I'm often pretty sure I'm the worst sister possible.

Because I don't know how to fix Eliot, and I've run out of energy to try, and when my mom says hopeful things I nod, and make noises that sound like I agree, and think, *Nothing will change, Mom. She'll lose those three pounds you're so excited that she just gained, and she'll drop an extra three for good measure, and you'll make some more calls, send some more emails, find a new doctor, cook some more food she won't eat, and nothing will change.*

In the spirit of harm reduction, I hold out my water bottle. "Hot work today," I say.

Eliot takes it. Sips. "Yeah, thanks."

While she's doing that, I peel the orange. My fingers piercing the skin release a sharp, citrusy scent. It drifts to my nose, and springs saliva to my mouth.

I pop a segment in my mouth and mutter, "Mmm ..." as the flavour explodes in my mouth. So good on a hot day.

Eliot's eyes have followed every orange-related move I've made. I've stopped walking to eat the orange, and my sister's come to a stop, too. She isn't even fidgeting, which says something about her level of concentration on my snack.

She takes another small sip of water, and I chew another orange segment. "Good run?" My mouth's still a little full and the words are muffled. I don't care.

"Hmm? Pardon me? Oh, yeah. Good." My heart seizes. Eliot, starving herself to death, fixated on the five-to-ten calories contained in each piece of orange I consume, is still even more polite than me. She never has to be reminded to say, "Pardon me."

Three-two-one ... I hope I'm timing this right. I lift my eyebrows, pause with a chunk of orange halfway to my mouth. "Oh, hey, I'm sorry, I've eaten most of it – did you want a piece?" I tip the segment I'm holding toward her, but I don't hold it out. She has to be the one to reach for it.

"Um ..." This is where I have a leg-up on our mom. I want Eliot to take it – of course I do – but if she doesn't, I'll just shrug and say, "OK." If she does take it, I'll also say, "OK," and hand it over, and that'll be it.

With my mom – with food, and Eliot, and my mom – there is no possible neutral response. Eliot would not be able to accept, or reject this portion of food from my mother without a five-minute monologue ensuing.

I get it. I understand all the frustrations and anxieties and – let's be frank – terrors, welling up and spilling out of my mom.

But part of me also gets the panic, and fear of loss of control, and rigid need to hang onto the inner rules she's set herself, that Eliot feels. Is it possible to have the in-built understanding of an eating disorder without the disorder actually being active? If so, that's me.

My sister takes the orange from my hand, and tears spring up so fast, I have to scrunch my nose against them. I wave my hand in front of my face, "Whoa, that sun makes me sneeze."

"Yeah, well, thanks for the water and the orange," Eliot says. She's still holding the orange. Hasn't eaten it. I don't know if she will. Won't see it if she does.

"Any time." *Stop running. Walk home. Eat something.* "Have a great run."

I wave, and step back, and watch my big sister swing back into her run. Watch the pumping of her knees; the insides discoloured from where one sharp knee will bump the opposite leg, bruising her white skin.

I want to run after her, tackle her, bring her to the soft grass on the side of the road and yell. "You are fine! You are beautiful! I'm going to lose you and I can't bear it!"

We used to do that at skiing – in the middle of our ski lessons – it was usually Eliot, diving onto me, popping me out of my bindings so I'd fall to the snow. Except she'd fall, too, and we'd roll and laugh until our ski instructor complained and we weren't allowed to be in the same lesson anymore.

But doing that now, I know – saying those things – would make me lose her for sure. That would be the end of her trusting me.

Everybody thinks my sister possesses the ultimate in willpower, but nobody knows how hard I fight to make her think I don't care, just so I can hold onto a tiny piece of her.

***

I'm walking back to the barn, with my mind following my sister up the exposed hill in the blazing sun, when my phone rings.

Manda gets bored, and she just has to call me.

I fumble the phone out of my back pocket, drop it, catch it before it hits the ground, and press it to my ear, gasping, “Hey you!”

A throat clears. “Uh, it’s me. Rand.”

“Oh. Of course.” I press my hand to my breastbone, give a deep exhale. “I’m really glad you called.”

“Not as glad as if I’d been that other person you were expecting.” There’s something churlish in his tone. Something that reminds me of Shaw complaining when I cuddled the neighbour’s baby, newly home from the hospital. “You like her more than me,” he’d said. Which was fine because, at the time, Shaw was four.

Rand is not four. “Now, now. It’s not a competition. I can be glad to hear from more than one person.” Before he can inject another sarcastic comment, I continue. “What will really make me happy to be hearing from you is if you say you’re coming up here to see about working with Jared.”

Silence. Then bang-shuffle-bump, then more silence.

“Rand?” I ask. “Are you there?”

“Just getting my shoes on.”

“So I’ll see you in a few minutes?”

“You just can’t wait to see me, can you?”

The devil rises up in me. “Well, I’d rather it was that other person I was expecting, but you’ll do ...”

I want to backpedal immediately. *Too far, Austen. Probably not funny.*

But Rand's bark travels down the line. "Geez Miss Goody-Two-Shoes, if you're not careful one of these days I might start liking you."

Relief stretches a smile across my face. "Oh yeah? Because I'm so funny?"

"Because you're a little bit like me."

The dead air of his ended call saves me from having to come up with a snappy reply. I hurry my steps to go tell Meg and Jared that Rand's on his way.

• RAND •

Chapter Sixteen

I'm struggling, and grunting, and standing on my pedals wondering what this Jared guy is like, and what kind of work he'll want me to do, and whether I have any hope of living up to his expectations.

Probably not, unless he needs someone to sweep all day.

And he's probably some country bumpkin who'll be all overly friendly, and want to take me hunting and fishing with him, and it'll probably drive me crazy to work with him all day.

So go home.

Yes, I could.

Just turn around and cycle back – downhill: bonus! – and nobody will ever know I was here.

The second that thought enters my mind, a resounding whinny rings through the air.

There's a horse, head lifted, nostrils flaring, staring at me. Or at least he sure looks like he's staring at me.

Departing incognito is clearly not an option now. A gaggle of little girls is approaching, saying, "Are you Austen's friend? Are you going to help build the new stalls? Does Mac know you?"

"Come with us!" the smallest one says, and my mom, with her theory that I have "authority issues," would be amazed to see me following this girl with pink and purple bows decorating the end of two long braids tied together behind her back.

"You can lean your bike there." The girl points at a tree, and waits while I obey, then starts walking again, making a clucking sound with her mouth. "Come on," she emphasizes.

The gravel widens into a large area with a barn on one edge, and a house on the other. "They're just in there," the girl points, then falls back with the other girls who have been following me, following her. In contrast to the bright sunshine, the interior of the barn is dark, and I can't see what I'm walking into, however the chorus of little-girl giggles behind me makes up my mind that I'd better just go forward and step inside.

I'm about to cross the threshold when I pick up the first words of the conversation taking place inside.

"... wish you'd checked with me first, Austen." It's a guy's voice, so it must be my new boss – Jared.

A girl – not Austen – answers. "I told Austen to call him, Jared. Don't be so stubborn. You've got a thousand dollars' worth of materials sitting there, and who knows how long before the weather turns, or something happens so you don't have time to get this thing built. Austen made one phone call, and Rand agreed to come, no hesitation."

"Well, maybe she should make another phone call ..."

"I can't!" Austen breaks in. "He doesn't have a cell phone, so I had to call him at his uncle's, and he's already left, so there's no way I can reach him."

The other girl's voice now. "Nobody needs to call Rand and tell him anything. He'll be here soon, and he'll do his best, and Jared can judge him for himself based on the work he does."

Suddenly, there's a push of small hands on my backside, and another round of high-pitched laughter, and I'm stumbling into the barn, blinking away the grainy dimness clouding my vision.

"Rand!" Austen steps forward and I feel this bizarre rush of relief, like when I was twelve and I had a fight in the school yard and, when I was called to the principal's office, my dad stood up from one of the chairs and I thought, *Well that's OK, because you're here.*

Except, really, I've only known Austen for twenty-four hours and a bit.

Then again, in that time she's already rescued me once.

The guy who must be Jared steps forward, and he doesn't look happy, and I'm doubtful Austen can rescue me this time.

"Hi," he says. "Rand?"

So, he's young. And doesn't have a beer belly – why did I think he'd have a beer belly? He's shorter than me, but his arms are more muscled. I wouldn't want to mess with him.

"Listen," he says. "I'm going to say this straight up. I've heard some bad things about you. And, yes, I need help on this job, but not at any cost. My mom's away, and I'm the only one in charge of this farm, and now our neighbour has his own place to fix after the storm. It's no help to me if I hire you to work with me, and things go wrong."

I'm not sure if I'm supposed to answer. I'm not sure what I'd say anyway, which is why I'm glad when he keeps talking.

Even if I don't exactly enjoy hearing what he has to say.

"If I decide to give you a chance, there can't be any drinking, no smoking ..." Both Austen and the other girl, who must be her boss, Meg, make these little choking noises. I guess smoking around barns is pretty bad. "... and I expect you to be totally honest with me. I don't want you cutting corners, I don't want anything going missing ..."

"Jared!" Both girls also say this at the same time. "Come on," Austen continues, and Meg says, "That's unnecessary."

I should probably hate this guy, but the looks he's now getting from Meg and Austen make me want to laugh. He is in *trou-ble*.

It sparks this weird solidarity in me. Not enough to make me get down on my knees and grovel and beg him for his job, but enough to make me nod, and say. "Understood."

"Yeah?" Jared asks.

"Yeah," I say.

He holds out his hand. "It's a deal, then. For now. Either one of us can pull out at any time."

I take his hand, shake it hard, once. "For now," I say.

I have a job.

***

"You gonna wear that?"

"You mean jeans?" I ask.

Jared shrugs. "Sure, I guess those are jeans."

OK, upon closer inspection, the fit of his are what you'd probably describe as "relaxed." I suspect the fabric has actually been faded by age and the sun, and the distress marks are probably real.

Mine are such a deep indigo my mom forbade me from wearing them on the white couch and, when I bought them six weeks ago, they came pre-distressed. They're skinny fit and I can't quite kneel all the way down in them.

Our t-shirts may belong to the same species, but Jared's green and yellow shirt declaring **John Deere Tractors and Plows: since 1837** is a different breed from my slimfit Abercrombie & Fitch.

Whatever. It's not like I care about these clothes. "I'm good to go," I say.

And we go.

He gets me to hold the end of a chalk line, while he snaps it, and that's the last easy thing I do.

"Today's all about digging," he says. "We need to make sure the grade's right, then we need post holes. Deep post holes." He lifts his baseball cap off his head before settling it back in place. "The frost line's deeper here than in Toronto," he says.

Screw you, I think. Then I make a mental note to wear a baseball cap tomorrow.

• AUSTEN •

Chapter Seventeen

Time for my therapy session.

It begins as I swing onto Mac's really-quite-narrow back. I love that he's so tall, but I can still wrap my legs around him. The few times I've ridden my coach's warmblood – the same height as Mac – I've walked bow-legged for a day after.

That's not the only way Mac fits me. His head carriage corresponds with the natural placement of my hands. His high energy and swinging forward stride match the way I like to move.

I smooth my hand along his neck. "Good boy."

It's how I always start my riding sessions – no matter the horse. There might be confusion and even disagreement ahead. There will be hard work – sometimes at cross purposes. There will be sweating and, occasionally, muttered curses, but we'll learn something from every single ride – even if it's what not to do next time.

During our no-stirrups warm-up, I let the worries of my day crowd into my head.

Eliot. Oh Eliot. She's a bit like Mac – I love her, but sometimes I want to shake her. I know, and believe, anorexia isn't a choice. The same little girl who once ate all the chocolates out of her Advent calendar in one day – and then blamed it on me – didn't develop this aversion to food because she wanted to. However, I also know part of her doesn't want to let go of it – not even a little bit – and that, sometimes, well ...

I direct Mac in an easy change-of-rein across the diagonal.

... well, it can be really hard when we all have to live with the consequences ...

"Trot!" I chirp it high and light, and the trot Mac gives me is equally floating and bouncy. There's nothing like the feel of posting in rhythm with a powerful horse. When we move together the motion is effortless; we could do this forever.

... like losing Tyler – except I'm starting to suspect Cleo wasn't the first time he cheated on me, so him being gone is definitely for the best ...

At some point, as always happens, all my extra thoughts melt away. It's like falling asleep – I never know when it happens; only know after when I wake up, *Oh, I fell asleep*.

In this case, Mac and I trot on the other rein, and I find the resistance we need to work on. It's like a knot – a spot, where he doesn't want to give – it's deep, and it's hard to get at, and he's *nearly* as good on this rein as on the other, and he's *almost* perfectly bent, and it's so, so tempting to just move past it and head into the canter, but that would be cheating.

"Come on. You know you'll feel better when you work through it." I'm talking as much to myself as to Mac. It's worth it. It can be better. We can get there.

We work in three or four-minute bursts of trot, with long-reined walk breaks in-between. I praise him for everything good he does. "Nice walk," "Good corner," "Excellent bend," but that's on his easy side. We're still chasing a breakthrough on his stiff side.

Finally, finally – just when I'm getting frustrated, and tensing up, which shortens my leg, and my hand, and my temper – I close my eyes and breathe deeply, and *feel* for the response I want from him.

And he gives it.

It's so profoundly different I can't believe I ever considered just letting it go.

He's carrying himself and me. We're dancing: floating.

"Good boy!" A scratch on the withers and I loosen everything and think, *Go!* He doesn't wait to be told twice. His ears sweep back, and he flicks his tail, and he rockets into a hand gallop, and I let him stretch his muscles around the outside track of the big sand ring, until he slows of his own accord, then I ride him forward to a walk and say, "That's how we do it!"

Meg laughs. "That was great!" I didn't even know she was there. Didn't think of anything in the world but my horse and how I was riding him, until right this moment. She adds, "I loved that give in the trot, right at the end."

"You saw it!" I say.

She nods. "Impossible to miss; his whole ribcage lifted. And nice reward after, too. Great work, Austen."

***

Meg and I are doing that barn thing – talking to each other over our shoulders without ever making eye contact because I'm busy grooming, and she's busy tidying up the tack room.

It's true we miss every third – or maybe second – word, so we can't exactly discuss anything deep, or meaningful, but it's companionable.

"It's exciting you're getting your lean-to," I say.

"Huh?" Meg's voice fades but I can still hear her. "Yeah, this camp's been a bigger success than I expected – I didn't think the girls would board their horses here. If I can have a few more stalls, it'll give me some more options."

A throat clears, and I spin to face Rand. "Uh, Meg?" he asks.

She sticks her head out of the tack room. "Yes?"

"Jared asked me to come get you. He's wondering about a few details in the lean-to."

She smiles. "Oh, sure. Thanks for letting me know."

She walks out of the barn, past Rand and me, and Rand goes quiet.

I poke him. "Hey – I can see you staring."

"I'm not staring. I'm just making sure she goes right over. Jared will probably somehow blame me if he has to wait for her." He lifts his hands in a show of innocence, and I notice the ridge running under his fingers is angry red and marked with rising blisters.

"Whatever." I snap Mac's lead shank on and Rand falls into step with us as we head for the paddock. "Make all the excuses you want. You pretend you don't covet your boss's girlfriend, and I'll pretend I believe you. It's all good."

I open Mac's gate and give him a light slap on the rump to send him out to the swaying grass. "Tell you what I covet is some Campfire ice cream."

"Campfire?" Rand asks.

I pull the gate closed and double-check the chain. I always have to; it's the only way to stave off a middle-of-the-night, heart-thumping, sit-up-in-bed awakening where I'll be convinced Mac's roaming free along the highway with the gate swinging open behind him. "Uh, yeah," I say. "Like roasted marshmallows? But in ice cream? Or don't they have roasted marshmallows in Toronto?"

"Wow, there's been a lot of dissing of Toronto today."

"You're right." I stop, bow in his direction. "I'm sorry. I can see that you and your Toronto hands, and your Toronto jeans –" faced with a coating of worksite dust and dirt the dark–dye denim has lightened several shades "– have worked very hard today. How can I make it up to you?"

"You can buy me a Campfire ice cream cone."

"Sure, next time I see you in the village I'll get right on that. Just remind me."

"No, now. Now is when I'm hot."

"I ... what?" I look at him sideways. "Is this you being serious? You do know it's nine K to the ice cream store, right? Then ten-and-a-half K all the way back home. And I haven't had dinner. And it'll be dark ..." I look at my watch.

He jumps in. "... in three hours. Which is lots of time for us to cycle there, and you to buy me a sandwich and an ice cream, and us to cycle back. Although I do hear they don't like being out after dark in Ottawa ..."

"Fine!" I say.

"Fine?"

"Yeah, fine. Except you buy the sandwiches, since that was your idea."

"OK, I'll make double-sure everything's clean, and meet you out front."

"Yeah, stay on Jared's good side. Or at least avoid getting deeper into his bad side."

I watch Rand walk away and bite my thumbnail, until I realize how caked with dirt it is.

This could be a problem.

This isn't pushing buttons, right?

I mean, pushing my mom's buttons would be sleeping in 'till noon because I was out most of the night before. Pushing buttons would be not working this summer, and asking for cash from my parents all the time. Pushing their buttons would be saying no when they ask me to rearrange my whole summer and come here, when they ask me to babysit my brother and get dinner started because they're at a doctor's appointment with Eliot. Button-pushing – come to think of it – would be borrowing a car without asking, getting drunk, and crashing it.

Which is kind of the problem. Because even though my mom doesn't have those details about Rand – at least

I don't think she does, but you never actually know in a place as small as this – she has sniffed out that one-of-these-things-is-not-like-the-other and that Rand isn't exactly like any of the squeaky-clean kids I ride and go to school with at home. Or, at least the kids that are good at looking squeaky clean on the surface, and have never been caught doing anything illegal.

Tyler was a master at shaking my dad's hand while he had a six-pack stashed in his backpack. At saying, "Austen and I are going to my cousin's for her birthday," and making it sound like cake-and-ice-cream at a five-year-old's house while in reality we danced grindingly close at a heaving university party and I half-carried him home after he funneled one-too-many beers. And, come to think of it, he was really good at blaming my sister's illness for our break-up, when he really just wanted a girl who was easier to get into bed with.

Why do parents always like the fake Tylers better than the blunt Rands?

It doesn't matter why – it just matters that they do; that my mom already doesn't like Rand – which means my mom will experience my very unusual request to go straight out from work, and not come home for dinner, as major boat-rocking / button-pushing, and she won't like it.

But ... Rand's questions from last night are fresh in my mind – his challenge for me to sit and enjoy my hot chocolate a bit longer – his queries about why I take on so much responsibility.

He's made me think differently – I guess, in reality, he has pushed at least one or two buttons in me – so I've already decided. I'm going out for ice cream tonight.

I take a deep breath, and while I'm still determined, and full of courage, I dial the cottage number. I visualize the phone in the kitchen ringing. Picture my mom, either chopping or stirring something; making dinner for Shaw. Making dinner for me.

I try to prepare, but my brain is pinging every which way and I can't decide how, exactly to bring it up – like should I ask, or should I inform, or what – and it takes me a minute to register when the voicemail picks up.

What?

Where is my mom?

Who cares? She's not on the other end of the line giving me grief. I exhale fast. "Oh, hey Mom. I'm up at work and we've decided to go into the village to get a sandwich and ice cream for dinner, so don't worry about keeping food for me, and also don't worry that I won't be home until later, because we're cycling. So it'll take a while. But I'll be home before dark. OK. Great. Later."

Done.

Easy.

"Ready to go?" Rand's standing behind me, tilting his head, squinting against the late afternoon sun shining in his eyes.

"Uh, yeah. I am."

So we go.

• RAND •

Chapter Eighteen

Although I blew off Austen's warning about the long bike ride into the village, a part of me thought, *Do I really want to do that again after cycling in this morning and working all day?* Or, at least, half of the day.

But it's fine. In fact, I quite enjoy the ride.

We pass deer grazing in a field who stop, stare at us, decide to be scared, and lift their white tails and bound away. At which point, two turn out to be three, "No, four!" Austen points. "No, look, five!"

Five white tails bobbing and weaving across the field.

Wild turkeys trot away from us – only taking wing at the last minute as though it's just occurred to them they have wings.

And, ahead of me, the muscles in Austen's legs flex and contract, flex and contract, with nothing to stop me from staring at the back pockets of the snug-fitting breeches she wore while I silently watched her make her big horse dance.

***

In the bakery Austen picks and chooses sandwich fillings. "Yes, lettuce, please ... No cucumber, thank you ... Sure, a bit of pepper, thanks."

She catches me staring at her. "What?" she asks.

"So goddamn polite," I mutter.

When the lady behind the counter asks, "Would you like a pickle with that?" I watch Austen try to just say, "Yes," but at the last minute she sneaks in a quick "please."

"Ha!" I say, and she sticks her tongue out at me.

I order my sandwich without saying either "please" or "thank-you" on purpose because, sure enough, Austen fills them in for me at the end of each of my requests.

"You just had to be rude, didn't you?" she asks.

"And you just had to be polite."

We sit cross-legged in the grass outside; napkins spread in our laps to catch all the falling bits of our overloaded sandwiches.

Austen takes a bite of her pickle, chews, swallows, and sighs.

"What was that?" I ask.

"What?"

"You sighed."

"No ..."

"You did. It was loud."

"I ..." She bites and takes her time through chewing (mouth closed, of course) and swallowing. "This is nice. Mealtimes are sometimes tense at our house."

"Hmm ..." I say. "Mealtimes have pretty much stopped being a thing at our house. Everyone mostly eats alone."

This is nice for me, too. I think it, but it seems too hard to say it out loud.

***

We eat our Campfire ice cream at the ferry dock, sitting on the breakwater, with our legs dangling over the edge; swinging against the concrete sides.

The girl who served us was from Ottawa and she and Austen got talking about neighbourhoods, and high schools.

"Isn't Ottawa the town that fun forgot?" I ask Austen now.

She laughs. "Because you're the expert in fun, right? It's not like Toronto has the best reputation: Toronto, The Good; Toronto, The Centre of the Universe."

"I don't want to go back." The words spill out before I can censor them. I give my head a quick shake. "I mean ... when I go back it'll be for boarding school, which I don't want, but which is still better than going back to my house, where my mom doesn't want me." I pinch my nose. "Sorry, we're not discussing my sob story – we should probably be talking about the CN Tower and the Maple Leafs."

Austen pushes a loose strand of hair back from her face. "No. It's fine. No need to discuss Canada's worst hockey team."

I seize on her change of subject with relief. "Sorry, when did the Senators win their last Stanley Cup?"

She grins. "I think we can both agree, at least we don't live in Edmonton right now."

There's a drip of ice cream threatening to run down my wrist. Austen watches as I lick it away, then says, "Campfire ice cream – discuss."

I close my eyes for a couple of seconds, and when I open them again say, "Unlike anything I've ever experienced before."

Her eyebrows lift. "In a good way?"

I watch her feet, freed from her dusty paddock boots, swing through the air. Travel my eyes along her long, lean legs and up her dust-and-horse-snot-slimed shirt to her face. Catch the gaze of this person I didn't even know a couple of short days ago, and hold it for a second. "To my surprise, yes."

"Oh," she says. "Yeah. It's funny how that can happen."

I have a deep urge to say, "We're not talking about ice cream, are we?" but I have a bigger fear of the implications if she answers either "Yes," or "No," so the next thing I say is, "I guess we'd better be getting back soon."

***

There's a frozen pizza in the oven – my stomach's empty again after the bike ride home – when the screen door swings open, nails scuffle behind me and a dog runs up and jams his nose between my knees. "Hey Dole." I ruffle the thick coat around his neck.

My uncle's right behind him. "Do I smell pizza?"

"Yeah," I say. "I picked it up today. Want to split it with me? It needs ten more minutes in the oven."

He rubs his hands together. "Sold! That gives me time to have a shower." He pauses in the doorway. "Thanks. I'm starving and I had no idea what I was going to eat."

"My pleasure," I say. And I don't even feel guilty because I used the cash Jared counted into my hand before I left today to replace the twenties I took out of the Mason jar that seems to serve as my uncle's ATM. I bought the food. I'm cooking – or at least *heating* – the food. I'm being helpful.

Checking my email will kill the next ten minutes. I wake my uncle's old laptop, grinding, and whirring, from its preferred sleep mode and login.

I work my way through my inbox, skimming, ignoring, and deleting, until I reach, in bold **Dan Pratten.**

My dad.

It's a reply to my message. The **I'm here** one.

Everything quickens – my pulse, breathing – I think I even blink faster. Why do I get so excited when he emails? It's probably nothing. It probably says **OK. Thanks.** Or, even just **THX.**

I don't dispute how busy my dad is; I just wish sometimes I could forget it.

I click his message open. It isn't one word. Or even one sentence. It's multiple paragraphs.

I know my dad can write this much – I've seen the occasional columns of his published in national newspapers – but I don't think he's ever written this much to me.

Hi Rand,

I have to say I was a bit surprised to get your message. Although – and maybe this is inappropriate – it did make me laugh a few times.

I'm sorry your uncle's not a great housekeeper, but I somehow doubt you're that worried about it. I'm happier to hear you're not bored there.

I'm glad you met a good-looking girl, and don't completely give up on her because she probably wouldn't spend time with you if she didn't like you. It's something it took me a while to figure out but, in general, people don't do things they don't want to do. Think about that.

With regards to her mom not liking you – well I'm not there, so I can't say if that's true or not – but as clichéd as this sounds, just be yourself, Rand. Or, at least, the best version of yourself, which I've seen many times. If you're not yourself it always shows, and if you just trust the cosmos, or the universe, or whatever, things will work out the way they're supposed to.

And, yes, as you point out, relationship advice is rich coming from me. I know things are a mess with your mom and me. I know that you know we've both contributed to that, but I feel like it's important for me to say it. It's not just her ... and Dan ... (you know I could have done without the detail about the breakfast bar. Seriously TMI).

I'm reading between the lines here, but it sounds almost as though you like it on the island. I'm embarrassed to say I don't really know what makes you happy, but I do want you to be happy.

As a father, I should probably call you out for such a rude and disrespectful message, but as a writer, I admire it. I didn't know you were so good with words. I'm sure there are more things you're good at that I don't know about.

I think you're right that my being there wouldn't solve everything but ... well ... I'm thinking about what you said.

If you have time to write back, let me know what's new with this girl, and your uncle and his island.

Thinking of you,

Dad

My mouth falls open with his mention of Austen. I cut that part out of my email. I cut out that, and the bit about my mom and Dan and, well ... everything. The note I sent was super-short and to the point.

Except ... I scroll down and, sure enough, back in the thread is my original message in all its sarcastic, profane, length. It is 100 per cent not appropriate for any son to send his father, much less me talking about my mom knobbing somebody else.

But it's there. And after the first rush of nervous cold sweat, no more comes. Because this is the longest reply I've ever had from my dad. Ever. And, yeah, maybe it would be nice if it came as the result of a nicer, kinder, more polite, more elevated piece of literature ... but it didn't.

It came from this. So whatever stupid thing I did to send the unedited version of my message, well – I guess it turned out OK.

Maybe one thing my dad said has already been proven true; "Things will work out the way they're supposed to."

"Ready?" My uncle, rubbing the moisture out of his hair with a towel, sticks his head into the room.

Either my stomach's been quiet for the last few minutes, or I've been too preoccupied to notice it, but it fills the room with a long, grinding growl now.

He grins. "Nice answer. I'll grab some clean cutlery – you check on the pizza."

***

That makes two meals I've shared today, and I've liked it. The freezer aisle pizza is surprisingly tasty and it's nice to eat with the dogs sprawled under the table and my uncle filling me in on the details of his day.

"What did you get up to today?" he asks.

He lifts his eyebrows when I tell him about going up to work for Jared. "Really? How'd you set that up?"

"Uh, Austen, you know from across the bay over there, she kind of set it up for me."

Austen, who I think is prettier every time I see her. Austen, who I probably have a major crush on.

I wonder if my uncle will razz me about her and that, as much as thinking about Austen, flames my cheeks. Then I wonder if he'll bug me about that, which warms my cheeks even more.

Fortunately, his mind's on another track. "Hmm ... I've got a new shed for the lodge on my to-do list for the summer – and there's a budget to pay someone to work on it – do you want to help me out when you're free?"

"I, uh, yeah ... sure, that would be great."

He stands, carries his plate to the sink. "Cool. Just give me a few days' notice so I can order the materials and we'll do it." He stretches and yawns. "Now I'm off to bed. Thanks for the grub."

I'm tempted to head straight to bed myself, but I've been thinking there's one more message I should probably send.

I select my mom's contact and type in a message:

Hi Mom,

I thought you'd like to know that I have a job. I got paid today.

The guy I'm working for knows about me – about what I did – he's not my number one fan, but at least he hired me.

One day down and I'm going back tomorrow, so something's going OK.

Bye,

Rand

On second thought I go back and add my dad's email address next to my mom's, and change the first line to: **Hi Mom and Dad.**

Then I log off and give in to the pull of my bed, and sleep.

***

I sleep, deep and true. Sending that email before bed freed my mind.

Because I slept so well, I also wake up, easily – refreshed – before my alarm goes off.

I stare at the ceiling; stretch out each limb – my legs all the way down to my toes, my arms to the tip of each finger. Then I think back to what my dad wrote – "I'm sure there are more things you're good at that I don't know about."

Maybe I was dreaming about it, but it seems like I have a fully detailed, three-dimensional plan for a porch swing in my head.

And, yeah, the one I'm thinking of would be called "The Austen" – it would be a swing to hold a girl and lift her toward her dreams – but it could also be modified into one that would look pretty darn good on the twice re-built porch of my parents' next-door neighbour.

I decide to head out to the barn with a measuring tape and a pencil and paper while "The Austen" is still fresh in my mind.

• AUSTEN •

Chapter Nineteen

That was fun. All of it. Deciding to do something unplanned at the last minute. Eating dinner out of my lap. Pedaling home as the sun's rays slanted horizontally across the highway and the evening breeze kicked up with a hint of coolness to it.

In fact, I only realize how much fun it was as I coast down the driveway to the cottage and tension starts to creep back in.

What to say to my mom?

Should I let on it was just Rand and me getting ice cream, or should I keep up the general "we" pretense and let my mom decide for herself – and hopefully assume – Meg and Jared were along?

I waffle back and forth between the truth that it's totally normal for a sixteen-year-old to make her own plans, and do her own thing, and the acknowledgment that, in our family, we don't do things on a whim. We're not good at spur-of-the-moment. My mom probably already had a portion of dinner made for me, which has now gone to waste. And she doesn't like Rand anyway.

I'm flip-flopping between defensive and angry, and trying to make sure angry's on top so I'll be strong when I walk into the house where my mom's waiting for me.

I walk into the house ... and it's quiet.

The front hall, kitchen counters, kitchen table, are all neat and tidy. At this time of night the entrance is usually full of flip-flops and floaties and every surface in the kitchen is usually covered with dishes and placemats because my mom has just, finally, gotten Shaw to sleep, and she's made herself a cup of tea before she attacks the day's mess.

The note on the counter glows white in the dim light from the vent hood.

Austen,

We were invited to the twins' for a pool party and barbecue. There should be lots in the fridge for you to eat. Sorry for the short notice. See you when we get home.

My eyes slide to the phone with its blinking message light. So, my mom never even knew I was out. My mom was the one who went out at the last minute.

Good. For her and for me.

And Eliot? Who knows ... I doubt she's gone with them. A barbecue isn't exactly her scene. More likely she's out tromping the gravel roads – racking up mileage to erase whatever mostly imaginary calories she's consumed today.

I put a mug of milk in the microwave for hot chocolate, then pick up the phone and dial in to erase the voicemail I left earlier.

While I'm holding the receiver, I dial Manda's number, leaving a message when she doesn't answer. "Hey you. I thought I'd give you a call tonight since the hay arrives tomorrow evening and you know what that means. Sorry I missed you. Give Bandit a carrot for me."

Then I sit in the quiet, and sip my hot chocolate – no marshmallows tonight, unfortunately – and think about Rand, and realize the reason I don't miss Tyler is probably that I never thought about him when we weren't together. Which, come to think of it, is probably weird, considering Rand's not in any way my boyfriend, and I just met him, but sitting here, right now, I can hear his barking laugh, and picture the shock of hair that must flop in his eyes when he's working with Jared. He should really wear a baseball cap ...

I should really go to bed.

I'm not a hundred per cent sure I have the place to myself. It wouldn't be unprecedented for Eliot to lurk upstairs, either sleeping, or just ignoring my rustles and bangings in the kitchen.

My ascent to the loft is hesitant – testing – but, when I get there, the low-cast yellow light of Eliot's bedside table shows her bed rumpled but empty.

I exhale. Even though it wasn't my choice, I do like being here. The countryside, Mac, the water, let me breathe. The cottage is a bit small for our whole family, though. Even one without the massive powder keg that is my sister at its centre.

It's nice to have the bedroom to myself, even if it's just for a while. The sun's nothing but an orange sliver of light on the horizon so if nothing else does it, the bugs should drive Eliot back soon but, for now, I can get changed without turning my back to her. I can toss and turn, and pillow-plump until my bed is perfectly comfortable without hearing, "Oh, lie still, would you? Those squeaky springs drive me crazy!"

I flick my bedside lamp on, and go to click my sister's off. It's on the far side of her bed so I'm leaning, shuffling, struggling to get close enough – I should just walk around the bed, but I'm too lazy – when something runs over my foot.

I clap my hand to my breastbone and snatch my foot up at the same time, which puts me completely off-balance, which sends me sprawling across my sister's bed, and I twist just in time to glance down and see the mouse running out the other side of the bed and scampering off to the eaves.

My heart's hammering; breath coming short and shallow. I can't believe I didn't yell.

I mostly like mice.

Not running across my feet, though.

Then again, it probably didn't like finding my feet in its way.

Which prompts the question of why it would venture out from the safety of the shadows rimming the low-roofed loft.

I think I know.

I don't really want to do this.

I stomp my feet on the floor a couple of times before resting them on the floor again. "Hey, little mouse."

Lowering to my hands and knees beside the bed doesn't do anything to bring my heart rate back to normal. "If you're still under there, just scoot on out."

I take a deep breath and duck my head down, below the bottom of the mattress.

Bingo.

I knew it.

I frigging *knew* it. My bloody sister. My mom-lying, food-hoarding, mouse-attracting goddamn sister.

There are bowls, and plates everywhere. Everywhere.

What a mess.

It takes me two trips with the serving tray we normally use for carrying condiments outside for barbecues for me to get Eliot's collection of dishes down to the kitchen. I scrape the cereal, and pasta, and sandwiches she took upstairs to pretend to eat, and the generous sprinkling of mouse poop that accompanies most of them, into the compost container.

When I've loaded the dirty plates into the dishwasher it's full enough to put on. I push a few buttons, close the door, and head upstairs.

Somebody should probably vacuum under the bed, but I've done enough; it's not going to be me.

***

It's funny how you think your fury will keep you awake all night but if your body is tired enough sleep just creeps in anyway.

I'm drifting in and out of awareness, so when Eliot mounts the stairs, I program the sound of her footfalls into a half-conscious dream about me in the water next to Rand's uncle's dock, and Rand walking toward me – his feet coming closer on the wooden surface. It makes me smile.

Until Eliot switches on her lamp, and pulls me further awake. Not in a happy way.

I squint, and pull my pillow across my light-sensitive eyes, and grunt.

"Whatever, Austen. It's not like you never wake me up."

"Yeah?" I mumble. "Well maybe I'd be less grumpy if I hadn't spent half-an-hour cleaning up your under-the-bed-buffet."

I don't have to look to know she's frozen on the spot. Even without the gasp she lets out, I know my sister well enough to picture her deer-caught-in-headlights reaction to confrontation.

I wait. The next move is hers.

"Are you going to tell Mom?"

The million-dollar question. The one I've been trying not to think about. The one I've faced too many times over the past few years – every time Eliot slipped her dessert onto my plate, when she gave me the new size four jeans my mom bought her so she could order herself a size zero without Mom knowing, and all the other times I've found food hidden in strange places.

What's right? What's wrong? What will help Eliot? What will hurt my family? As if I know ...

"If I ever see another mouse up here I will."

She exhales. "OK. Thanks."

"Don't thank me yet. There are a lot of mice around here and I can't promise I got every crumb. I'd sweep under the bed if I were you."

It's been a long day. My words are slurring. I hear Eliot head back downstairs but I'm asleep before I can hear her come back up carrying the broom.

• RAND •

Chapter Twenty

My hands still hurt – maybe more, since a couple of the blisters have popped and the yellowish dead skin around them is stiff and crackly.

Jared is still not my number-one fan. When he re-checks the post we've already spent half-an-hour leveling and I make the mistake of sighing, he stops, lets go – *great,* now we're back to not-level-at-all – and says, "Is there something you'd like to say, Rand? Because I much prefer it when people just say what they mean – you know; when they're honest."

Ouch.

"And, if you can't learn to get the basics right, you'll never build a single straight structure. So, if you're quite ready, let's get this post level."

"Yessir."

He looks at me like he's not sure whether to punch me, or push the post over on me.

The battered skin on my hands loosens up, the post gets leveled, and I'm starting to see the basic outline of the lean-to by the time Jared grunts, "Lunch," and starts for the house, where a couple of hundred feet ahead of us Austen and Meg are disappearing through the door.

When we get to the doorway, I hesitate, but Jared walks right over to Meg who's standing at the sink. He circles his arms around her waist, and kisses her neck, and she laughs. "These berries were clean and you made me drop them back in the sink."

He reaches in, picks one up and pops it in his mouth. "I guess I'll just have to take my chances with possibly dirty strawberries."

He's a different guy than the one I worked with for the last couple of hours. There's a joke in his voice, and his smile stretches to his cheeks and eyes.

He must really love her.

Or, he must really not like me.

It worries me for a second until Austen's voice snaps my attention to the refrigerator. She appears to be looking for something in the bottom of the fridge; she's straight-legged, bum toward me, and how – seriously, *how* – am I not supposed to stare at it. "Are you sure it's in here, Meg?"

Meg twists away from Jared, and before she can catch my eyes on Austen's backside I spot a door off to the side with a sink and toilet beyond it. "May I ...?" I ask, and Meg waves her hand. "Of course, please make yourself at home," before stepping behind Austen, "It's definitely in there. I just put it away last night ..."

While I'm washing my hands there's a fluttering tap on the powder room door. Austen's voice says, "We're going to sit outside to eat. You know, for when you're finished prettying yourself up."

Cool. Good. Great. I'm hungry.

The door squeaks as I open it, and I freeze. *Oh crap.*

I didn't bring lunch.

The simple truth is, I didn't think of it. My mom's voice – *"Par for the course, Rand"* – jumps into my head. Not thinking, not taking responsibility, not stepping up – these are her favourite themes to lecture me on. Even though this doesn't compare to car theft and drunk driving it would be, for her, another example of thoughtlessness, just like walking past the empty garbage cans at the end of the driveway without rolling them up to the garage, or using the last bit of milk without buying more myself, or even telling her it was gone.

I stand alone in the middle of the kitchen. My stomach twists. I. Am. Starving.

In addition to the hunger boring a hole into my gut is the embarrassment of walking out there to face three people who've planned ahead, and made their own food, while I sit down like a kindergarten kid who forgot his lunch.

Starving and stupid.

It might not be sex, drugs, or criminal activity, but it won't impress Jared.

Even as I'm thinking about it, my stomach rumbles and growls in the quiet of the kitchen. Which it will definitely do right after I shrug, and lie: "I'm never hungry for lunch."

The spring on the screen door protests as Austen sticks her head inside. "What are you still doing in here? It's cooler outside in the breeze, you know."

I don't want to look at her. Don't want to answer her. I'm eleven years old again, at Scout Camp, paralyzingly, floodingly, overwhelmingly homesick. Nothing is right. It's been raining, and everything's soaking, and one of my tent mates tells terrible, twisted horror stories every night, and the food is terrible and I just want to go home, but I can't because my dad's on an assignment, and my mom's on a business trip, and they've sent my sister and me to different camps while they're away, and I'm out of options.

That's me right now. Out of options. It's even worse than when I was at Scout Camp, because then I just couldn't go home for a few days – now I don't have a proper home anymore. The thought spears a deep ache through me. To not have a home ... it's the worst feeling ever. This place is pretty much my only chance, and I'm screwing up here. Jared hates me. I make lots of mistakes working with him. And now this – I can't get the simplest thing right. I'm stupid, stupid, stupid, and the one person who might not have thought so is standing in front of me, watching me disintegrate.

"Rand?" Austen asks.

I blink hard. "Just leave me alone." I say it with the same vehemence I put behind my words yesterday – "I don't want to go back" – except this time I snarl a bit; mostly so I won't cry. Her nostrils flare, and she bites her lips. She takes one step toward the door, then stops, and takes the same step back. "Are you hungry?"

"What?"

"Here." She grabs an apple from the fruit bowl. "Bite this."

I'm about to say it again – "Leave me alone" – but the apple is beautiful. I bite it. It's tart, sweet, explosive.

"Chew," Austen says. "Swallow. Now, do it again."

I do, and suddenly, I don't want her to leave me alone anymore. I remember that, in the end, I helped Jared get quite a few posts in straight. I look down at my jeans, a pair I found that are loose, and faded, and good for work. I think, maybe, the world isn't ending.

Austen nods. "So, now that we're past that, are you coming out to sit with us, or what?"

"I, uh ..." I lift both hands, palms up. "I didn't actually bring anything to eat. So I guess I'll just get back to work."

"I figured that out, Boy Wonder. Why do you think I force fed you the apple? Listen, you can't work all day in this heat and not eat. My mom was at a barbecue last night and they sent a ton of food home with her. Potato salad, pasta salad, black bean salad ..." She ticks them off on her fingers. "There's no way I can eat everything she packed up for me. So, help me out?"

"How did you know?" I ask.

"How did I know what?"

"That I was hungry."

She bites her lip again, but quickly, then gives a smile that doesn't come near to hitting her eyes. "Let's just say I'm pretty good at figuring out people, and food, and when they haven't had enough." She gives her head a quick shake. "Speaking of which, I haven't had anything to eat, so let's go."

***

As always, Meg and Austen have lots to talk about, and new, easy-going, happy Jared is all smiles as they chitchat, so Austen handing me each of her dishes in turn and saying, "Here, scoop some out," just gets lost in the flow. The food is delicious, and there's lots of it, and while everybody else talks I can stay head down eating, which is fine with me. When the conversation stops, I look up to see Meg's reached across the table and trapped Austen's hand.

She squeezes it, and looks Austen in the eye, and says, "Eliot."

Austen's head whips toward the road. "Oh, God. Oh no," she says.

She grabs a drink can, and an apple and swings her legs over the bench. "I'll be back." Her lips are set; voice grim.

We all watch as she takes the steps two-at-a-time, then runs toward the end of the driveway to intercept the slight figure of a girl running along the road.

Eliot, Meg said. The sister. The one I've never seen.

Weird time to run.

"Weird time to run."

Stupid, Rand. It's none of your business.

The longer the silence following my declaration stretches, the clearer it is to me that it's none of my business.

"Sorry," I say. "That was a dumb thing for me to say. It's none of my business."

"No," Jared squints up at the sun beaming straight overhead. "You're right. It is a weird time to run."

I'm surprised he's the one letting me off the hook.

"She's sick," Meg says.

"Sick?" I ask.

Meg shakes her head. "Now I'm the one saying things maybe I shouldn't." She sighs. "I can say this much – it has to be hard on Austen."

She's looking at me, like that statement should mean something to me.

And I'm nodding, like *Yeah, I got it.* Like, *Sure, count on me*. Even though I don't have a real clue what's going on.

Jared stacks a bunch of dishes together in front of him; pushes his chair back. "We should get going again."

Meg's standing now, too, clutching her own armful of mustard and mayo, clutching a bag of chips. "I've got a few minutes. If you each bring in a load, I'll put everything away."

I follow Jared back to the worksite on the far side of the barn – taking frequent glances at the two girls standing on the exposed road under the baking midday sun.

Why? What? Who? I'm flooded with questions about this sick girl, who apparently can still run.

My chest tightens, and a shadow of that fear I felt yesterday, watching Austen's bike skid across the road – desperate for her not to be hurt – seeps into me again.

I don't like it.

Just like I didn't like the way her face tightened when I asked her how she knew I was hungry.

There's something there – something I feel like I should know about, or understand – but I'm not quite getting it.

What I do know is for a girl who can be so funny, Austen sure seems to take a lot on her shoulders. Or maybe it's the other way around – for a girl who worries so much about other people – Austen's still amazingly fun to hang out with.

That's what I want to see more of – the fun, *funny* side of her.

If there was a way to give it to her …

Her face lit up with happiness, staring at the moon, swayed by the swing flashes back to me. Maybe it's naive – maybe I'm being simplistic – but at least I can give her that.

At least I think I can. I've measured everything twice and I'm ready to start cutting when I get home tonight.

I'm feeling pretty confident.

Until I get back to Jared and the construction site.

He's studying the marks I've made on the two-by-four that will form the bottom plate of the wall. "Are these marks for your studs?"

Butterflies sweep my stomach. Why am I nervous? This isn't a trick question. *Don't show him you're worried.* "Yes." In masking my uncertainty something that sounds very much like defiance comes through in the word.

Jared gives me a quick, sharp glance. "Are they sixteen-inch on centre?"

Take it down a notch this time, Rand. "Yes."

He nods, bends to lay a measuring tape alongside a couple of the marks, nods again. "OK. Good."

Jared straightens. "I'm supposed to go look at some cattle this afternoon. Do you feel like you could frame up this wall without me?"

"Yes!" This time there's excitement bubbling into the word, and the smile that flits across his face tells me he hears it too.

"OK," he says.

That's it. "OK." I wish he'd said "Thanks," or "I appreciate it," or, even, "You'll do fine."

Then again, I guess there are people who wish I'd said certain things I've never quite gotten out. Like, "I'm sorry," or "I made a mistake."

I think about that as I gather up my measuring tape, and pencil, and framing square and make a mental promise to measure, not just twice, but three times, before I even contemplate making my first cut.

***

Back at my uncle's another pizza is cooking in the oven, the sun's fizzing low over the horizon, the bugs are starting to gather, and I'm in the barn, cutting three-times-measured lengths of barnboard.

Sawdust explodes into the air in a cloud, thinning to wisps, and then just motes. The blade of the saw releases the smell of wood that's been rain-washed, sun-baked, weathered-grey, and that – right at its core – still has just a hint of fresh, never-exposed-to-the-air newness to it.

The grain is rugged, pronounced. I run my hand over the ridges. I don't want to smooth them right away. Maybe just to take the roughness from the boards, but still leave ripples behind.

I'll treat them with something that won't alter the silvered tones of the wood – just something to protect the surface from the elements. Something like shellac; smooth to fingertips and the soft skin on the back of thighs.

Dole watches me from his position flat-out on the hard-packed dirt floor, tail thumping every time I have to step over him.

Then, when I'm nowhere near him, his tail double-thumps and he makes the effort to produce a low whine and, sure enough, my uncle steps into the doorway.

"Hey," he says.

"Hey."

"You good?"

"Uh-huh," I say. "Dinner's in the oven if you're hungry. Another pizza."

He rubs his stomach. "I was hoping you'd say that." He squints into the barn. "What are you working on?"

"Oh." From one second to the next all the calm confidence I had – the steady sense of purpose as I measured, and cut, and visualized my next steps – drains away. Still ... I have to tell him. I stack the length I just cut. "You know this barnboard I asked if I could use?"

He nods.

I walk over to the milk crate just inside the barn door where I have my plans tucked away. Pull them out and hand them to him. "This is what I'm making – well, trying to make."

He takes them and turns sideways so the last rays of the sun illuminate the paper. He traces lines with his fingers. Then he steps inside and looks over the stacks of wood I've already created.

"Hmmm ..." he says. "No 'trying' about it. I'd say you're making it. More than one, from the looks of it."

"Two," I confirm. "A few differences, but the same main design."

He jerks his thumb over his shoulder toward the house. "Based on the old swing over there?"

"That's right."

"But better, I see. Nicer lines." He hands the plans back to me. "You've got a good eye."

"I ... uh ... thanks." The confidence that returns to me is even stronger for being validated by someone else. Someone who, as it turns out, I'm starting to respect quite a bit.

"If you need help as you go along, just let me know."

"Great," I say. "Will do."

But first I'm going to eat some pizza.

• AUSTEN •

Chapter Twenty-One

Heat waves don't come often on the island. There are the non-stop breezes and, of course, the water always within walking distance, and just the fact of being far away from a big city. Nothing is as wiltingly humid as Ottawa, or Toronto, when the temperature soars mid-summer. Here there's always space to move – to breathe – but, these days I have to admit, it's getting hotter and sweatier to work during the day, and stickier and more uncomfortable to sleep at night.

During the after-lunch lesson one of the girls rides over to me to complain about the heat and, when I reach to stroke her pony, his dark coat is almost too hot for me to touch.

For a brief second an image of Eliot flashes into my head; this is the heat my sister chooses to run in. But there's nothing I can do about that, so I try to push it out of my mind and focus on the here and now; four ponies dozing in the breezy barn, and four girls sitting cross-legged on the cool concrete floor with bowls of rapidly melting ice cream in front of them.

Stable management was invented for days like this.

Nutrition. Before Meg's even finished writing the word on the blackboard in the shady barn, four hands have popped up. The girls start yelling, "Hay!" "Sweet-feed!" "Bran mash!" "Beet pulp!" "Grass!"

Meg's writing furiously. She throws her hands up. "Let's talk about the pros and cons of all these feeds. Why, for example, are your four ponies not out right now in that field where they'd be knee-deep in beautiful grass?"

"Oh! Oh! Oh!" The girl who owns the chunky grey pony stretches her hand up as high as she can. "Because they'd get too fat?"

"Well, partly," Meg says. "Has anybody here heard of laminitis?"

Meg starts writing down the signs and symptoms of laminitis and I look around at the girls' rapt faces. As much as you'd think they're just in it for the riding, it's amazing how much they love having the chance to learn about their horses, too. I suspect there will be some dinner table conversations tonight about coffin bones, and cresty necks, and corrective shoeing.

And who can blame them? I'm still fascinated by it myself. Meg's talking now about a cluster of flies forming around the horse's withers as a warning sign of a laminitis attack.

"Really?" I say.

She nods. "Apparently, so. I heard it at a clinic a long time ago and, as much as it sounds like an old wives' tale, our vet says it could be true. Maybe something to do with excessive glucose being released through the horse's system?" She shrugs. "At any rate, doesn't hurt to pay attention if you ever see anything like that."

When the ice cream's long gone, and even the barn floor's starting to feel warm, and the girls are getting twitchy from too much sitting, and not enough doing, we take the ponies out for baths following the theory that being wet is the best way to keep body temperatures in check for both humans and equines.

It's so hot that even the normally ice-cold well water is bearable, and the girls hand the hose around punctuated by quite a few accidental-on-purpose sprayings.

Mac's bay coat always looks good, but I only realize how dirty his white socks were as I scrub them clean.

I take a step back to get a good look at the gleaming horse. It also gives me a view past him to where Rand's driving nails into boards with strong, efficient strokes. My first impression was that he's thin, but I can see a pull and release of long, strong muscles through his arms. I imagine them rippling across his back, under his t-shirt. "Hmm ... nice ..."

"He does look good," I whirl around to see Meg standing beside me. *Don't blush Austen. She means the horse. She thinks you meant the horse. Breathe.*

I breathe.

"Listen, Austen ..." Meg lays a hand on my shoulder, and the gentleness in her voice and her touch, send a shock of worry through me. There's nothing tragic in a clean horse, so this is about something else. "Angie just called. She's coming through town. She'd like to see him."

"Oh." Angie, Mac's owner. Angie will want to know if Mac is ready to go back to work. Back to eventing. Back with her. "I think he's made progress."

"I think so, too." The bittersweet undertone in Meg's words tells me I don't have to explain anything to her.

We want him to be better – to be happier; to want to work – of course we do. But we'll miss him.

Meg bumps my hip. "It might not mean anything. It could be just a check-in. But, still, I think we should pop him over a few fences before Angie shows up, just to gauge how he's feeling. Don't you think?"

As consolation prizes go, it's a pretty good one. I can't keep the horse – was never going to be able to keep the horse – but having a chance to jump a horse as nice as he is ... I smile. "I think it only makes sense."

"Great. Tomorrow in the morning. Before it gets too hot."

"Deal." I step back to Mac, find his favourite always-itchy spot on his shoulder, and scratch until he stretches out his neck, cocks his head, and closes his big dark eyes, then lead him to his paddock.

The first thing he does is paw the dusty area near the gate, circle a few times, drop to his knees and, pushing his withers into the ground, kneading his muscles and satisfying more itches than my fingers can ever find, he rolls. He grunts, and farts, and dust clouds fly out around him. So much for bath time.

"Oh well," I say. "Getting dirty right after your bath definitely qualifies as 'just being a horse.' Good job buddy."

While the girls get ready to go, I head up to the hayloft to make sure it's swept up nice and clean and ready for the new hay to arrive.

What's left of last year's hay is near the hatch, so we'll throw it down and use it up first, and the rest of the space is neat and tidy. I take one last scanning look around, and as I glance out the double doors facing the paddocks I see it.

"Whoa!" I drop through the hatch and all but slide down the ladder, missing rungs, risking splinters.

As I belt out the barn doors, Meg's voice floats after me, but I don't have time to stop. My eye is on the little girl holding a lead rope while her pony tears at the lush green grass on the outside of the paddock fences. The succulent shoots the horses can't reach, even when they stick their heads between the boards and reach, stretch, strain.

No such effort required now for the chunky pony who's grabbing, ripping, chewing, and swallowing as fast as he can.

Halfway there I yell. "Vanessa!"

She turns big, blue eyes to me. "Yes?"

"Vanessa, you can't do this!" I close the distance between us, make a swipe for the lead dangling from the pony's halter and, catching it, lift his head high, pulling hunks of grass from the corners of his munching mouth.

"What?" she asks.

"He can't eat this grass." I start leading the pony out of the grass so high it's tickling the bottom of his belly. He rolls his eyes back in his head, pins his ears, and leans back with every step – just in case I change my mind – but he comes with me.

I turn to talk to the girl following us. "This is exactly what we were talking about this afternoon. Laminitis – remember?" We emerge onto the mowed edge along the driveway. "Here. Put your hand right here on his neck. Feel how thick that is? Horses built like him have a really high chance of foundering, and foundering is terrible. To be safe he needs to stick to eating the hay Meg gives him."

"But, he loves grass so much." The girl's eyes are wide. "What's the point of being a pony if you can't eat grass?"

"Vanessa, I know it's hard to understand but, trust me, you don't want him to founder. He'd be in a lot of pain, and you don't want that, do you?"

She sighs. "I guess not."

A car pulls into the driveway. Vanessa's mom. "Listen, I'll put him back in his stall. You get going. Have a good night and we'll see you in the morning."

As I lead the pony into the barn, Meg asks. "What was that all about?"

I point to the green foam dripping from his mouth. "Vanessa was grazing him out there in the waist-deep grass."

"Yikes!"

"Exactly. I'm not even sure how long they'd been there."

"Well, good catch. We'll keep an eye on him." She juts her chin into the yard where Jared's manoeuvered the elevator up against the open loft doors. "In the meantime we have some work to do."

Jared and Rand are fiddling with something at the base of the elevator – "Hold that steady so I can slip the bolt in," Jared says, and the heat has his fuse short too. "Steady, as in not moving. Try again." Rand must eventually do it right, because Jared finally says, "Fine. Thanks."

Rand glances at me, and if I wasn't roasting hot, worried about my sister, and annoyed by Vanessa, I'd throw him a bone – roll my eyes, or wrinkle my nose to let him know, *yes, Jared's being an ass; just hang in there* – but since I'm so grumpy myself, I say, "So, does this mean you're going to make yourself useful and help load the hay in the loft?" Then, before he can answer, I add, "Although I'm sure it'd be quicker for me to do it myself."

This thing happens then. This slow-but-definite spread of a grin across Rand's face.

Despite everything – despite my wound-tight nerves and my hair-trigger temper – something in my gut does an equally slow-but-definite flip-flop in response. Oh my – wow – he is so good-looking. How did I never notice before how his skin crinkles under his eyes near his nose, and how his eyes are this brown so light, it's almost gold?

I'm so distracted I almost don't understand the words he's saying. "Never let it be said that I make things easy for you. If it's harder for you to work with me around, I guess I'll just have to stay."

Stay. That's nice. I mean, it's nice that we'll have more help with the hay. And it should make Jared like him. And Rand needs this job. So – for all those reasons – nice.

Meg's snapping her fingers in front of my face.

"Huh?" I ask. "What?"

"Come get a pitcher of lemonade with me. We all need a cold drink before we start doing the hay."

***

"So ... Rand." Meg's reaching into the high kitchen cabinets, hunting for the unbreakable cups Jared's mom keeps for taking drinks outside on hot days like this. "What was that back there?"

I'm stacking the cups as she hands them out to me. "What was what?"

"Zing," she says. "Sparks, chemistry, whatever you want to call it."

"No." I shake my head. "That was this little thing called annoyance. I can understand why you don't recognize it; people don't get annoyed with you."

"Except you, now?"

"I'm not annoyed ..."

She breaks in, "No, you're in denial." Then flashes me a huge grin. "Am I annoying you yet?"

She eases herself down from the counter. "It's fine, Austen. It's great. If you don't like him, then just write me off as an interfering idiot. And if you do ... well, there's something about him I like, too."

I snort. "Jared doesn't."

Meg opens the fridge and pulls the lemonade out, gripped in two hands. "Jared has a pretty limited comfort zone. It's something I learned about him the first summer I met him. He tends to cling to what he knows."

"And what he knows about Rand isn't good."

She nods toward the door for me to open it. "What he's *heard* about Rand isn't good. Knowing Rand is different – that'll come from what he shows him." She smiles. "Which, I'm sure will be fine."

***

"You two are up." Jared points at me, then Rand, then the loft. "I need to stay close to the temperamental end of this thing." He kicks the ancient elevator, but with affection. We'd be in big trouble without it.

He doesn't have to say it twice. Up in the hay loft is my favourite place to be.

"How do we get up there?" Rand asks.

"Follow me." I run to the ladder, rest my foot on the first rung, then stop. That thing sweeps me again – what did Meg call it? A zing. It takes away my breath. It scares me. It sweeps me full of awkward self-consciousness. "On second thought, I'll follow you."

"You just want to check out my butt while I climb," Rand says.

If only he knew ... keep it light. "Well, my reasoning does have something to do with people checking out other people's backsides – that I admit."

"Whatever – try not to get too excited." He mounts the ladder and, of course, now I can't not look at his butt. Thankfully the loft is hot enough to account for the flush in my face.

"So, what exactly do we do?" Rand asks.

I'm about to give him my entire theory of proper hay stacking and storage, when the rattle-growl of the elevator starts up. No way can I make myself heard at this point. Instead I shrug, and yell, "Time to get to work!"

It's hard, sweaty, muscle-intensive work. But it's satisfying. And the loft just smells better and better the more hay we load into it.

Rand catches the rhythm almost right away. He figures out where to grip the bales, and how to balance them so their momentum actually helps him move them. The muscles in his arms tense and slide, but the never-ending stream of bales arriving at the top of the conveyor keeps me from staring at them. Much.

Halfway through the noisy engine sputters to a halt and Jared sticks his head up. He places a full bottle of water on the loft floor beside the hatch, looks around, nods once, and says, "OK."

I bow. "Your words of praise are overwhelming."

He's halfway down the ladder when, "Good job, kids," drifts back up. Followed by, "Five minutes, OK?"

I grab the bottle and gulp half of it down.

"That's fine," Rand says. "I wasn't thirsty."

"I left you half!" I'm indignant. I would never not share. I always do with Shaw, and Eliot, and Manda. Then I realize, I'm related to two of those people, and have swapped spit with the third.

"Whoops." I wrinkle my nose. "I kind of forgot you're not my brother."

"I'd hope not," Rand says. "The way you threw yourself at me the other night. Dripping bathing suit, super-hot après-swim outfit ..."

"OK, OK, Jared's going to start the elevator in about two minutes. Do you want a drink or not? Last time I checked I didn't have cooties."

I hold the bottle out, and he takes it. "I guess I'll have to take my chances, won't I?" He keeps eye contact with me while he closes his mouth over the lip where I just drank and, there it goes again – my stomach takes one big flip up, followed by one big flop down.

It's a relief when the elevator engine rumbles to life again, and we're back to the continuous cadence of the bales arriving in front of us; needing our attention.

The time that I stick my head back out the doors to wait for my next bale, and a drop of sweat actually falls off my forehead and splashes on the floor, is the time that Jared yells, "Last one!"

Last one. Hard to believe, until I turn around and note the now-full loft. How muffled the air is by the stacks of bales.

We did all this.

The elevator noise dies again and, "We're done," I tell Rand. I move to the doors to catch the breeze. Below Meg's forking all the scattered hay under the elevator into a wheelbarrow. The ponies will get it tonight.

I stand, bent double, hands on my knees and think I'm probably just as wet now as I was when Rand pulled me out of the river the other night. My underwear and bra are soaked, and there are patches of sweat wherever my outer clothes have touched my skin. *Yuck.*

I glance over at Rand, only to catch him looking at me. "What are you looking at?" he asks.

"Just wondering why guys look good sweaty, and girls just look mucky." I shake my head. "It's unfair."

His signature laugh barks out. "Miss Austen, I do believe you just gave me a compliment."

I bury my face in my hands and mumble through my fingers. "Oh Lord! I certainly didn't mean to. Just put it down to me being in a weakened state." I lift my face and fling my arms wide. "I know not what I say!"

I ease my way back to standing. "Come on. Now that the sun's heading down, it'll be much cooler out there."

As I lower myself through the hatch, right foot fishing for the next rung on the ladder, Rand says, "By the way, who says girls don't look good sweaty?"

"Watch out," I say, "You might just charm me right off the ladder and then my parents would sue you for my untimely death."

The pulse thrumming through my neck threatens to quiver my voice but somehow I manage to make the words come out light and teasing. At least I think I do.

I'm glad Meg's not here right now. I'm not sure I could write this flash of chemistry off as annoyance.

• RAND •

Chapter Twenty-Two

I've probably never done such intensely hot, sweaty work.

It was also, however, incredibly satisfying.

Even though the open air of the barnyard feels cool by comparison to the loft, now hemmed in with freshly stacked hay, it doesn't take long for my body to tell me, *no buddy, it's still pretty hot out here*.

All four of us have hay in our hair, hay stuck to any exposed skin, and hay falling out of folds of our clothes every time we move.

Meg pours more lemonade into the cups we all left down here and, as we gulp it down, says, "Ice cream, I think. Yeah?"

"Definitely," Jared says. "We got that done way faster than I expected, so let's go now, then I'll move the elevator later."

I've been following Austen's lead all along, so I decide to just keep following it now. If she goes for ice cream, I guess I will, too. If not, I'll stick with her.

It never occurs to me the decision won't be left to me.

"Alright, hop in Meg, Austen," Jared says. "Meg, if you want to go ahead and start the engine, I think we could use the AC tonight."

He walks over to me, pulls his wallet out of his back pocket and counts out bills, just like he's done every day so far, with a few extra for the additional hours I worked today. "Thanks for staying later today. It helped us get done quickly."

Austen, halfway to the truck, turns and says, "Do you want to ride in the cab or the back, Rand?"

"I ... uh ..." I've been tripped, kicked, and punched in the schoolyard, I took a basketball to the head once – flung on purpose, from short range – but nothing has ever cut me like this. Oh. Wow. Jared has just completely iced me out.

"Rand's good, Austen," Jared says. "I've paid him. He can get going."

She stops dead. "Excuse me?"

Jared walks up to her. "Come on. Meg's got the truck running. Let's go."

He's standing between us now, blocking my view of Austen. I can hear her, though. "No, no, no. Rand worked with us, he comes with us." She's saying it the way I'd expect her to explain this situation to her little brother – as though Jared doesn't quite get it; like he made a mistake, which she's pointing out. Her voice lifts at the end, leaving him the chance to turn to me and say, 'Of course, if you want to come, jump in.'

He doesn't, though. He says, "Austen, the truck's leaving in thirty seconds, with or without you."

The lift is gone from her voice now, replaced by steel. "I'll take *without*."

She steps past him, then does a half-turn back. "I'm really angry with you right now," she says. I'm rocked by her sheer guts. She doesn't swear. She isn't rude. She's just direct and accurate: *I'm really angry*. Wow. I wonder what would happen if I was that direct with people?

Jared folds his arms. "Ditto."

"Well then I'd say it's better for us not to go for ice cream together, wouldn't you?" Austen walks over to me, hooks her arm through mine, and says, "Let's go swimming. OK?"

It's like two things at once – it's like one of those moments in a movie, when the music swells, and the underdog wins and, at the exact same time, it's like one of dozens of tiny moments in gym class, or on the schoolyard, when teams are being picked and the captain looks between you and somebody else, and chooses you. Austen's gesture is huge, and small, and it embarrasses me a bit, but I'm also deeply grateful for the strength of her lean, tanned arm through mine.

Meanwhile Meg swings the truck door open. "What's going on out here? I'm going to get carbon monoxide poisoning waiting for you guys."

Austen shades her eyes, and calls to Meg. "Rand and I aren't coming."

Meg steps to the ground, takes a half-step forward. "Why-y-y?"

"Jared will explain!" Austen says. "But now we're going to go swimming before I melt. See ya!"

I should probably hate Jared. For a few seconds there, I definitely did. But more than hating him, right now I'd hate to be him, as I watch him climb into the truck next to Meg, and Meg turn to him with her palms up. I have a feeling Meg might also be very angry with Jared, and I have a feeling he's going to hear about it.

I don't have time to dwell on it, though, because Austen's already on her bike, and a swim really does sound great right about now.

***

Austen's slight form, wheeling out of the driveway, beating me out of the gate, bubbles that competitive instinct in me – the urges to win that I've had no outlet for since I stopped playing basketball – and I race after her. I. Am. Going. To. Catch. Her.

I manage it right before the highway; mostly because my legs are about four inches longer than hers, but that doesn't stop me from gloating. "Ha! Caught you!"

She shakes her head. "Well, that was kind of the idea, right? For us to swim *together*?"

I'm rushed with shame. She stuck her neck out for me. Told big, bad Jared she was *angry* with him, and I haven't even said thank you. I'm just focused on pedaling faster than her.

"Yeah, listen, about that Austen. That was really cool of you. I ..."

She cups her hand behind her ear. "Sorry, what was that?" And with a flurry of pedaling and a burst of speed, pulls ahead of me, calling, "Ha! I'm going to beat you!" over her shoulder.

• AUSTEN •

Chapter Twenty-Three

We're coasting down the final bit of Rand's driveway, and the only reason he's still behind me is the drive was too rough and narrow for him to pass, but up ahead it widens and he's going to pass me. I know he is, and I don't want him to, and there's only one way I can think of to stay ahead of him.

I sight up the dock. It extends straight out level with the lawn. My brain goes into jumping mode. The dock is a jump, and if I get the right approach, the jump will take care of itself.

I line up my tire with the centre, tap my brakes, stand on the pedals so I float above the saddle and absorb the bumps of the terrain change from grass to wood, and, as soon as I hit the dock, with the deck boards thumping at regular intervals under my tires, I sit down and pedal hard.

Behind me Rand's yelling, "What are you doing?" but I'm going. I can't stop now even if, for a small second it seems like the prudent thing to do. I left prudence somewhere back on the lawn.

Pump, pump, pedal, pedal, then stand, and lift, and the bike flies off the end of the dock, with me on it, and we both sink into the river and, "Oh God! This feels amazing!" I yell.

"Are you nuts?" Rand's on the end of the dock. "Are you totally crazy? What were you thinking?"

I can touch bottom here: just. I stand, holding my bike upright under the water, and say, "I was thinking it would be fun. And it was. Why don't you try it?"

"But ... but ... your bike ..."

"Hmmph ..." I say. "I've left it out in the rain before. It'll dry off tonight. It'll be fine. And your bike ... well ... are you really worried about *it*? I'm sorry to say this, Rand, but it's kind of a piece of crap."

When he doesn't move I start wheeling my bike out.

"What are you doing?" he asks.

"I'm going to go again." I'm up alongside him now, where it's quite shallow. "Here, help me lift this out."

He leans over, and I splash him with as big an armful of river water as I can.

"Austen!" he jumps back.

"Now you're mostly wet. You might as well get all wet. Or ..." I'm making my best chicken noises. "If you're too scared, that's fine. I get it. More turns for me."

"I'm not scared."

"Show me."

"I'm not."

"Uh-huh. Well I'm going to go again before you've even gone once."

"Fine," he says.

"Fine what?"

"Fine, I'm going to go."

"Oh, yay!" I jump up and down. "I'm not sure if I should be encouraging you to buckle to peer pressure, but I'm excited you are."

He's settling on his bike. "Oh, don't worry – the drinking and driving was all me – no peer pressure. That's not my weakness."

Before I can answer he's released his brakes and he's going.

"Pedal!" I yell. "Get up some speed! Go, go, go!"

He flies off the end of the dock and it really does look weird – I can see why he was freaked out by me doing it. I run to the end and look down at him. "So?"

He grins up at me. "So, that was the most fun I've had sober for a really long time."

I laugh. "Let's swap bikes and try it again!"

***

It's a still night, and sound always carries well across the water when the bay's flat and there's no wind to compete with.

I guess we're making a lot of noise with our splashing, and laughing, and yelling because, in a lull when we're both quiet for a minute, a whistle from across the bay snaps my attention to the shoreline of our cottage.

It's only as I'm squinting over that I realize how low the sun is. The light's gone grainy and it's nearly impossible to make out any details. All I can see is a figure, waving one of our brightly striped beach towels – those are easy to spot.

I glance at my – fortunately – waterproof watch. "Oh! I had no idea it was so late. I guess I should go."

Rand hauls my bike out of the water. "I'll ride partway with you."

I reach for it. "You're not going to tell me not to go this time? Tell me I'm old enough to stay out as long as I like?"

He grins. "Well, this time I'd say you've probably actually had quite enough fun." As soon as he stops talking, his stomach rumbles loud and long.

I laugh. "That ... and once I'm gone you can eat."

His stomach growls again, and he presses his hand to the cotton of his soaking shirt. "I'm so hungry I can *feel* the rumbles."

I stretch my hand out toward his shirt, his abs, his body, then snatch it back, shaking my head. "Sorry ..."

"No," he says. "It's fine." We meet eyes for a second then both glance away. "I mean, of course you probably don't want to touch my wet, dirty shirt, but if you did it would be OK." He shakes his head, still no eye contact. "I mean ..."

I swing my leg over my bike cross-bar, lift one hand. "It's good. It's fine. I think we're both delirious with hunger. You go eat, and I will too."

I've got to go. I'm definitely borderline delirious, but I don't think it's because I'm hungry.

"Austen?"

"Yeah?"

"That was super-fun."

I nod. "Yup. It was."

"Maybe I'll see you on the way to work in the morning?"

"Possibly," I say. Then, without really thinking, I lean over and kiss Rand's cheek. It's what I do when I say good-bye to Shaw. I used to do it before Tyler and I went our separate ways into school in the mornings. But Rand isn't my little brother, or my ex-boyfriend. With my lips still on his skin, my insides explode with butterflies. I scramble to cover up. "Ha! Just wanted to drip on you one last time. Gotta go!"

And I'm off, pedaling hard.

I am so not angry at Jared anymore. Who knew him cutting Rand out of the ice cream trip would be the best thing he could possibly do?

***

Me: **You know, I don't think I really liked Tyler after all.**

Manda: **Well, that makes two of us :)**

Me: **Seriously, how can you tell when you really like someone?**

Manda: **That's easy – they make you smile, and feel good, and you want to make them feel good, too. You'd do anything for them.**

Me: **Thanks. That's a super-nice description.**

Manda: **My pleasure. I'd do anything for you ;)**

• RAND •

Chapter Twenty-Four

I should have gone with her.

• AUSTEN •

Chapter Twenty-Five

I should have let him come with me.

• RAND •

Chapter Twenty-Six

I'm probably being ridiculous, but as Austen disappears into the gloom of the driveway the gathering dusk suddenly makes everything seem ominous – like anything could happen. I frown. Maybe she shouldn't be alone.

I shake my head. She'll be home in a few minutes. I'll be able to look across the bay and see her bike. She was right – I'm delirious – it's making me paranoid.

I mount the porch stairs, and the phone starts ringing. I'm tired, and hungry, and I have to pee – and I have that niggling feeling that I should be out on my bike watching Austen get safely home right now.

I answer the phone anyway.

Which is stupid.

But it's my uncle's phone. What if it's important? What if it's him? I don't feel like I can just let it ring.

"Hello?"

"Rand?"

It's my mom. For just a second, a balloon of happiness starts to inflate in me. Because she's my mom. I've had a decent couple of days. Maybe she's calling to congratulate me on my job.

"Yeah, hi. It's me."

"Where have you been?"

"Well, um, working. At the job I told you about. And today I helped load hay into the hay loft, which was the first time I've ever done anything like that ..."

"Rand! I've sent you emails. I've called several times today. I had an email from the school yesterday that they still haven't received your boarding questionnaire back. You know it was due yesterday. I reminded you dozens of times. You had a self-addressed stamped envelope to use. What is wrong with you? Why are you so selfish you can't do one simple thing that I ask?"

Oh, yeah. I forgot. She's my *mom*. The woman who can most consistently send my anger zero-to-sixty. My number-one critic.

The tension whooshes into my body; fills all the pressure points and finds no outlets except in words. Not the relatively safe words I've been putting down on paper;

the hot, uncensored ones right at the front of my brain; on the tip of my tongue.

"Selfish? I'm selfish? You only want me to send that questionnaire in so the house is empty for you to keep shagging my basketball coach whenever you feel like it."

"What did you just say to me?"

"Do you think I'm an idiot, Mom? Oh, God, yeah – you're the new communications rep for the team; that's why you have to be with Dan all the time. You two are working on your oral messaging, right? It makes me sick. No wonder I started drinking – so I wouldn't have to think about my mother cheating on my father with some pathetic has-been who can't even coach basketball to save his life. So if you don't like your drunk, criminal of a son, just think about who made him that way."

Click. Crackle. Dial tone.

I guess she's thinking about it.

Oh shit. This could be bad.

***

I know what would make me forget.

I open the fridge. Still no beer. Not even the chance of one lurking behind a carton of milk, or a leftover casserole, because that would require having groceries in this fridge which, once again, is almost empty.

Just one bottle – or maybe two – would be nice. It would be enough to relax me. Enough to make me forget that really, quite, enormously bad phone call.

Shit.

I grab a jar of peanut butter instead. There are no clean knives, so I use a spoon to glom PB on the two heel pieces of bread left in the bread bag. Fortunately they're fairly stale, or the way I'm stabbing at them would tear them to shreds.

I walk out to the barn, chewing as I go. Halfway there, I turn back and grab the peanut butter jar and the spoon to bring with me.

Even if nothing else is coming together for me, these lengths of wood do – perfectly.

I unstack them and lay them out – both the original, more compact, *friendlier* swing I designed for Austen – and the longer, more substantial one I'm hoping will look great on Joe's huge custom porch.

Once all the pieces are in place on the dirt floor, I gouge a scoop of peanut butter from the jar and work it off the spoon in sticky mouthfuls, while I walk around both not-yet-assembled swings.

They're going to come together.

I can actually see it now. I mean, it was clear in my head before, and it even looked reasonably convincing on paper, but this is the moment where I know for sure that this lumber – for the second time in its woody life – will soon be assembled into something beautiful and useful.

I take a deep breath, assemble the drill, a screwdriver, and some screws, and start building a swing. Austen first, of course.

The smell of metal boring into dry wood is soothing.

When the cordless drill dies, I dig around until I find an old, corded one and an extension cord.

The whine of the drill is hypnotic, and I know how far the screw's gone in from the changing tone of the drill alone.

When I make one clearly bad join, I take a deep breath, and a fresh spoonful of peanut butter, and reverse the screw out, re-align everything, and try again.

A mistake is not forever. A mistake can be undone. I can do this.

When the first bug bites, I flinch. When the second one bites, I slap at it. Then, three more bites come in quick succession, and I lay the drill down – *shit!* – run my hands through my hair and over my arms and the high-pitched drone of mosquitos fills my ears.

Reluctantly, resentfully, I tidy up the tools.

Don't think about that phone call.

But the farther I get from the partially put-together swing, and the neatly stowed tools, the more it knocks at my brain. *That was bad, Rand.*

As I push through the screen door, I wish this wasn't one of those times my uncle's taken the dogs with him. I could use them here, now. I'd welcome their tail-wagging, tongue-lolling delight in life. I could scratch their bellies. I could feed them peanut butter and watch them try to unstick their tongues from the roofs of their mouths. At least they'd be some company.

Oh God. Those things I said.

My gut takes turns rumbling and twisting. I'm not hungry anymore, which tells me it's pure anxiety.

A drink would help.

I look at the now-dark square of window facing the barn. Even if it wasn't too dark, too late, too buggy to head back out there, the compulsion to build is gone.

I pace, and try to talk myself down. What's my mom going to do anyway? Yeah, I said some stupid things, but they're just words. Come to think of it, when I accidentally sent that blunt email to my dad, it helped. Maybe that call was just what my mom and I needed to clear the air, once and for all. Maybe once we've both cooled down, we'll decide it was a good thing.

That's probably it. I'm probably right. Maybe I should just login and send her an email. Tell her I took it too far. Apologize.

She'll like that – right? That's what moms like?

It's true my inbox is full of old reminder emails from my mom with the subject lines **Questionnaire** and **Have you sent in the questionnaire?** When I look at them altogether, there are actually quite a few. I'll apologize for that – I'll fill the questionnaire in tonight. I'm sure the school didn't mean yesterday was an absolute cut-off. More of a guideline – a would-be-nice.

Here's a new one, though. I squint at the screen. Sent in the last hour.

It doesn't contain a subject which, for some reason, seems really ominous to me. She's also copied my dad, which she never does. Which also freaks me out a bit.

Kind of like the time my report card came in the mail and I knew if I hadn't failed World Issues, it was only because I'd earned fifty-one per cent, and I both did, and didn't, want to open it at the exact same time – that's how I feel right now.

I cross my fingers and double-click to read:

Rand and Daniel,

Rand, you've taken it a step too far.

I don't know what to do with you anymore. It's obvious from the phone call we just had that your attitude hasn't improved at all while you've been with your uncle.

Given that, I can't in good conscience leave you for him to deal with.

I have no idea what to do with you, but the island experiment hasn't worked, so we'll have to think of something else. You probably won't like whatever it is but, not surprisingly, I don't care.

Daniel, it's time for you to step up. I can't do this alone. I don't even know if I can deal with Rand at all anymore.

Rand, your father and I will let you know when the arrangements are made – one of us will pick you up within the week.

Crap. Shit. Damn.

The island experiment. I didn't know it was an experiment. I didn't know I could fail at it.

I didn't know how badly I don't want to, until right now.

I don't want to leave.

Also, to my surprise, I can see how I put myself in this position. I understand why my mom's freaking out.

I just wish I knew how to stop her.

I want to talk to Austen about this.

But she's not here.

What I'm pretty sure is here – *somewhere* – is at least some kind of booze.

Almost everyone keeps some alcohol around, for when visitors drop in, or for special occasions, or just because someone gave them a bottle for Christmas.

I go hunting for my uncle's liquor stash.

I find it at the top of a closet on the landing to the basement stairs where most people might keep cleaning supplies.

There are a few "normal" bottles – whiskey, rum, and gin – the kind you might use to mix someone a drink if they ask for a rum and coke, or a gin and tonic. I keep looking and right at the back, jammed into the corner are two mostly full bottles – one Peach, one Peppermint Schnapps.

I bet you they're old, and I bet you they were gifts, and I bet you my uncle has forgotten they're even there.

Score.

Yuck.

Eenie-meenie-miney-mo. Peppermint Schnapps wins.

The first swig is strange. It tastes like candy canes – out-of-place during a midsummer heat wave.

The second swig is truly disgusting.

The third one is marginally better.

I sit on the basement steps, in the semi-gloom, all alone, drinking pilfered Peppermint Schnapps, and am horrified by myself.

This is pathetic. This is living up – or down – to everybody's worst expectations of me. Austen would hate to see me like this.

On the other hand my stomach's warming, and not roiling anymore. There's a fuzz seeping into my brain; taking the lingering edge off the aftermath of the phone call. And, perversely, the very fact that I've already let myself down by starting to drink, makes me feel like I might as well just drink some more. Jump right in with both feet.

My hand is wrapped around the skin-warmed neck of the bottle.

Should I? Shouldn't I?

I flex, then release my fingers. Flex, and release.

Will I? Won't I?

Behind and above me there's a crash, and a thud, then a bulky shadow falls over me at the same time as there's a massive retching sound.

I leap off the step, knock the Schnapps flying, scramble to pick it up before the entire staircase smells like a toothpaste factory, and whirl to face Dole, legs spread wide, head down, heaving once, heaving twice, then opening his mouth and vomiting.

"Oh yuck!" I yell. "Oh gross!"

The steaming liquid slides over the edge of the floor, onto the first step, then starts seeping toward the next one.

"Oh geez, Dole! Seriously? You are the most disgusting dog ..."

I stop. Take a deep breath.

At least my decision is clear. Dole needs to be looked after. And I can't look after him if I sit here getting hammered.

I screw the top back on the bottle, tuck it back in the corner where I found it and, plugging my nose as I step around the groaning dog and his pool of vomit, I think at least the odour of puke masks the smell of spilled Peppermint Schnapps very effectively.

***

There's something wet and warm nudging my neck.

I'm conscious enough to know it's not something nice and wet and warm – not like Austen's lips on my cheek after our bike diving – rather it's something sloppy, and slobbery, and ... I open one eye. "Coal!"

Oh wow. I'm a mess. My back and bum are cold from being slumped on the kitchen floor, propped up against the kitchen wall.

My legs are too hot, from the huge dog spread prone across them. They're also completely asleep.

The good news, as I open the other eye and scan the immediate surrounding area, is that there are no fresh pools of dog puke. Not that I can see, anyway.

That means after Dole threw up the first four times, and I finally gave up and just decided to collapse with him in the kitchen, since it has the easiest-to-clean floor in the whole house, he hasn't been sick again.

How long is that? I'm too disoriented to know.

Coal. Coal's here. That means my uncle must be here.

I try to scramble to my feet and, literally, nothing happens. It's as though the message can't even travel from my brain through my dog-crushed nerves to my legs.

So I'm stuck on the floor, calling "Uncle Kurt?"

He pushes through the screen door carrying a heap of linen, which he drops on the floor when he sees me. "It's the middle of the night, Rand. What are you doing?"

My arms work well enough to straighten me to a more upright position. "Your dog ..." Dole's tail thumps hard on the linoleum floor demonstrating that while his weight across my legs is dead, he's still alive. "... has been heaving out his guts since about nine o'clock."

I rub my eyes. Bad idea; my hands smell like dog stomach juices. "I don't know what he ate – he must have found something long-dead in the woodlot. He wasn't around when I got home – I figured you had him – then he trotted in, opened his mouth, and deposited something half-decayed, and partially digested on the floor."

"Which you've been cleaning up ever since."

I nod. "At twenty-minute intervals. Except ..." I squint up at Kurt hopefully, "... not for a while now. I don't know how long I was asleep but he hasn't been sick once. So maybe he's done."

At which point Dole rolls over just enough to raise his head off the floor, and makes a familiar retching sound, and deposits a new supply of warm bile on my legs.

I bang my head back against the wall. "Forget it. Stupid me. Why did I say anything?"

My uncle shakes his head. "I'm so sorry Rand. And any other night I'd take him off your hands, but I'm actually here because one of the guys at the lodge is sick as a dog." He raises his eyebrows at Dole. "I came back here to find some Gravol, grab some extra sheets, and throw these ones in the wash. I have to go back."

I sigh. "Yeah, it's OK. I understand. I don't really need to sleep tonight anyway." I blink a couple of times, then ask. "Do you think he needs to go to the vet?"

"Well, the vet's a ferry ride away, so there's no way he's seeing one tonight. Let's ride out the night and see how he is in the morning. Then we'll decide."

Ride out the night.

OK. I can do it.

And as I fill the bucket with fresh water, and dip the cloth in it yet again, a funny thought flits through my mind, that I'd rather be spending the night cleaning up somebody else's sick than being sick myself.

There's a reward in being there for somebody else – even if that somebody is a dog.

Who knew?

• AUSTEN •

Chapter Twenty-Seven

Oh, wow, it's a beautiful morning.

I tumbled into bed feeling fresh and river-washed, and the air this morning is crisp enough that I still feel that way.

I mean, yeah, after a couple of hours of mucking out stalls, and sweeping, and chasing reluctant ponies into the canter, I'll feel pretty disgusting, but for now ... heaven.

It was Eliot waving me home last night. Eliot coming back from one of her late-night rambles, recognizing my giggles floating across the bay, figuring I might want to get in before my mom noticed it was pretty late to be haying and wondered where, exactly, I was, only to find I was flinging myself – and my thousand-dollar mountain bike – off her not-favourite-neighbour's dock.

It's Eliot's way of paying me back for not ratting her out about the food under her bed and, in return, if I see her running at high noon again today, I probably won't tell my mother.

I'm watching Rand's driveway as I cycle toward it. He said he might see me this morning. I'm trying to figure out if it's better, or worse, for us to arrive at work together after yesterday's showdown with Jared.

I'm not sure. I'm just hoping Meg told Jared off and things will get better from here on in. From what I can see the lean-to's been going well – even if Jared doesn't want to admit it just yet. I figure Jared has to give Rand credit for a good finished product. Maybe if Rand can get a reference, he can send it to his parents, maybe they'll back off on the boarding school threat. Maybe he can stay here; at least until the end of the summer. At least as long as I'm here ...

A truck's rumbling out of the driveway. It slows, and the passenger side window glides down. I walk my bike over to it.

"Morning!" I greet Rand's uncle.

"Hi Mr. Nickelsen," I say. "Nice to see you this morning."

He smiles. "I am so not Mr. Nickelsen; just call me Kurt. I hear you've been busy working up at Strickland's and helping Rand get work there, too."

I shrug. "I just introduced Rand. But he's the one doing the hard work."

Kurt frowns, and looks at his dashboard. "Speaking of work, he had a bad night. He's still not up."

My heart catches. A dozen assumptions jump to my mind and none of them is good. But I can't let his uncle know that. "Oh, he isn't?" *Light voice. Casual tone.*

He taps the steering wheel. "He only got to bed a couple of hours ago. I didn't have the heart to wake him up."

Jared's going to freak. Jared's going to say 'I told you so.' Jared's going to fire him.

Breathe, Austen. Smile, Austen. Pretend everything's OK, Austen. "Hmm ... well, the thing is, I think there were a couple of things he and Jared were going to work on today that he wouldn't want to miss. Maybe I should go see if I can get him up?"

"Help yourself darlin'! If you can get an exhausted seventeen-year-old boy out of bed, you're a stronger person than me." Kurt tugs on the peak of his cap and adds, "Although I think that Strickland boy could cut him some slack."

"Oh, I'm sure he would," I lie, "But I think Rand would want to be there for this part of the project. I'll at least ask him."

Kurt winks. "Like I say, do your best! Nice to meet you!" And he's off with a spurt of gravel, and the volume turned up on crashing classical music. Not what I expected, but maybe I should just learn not to have expectations when it comes to Kurt and his nephew.

I ride away, calmly, until he's out of sight, then churn my pedals. What is 'a bad night' supposed to mean? Why isn't Rand up? I don't want to think the worst of him but there's no denying I already am.

***

I decide I don't have time to be polite. Kurt said I could go, so I'm going – straight in.

I step onto the mat I dripped bay water on just a few days ago. I can't believe it was so recent.

"Rand? Rand!"

Nothing. So he still hasn't made it downstairs. I guess I'm going up.

I step over the chunky yellow dog, stretched out on his side on the kitchen floor. He doesn't even lift his head, but his tail does twitch when I say, "Hey boy." I bend down to stroke his ear and wrinkle my nose. "Oh, you smell *funky* – and not in a good way."

I straighten. “Rand! I’m in the house. I’m coming to get you.”

I climb the stairs.

“Rand! If you’re not decent, you’d better get decent because I’m at the top of the stairs!”

I have no idea which of the several doors opening off the hallway is his bedroom. I stop, hold my breath, wait. Sure enough, the long, slow saw of a snore reaches me from two doors down.

The door creaks when I push it – this is an old farmhouse after all – but all Rand does is twitch and start in on a new snore.

“Rand.”

Twitch again.

“Rand. Rand!” I lay my hand on a sheet-covered bump that must be his arm.

Now that I’m closer to him, there’s something. A smell. Familiar, but I can’t quite peg it. Not pleasant, but not booze. At least not that.

The tick of an old analog clock thunks into the dead air space between snores. The time’s wrong – I know it’s not 2:15, a.m. *or* p.m., but it reminds me time’s passing. We need to go.

I take a deep breath and shake the lump. “Rand! Get up! Now!”

“What the?” He opens one eye. “M’ so tired ...”

I lean down low so my mouth lines up with his ear. "It doesn't matter. You have to wake up."

In a sudden flurry of movement, he hooks his arm around my neck and pulls me down, so I'm sprawled next to him.

He splays his fingers through my hair. "There. That's better. Just lie with me."

My head's against his chest. His heart thumps through bone, and muscle, and warm skin, and thin cotton, right into my ear.

For a second – OK, maybe two, or three – I give in. Relax against him. Feel the sucking temptation to just lie in this messy, soft bed, with this warm body next to me.

To my surprise it's Rand who keeps us both awake. "I had a bad night," he says. Because he's lying on his back, his words float into the air above us. I picture them, like a canopy overhead. I see the two of us lying under them and I see this as a moment of opportunity. Those words have been put out there, and I can pay attention to them, and do something with them, or I can ignore them and they'll disintegrate and disappear, like clouds being blown away in the wind.

Tick-tock. Time. Clock. Work. I give a mental shrug – accept the time I'd built in to ride Mac before work is now gone – and say, "OK. So tell me about it."

He takes a long, deep breath, and I wonder if he's going to say, 'Nah, forget it,' but instead he struggles up on his elbows so he's upright against the headboard.

I do the same thing, and once I'm up I nudge him with my shoulder, then I just wait, while the clock ticks.

We're both staring straight ahead, and maybe that makes it easier for him because, without looking at me, he starts: "After you left I was out of sorts. Hungry. Tired, I guess. I felt like I should have cycled home with you."

I was fine. I bite my tongue hard and don't say it. This is Rand's story.

"So, I was in a bad mood and my mom called," he pauses. "I was a bit snappish."

"A bit snappish?" I prompt.

He slides me a sideways glance. "OK, completely rude. And she emailed me back, and she was so, so angry, Austen – she wants to take me back to the city – and I didn't handle it well; I went looking for something to drink ..."

Back to the city, something to drink – I suck in my breath at the words, then literally pinch myself; twisting a fold of skin between my thumb and index finger until it stings. *Shut up, Austen.* He's talking. Let him talk.

He waits, and I wonder if I've put an end to the flow of words, but he continues. "I found this bottle of – yuck – Peppermint Schnapps, which I was pretty sure my uncle wouldn't miss. I had a sip, and then another one, and I was sitting there all alone on the basement stairs, like the saddest person on earth, trying to decide what to do – whether to keep drinking ..."

"... and?" I ask.

"And then Dole came in fresh from some disgusting feast on a rotting animal corpse, and threw up everywhere and I kind of forgot about drinking."

"Oh!" *That's* the smell. I place it now. Funky dog, funky boy. So, so much better than the smell of Peppermint Schnapps, though.

"What?" Rand asks.

"The dog. I saw him downstairs. He stinks."

Rand nods. "Yeah, I probably do, too. I lost count after I cleaned up his eighth pool of puke. He stopped around four in the morning and I was way too bagged to bath him, or me. I just flopped in bed."

"Good for you," I say.

He shakes his head. "Not really. If it wasn't for him I might have downed that whole bottle."

"But you didn't."

"Of course I didn't. The dog needed to be taken care of."

"You do realize some people would have just locked the dog out of the house and kept on drinking?"

I wait for him to make a joke. To say, 'Why didn't I think of that?' But, for once, he's dead serious. "No way. I could never. That would be terrible. He's an animal. He needed help."

"Rand, just the fact that you see that – that you think that – you're fine."

I think of Eliot – of how on Shaw's nursery school graduation day she made us all late because she was determined to run before the ceremony, and we all ended up sitting in the car, ready to go, waiting for her to finish her shower. Of how she won't eat anything for days – weeks it feels like – but the last time my mom baked her food-porn-gorgeous, world-famous chocolate cake for a dinner party, Eliot decided she'd like a slice. My mom – unable to say no in the face of my sister actually requesting food – took the cake to the party with a slice already out of it, rehearsing explanations for the gap. Later I found the slice, crumbled and pushed around the plate, but not eaten, on my sister's chest of drawers.

I'm not saying it's Eliot's fault – not entirely – but I do know her personal addiction runs so deep she doesn't have any perspective or control over it.

"Seriously, Rand. I know things have been hard for you. I know you hit a bad patch. But since I've known you, I've seen someone who's thoughtful and someone who makes good choices."

It's amazing the things you can say when you don't have to look the other person in the eye. Actually, it's borderline terrifying, the things you can say.

What did Rand call me? Miss-Dry-Between-Her-Toes, Goody-Two-Shoes? Sounds about right when I go around preaching like that.

"Wow, Austen, I knew you thought I was hot – I mean who wouldn't? – but I had no idea it was as wild as that. Thoughtful and good choices ... how are you not ripping my clothes off right now?"

There's laughter in his voice ... I *think*. I sneak a sideways look to double-check and, sure enough, he's grinning.

I grin back.

He nudges me in the ribs.

I nudge him back.

"OK," I say. "I take it back. You're a self-absorbed asshole."

He laugh-barks. "Well, based on my past experience with girls, that's far more likely to get me laid."

The sound of a distant siren drifts in through the open window. It's the whistle from Cape Vincent – across the river in New York. It normally blows at noon, but also sounds to call the volunteer fire department or for other occasions.

"What's that for?" Rand asks.

"Telling us it's time for work?"

He sighs. "Yeah. Work."

"Are you going?"

He grimaces. "Well, I know how much Jared would miss me if I don't so, yeah, I guess I am."

• RAND •

Chapter Twenty-Eight

Austen informs me a shower is non-negotiable. "You really do smell awful, and it's only going to get worse if you get hot and sweaty."

"Yeah, OK, fine. Maybe it'll help wake me up."

Thanks to my uncle's temperamental hot water heater, the shower's mostly cold so I'm definitely awake by the time I get downstairs. I smell better, too, so success on both fronts.

"Wow. You clean up well. I don't think I could pull that off." Austen turns to me holding out a plastic-wrapped sandwich. "I found an old hamburger bun –" she makes a face "– and made you a sort-of sandwich. By the way, what's up with your peanut butter? It had the weirdest marks in it ..."

How many times have I seen her like this? Face lit up, grinning, making a joke of something, but always doing something for somebody else. For the little horseback riding girls, for Meg, for that big horse of hers. For me – filling gas tanks, making me hot chocolate, getting me a job. I know she's missing her morning ride by being here to wake me up. I know she's risking being late for work. Yet, still, she's standing in my uncle's not-exactly-gourmet kitchen, making me food.

Her brow furrows. "What is it? You're not allergic to peanuts are you?"

I shake my head. "No. I ... just ... you don't need to do this, you know. It's not your job."

"What?" Her face goes white except for two spots of red that bloom on her cheeks. She claps her hand over her breastbone and instinctively I touch the same spot on myself. There's a spot there that always feels like it's been punched, dead centre, with something hard, when my feelings are hurt, when I'm hit with a bad surprise, when I'm about to cry.

Oh no. I think Austen's about to cry.

She turns away from me, back to the counter, and places the plastic-wrapped sandwich there. "Sorry." She says. "I thought it would be nice."

Instead of turning back to face me, she twists awkwardly and heads to the door without meeting my eyes.

She steps over Dole. He still stinks – I can smell him from where I'm standing. She clomps down the stairs to her bike, and hauls it up by the handlebars, and I'm already chasing her.

"Austen, where are you going?"

She's actively avoiding my eyes, and she's sniffing, and – yup – I've done it. I've made the happiest girl I've ever known cry. *Great work, Rand.*

I lay my hand on her arm and pray she won't snatch it away. "Look at me, Austen. Answer me. What's up?"

One sniff, two sniffs, and then a sob. "I'm an idiot. I've just realized it. It's always me coming over here, isn't it? It's me, barging in, telling you what to do. I'll stop. That's fine."

"No!" I say. *No, no, no.* "That's not what I said – that's not it at all. It's you doing nice things for me all the time. Getting me a job, sticking up for me, helping me keep my job ... It seems like you always do things for other people, and I don't want you to feel like you have to for me. I don't want to be a pain. Helping me isn't your job – *that's* what I said."

She finally meets my eyes. Blinks a few times in quick succession. "But you don't ... you're not ... I *like* doing stuff for you – with you – you've never asked me for anything. Not like ..." she tails off.

I think of the weird sick-but-still-running sister. Of Meg saying "It's got to be hard on Austen." There are things I don't know, but I do know Austen likes to help and I can easily imagine people taking advantage of that. And I don't want to be one of those people.

She swallows hard. "Besides, you've given me stuff, too."

"Oh yeah? Like what?"

She smiles again, even if it is through the remnants of her tears. "Like fun. Like laughing more than I can remember laughing before. Like giving me a break from thinking about all the other people who want my help."

It doesn't sound like much to me, but I'm just relieved she's stopped crying. "OK, then."

"OK, what?" she asks.

"Well, I don't necessarily think that's a fair trade, but if you do, I'll take it."

I hold out my hand and she slips her own warm, strong hand into mine. I'd much prefer to slide my whole body right up against hers if her bike wasn't between us, if I wasn't scared it would freak her out, and if it wouldn't make us even later ... and then Austen takes care of it.

She reaches out and circles her arm around me, and we're in this awkward bike-in-the-middle clinch, but it's still one of the nicest hugs I've ever had. There's something supremely comforting about the warmth of her head resting against my chest, and I realize this is the first time somebody's touched me in a truly affectionate way, for a really, really long time.

In fact, I can't remember the last time it happened.

Now my breastbone really is starting to ache, and to relieve the pressure, I talk. "You said I was thoughtful, but maybe you were wrong – I made you cry, after all. You should talk to my mom – she'll tell you all my faults."

Austen's laugh is muffled, then she lifts her head away from me, and the spot where it was resting feels cold and empty. "Rand?"

"Yeah?"

"Think about the day I met you."

The smell of gas comes to mind. The clench of uncertainty in my gut. "I'm thinking about it."

"Do you think maybe I knew you weren't perfect that very day?"

I was pretty grumpy. I was, actually, quite rude.

"Hmm ... possibly ..."

"And I like you anyway – faults and all."

"Oh," I say. *Wow,* I think.

"Now, come on, because if there's one fault I can't stand, it's being late."

• AUSTEN •

Chapter Twenty-Nine

I haven't missed my ride on Mac after all, because Meg's built it into the girls' day.

She's told them I'll be jumping Mac and there's a zing of excitement in the air – from them, from Meg, and now it's seeping into me, too.

It's the first time I've ever ridden Mac in his full jumping gear. Not that he wears anything over the top, but he has a really expensive bridle and saddle – I smooth my hand over the buttery leather – and I've put on his breastplate and boots.

Although he stands still for me to mount, little shivers run under his skin, ending here and there in tiny tics. Once I'm in the saddle he minces sideways. "Hup!" I warn, and he stops, but it's nearly impossible to believe this is the same horse I've been hacking around on, and that little girls have swarmed while swaddling him in bandages.

I ride him in big, sweeping trot circles while Meg guides the girls in setting up our jumps.

The girls had a million questions about Mac's boots. "What are they for?" "How do they go on?" "Do they come in prettier colours than that?" "Can I try putting one on?" and now they're headed off to pace out distances, and lug standards and poles into place, and are full of questions about that. "Do they all need ground lines?" "How many steps for four strides?" "How many for six?"

Wow, this horse is *on*. There's an energy in his step I've never felt before. I thought I knew him, but it takes me several seconds to sync my posting to the new coiled-spring power of his trot.

Meg and the girls have arranged several jumps in the classic hunter side-diagonal-side formation. There are dozens of possible courses to take through these few jumps, and they've set them up so we can approach them from either direction.

"Any particular plans for me to tackle this?" I ask Meg as I sink every ounce of my weight into my heels; concentrate on keeping my shoulders back. I can't outmuscle this horse, so I've got to dazzle him with technique. The stronger he gets the more important my position – and my ability to remain calm – will be.

She shades her eyes against the quickly rising sun. "How about one jump at a time?"

Excellent suggestion.

OK, so here we go. Pick a jump and go.

Mac's so sensitive, and so hyped, that's literally all I do. I pick the jump, look at it, and think *go*, and he goes.

He's bouncing, quivering, eager. He listens to me until he just can't listen anymore. His ears sweep forward and he takes a massive long spot and soars the jump twice as big, twice as wide as it really is.

My whole job for a few seconds is not to reef him in the mouth. It's the only thing I'm thinking of. We've spent weeks resetting this horse, letting him enjoy life, letting him miss jumping, letting him decide he wants to do it again. There is no way I want to undo all that with a double-barreled yank on his sensitive mouth. I grab his mane – I'm not proud – and when he lands there's a loop in the reins and I breathe a sigh of relief until I notice how fast we're bearing down on the perimeter fence.

The way he feels right now, he'd jump that in a heartbeat. So now my job is to tell him "No, not that, please. How about this jump over here?"

Far from one jump at a time, I'm riding one stride at a time, one second at a time. It's exhilarating, and exciting and when we finish a sequence of jumps and I walk him in a circle in front of Meg, I realize it's been breath-taking too. My breastbone's rising and falling, lungs heaving, the tattoo of my heart jibing with the rhythm of Mac's footfalls between jumps.

"How does he look?" I ask her.

"How does he feel?" she asks.

"He looks super-freaking-crazy-amazing!" one of the camp girls yells, and the others echo, "Crazy!" "Amazing!" "Can we jump after?"

Meg laughs. "I'm going to raise the jumps, and get Austen and Mac to do one more course, then that's enough for Mac, and you girls can do some jumping."

"Over the big jumps?" It's the girl with the smallest pony asking.

"We'll make the jumps as big to your pony as these ones are to Mac."

There's a moment of silence while four pairs of eyes slide along Mac's tall legs and long body, followed by nods. "Deal," the little girl says.

Once Meg gives me the thumbs up, I take Mac back into a trot. We flex and bend through the gaps between the jumps and, again, just with the slightest thought from me, he picks up a canter.

Meg wants me to do a very basic course with him – simple and straightforward. It's side-diagonal-side-diagonal. The first three lines each contain two jumps with varying strides between them. The final diagonal holds a single jump.

Mac is still fast and eager – he covers each line in one stride less than I'd ever expect to do them on the horses I usually ride at home – but he's in control. I'm not scared – just buzzing. My heart lifts over the first jump and it stays up, floating, the whole time we're on the course.

As we approach the final jump, he's stronger, and I'm a little tired, and it's a single vertical – which, although it may seem counter-intuitive, is actually quite a lot harder to ride than a combination of jumps. There's no benchmark here – no other obstacles to regulate our pace – just this one fairly tall jump placed in the middle of a long stretch of the sand ring.

He sneaks in a little extra speed, and I let him get away with it, and we're going to hit it at an awkward spot – it's going to be go long, or chip in – and he decides for us: go long. His hindquarters thrust, and we're launched and rocketing, and once again I'm grabbing mane, and he lands and I want to yell, want to whoop, and that's when I remember what the horsey version of a whoop is.

He's going to buck.

I know I shouldn't like it, but I do. The exuberant gathering of muscle power, the way it corkscrews through the horse, the way it flies free out of his heels. It's a freeing feeling. Of course, it's especially freeing if it liberates you from the saddle and you go flying – *free* – through the air.

Lean back, lean back, lean back. Mac drops his head between his knees. *Heels down, heels down, heels down.* His muscles screw up tight, pulling in the energy, holding it close. *You're going to have to ride this out, Austen* ... and he lets go, his body unfurling in a long, fast whiplash ... *go with him, be flexible,* and I throw one arm up and back and give myself up to whatever's going to happen next.

***

I'm on, I'm on, I'm on, and then I'm not; I'm flying through the air, over Mac's left shoulder.

Most of my falls before have happened in a blink. I'm on, then I'm off, because of a sneaky dip from a pony's shoulder, or a couple of times, because of the horse going down.

This time I'm ninety-nine per cent sure I'm going before I actually go and it puts the whole process in slow motion.

I have time to think, time to reason, time to stretch my legs out, angled down and in front of me ... and time to land on my feet; hitting the ground with a spray of sand, and sticking the landing.

No way.

I did not just do that.

Everybody – Meg, Mac, the watching girls – is silent.

I look down at the ground solid under my feet.

I did.

I do the next logical thing: I bow.

The girls giggle.

While I'm turned to them, Mac moves behind me and nudges me with his nose, and that's what finally sends me toppling into the sand.

Meg laughs out loud.

I scramble to my feet, brushing at my legs. "Great! Just when I thought I was going to get away without having to wash my breeches tonight!"

"I got that on video!" Vanessa yells, holding up her phone.

Meg lifts her eyebrows. "Well, in that case, I guess I can't give you a hard time for having the phone at the barn. Now you can film Austen getting back on and doing one more jump, and staying in the saddle."

***

The girls are eating lunch in front of the blackboard; taking turns drawing outlandish jumping courses even Big Ben and Ian Millar couldn't have come through with no faults.

Meg walks to the paddock with me while I turn Mac out.

"So," she says. "Angie's planning to come tomorrow. You good with that?"

"Huh? Oh, yeah, sure."

She bumps me with her hip. "When you untacked Mac, then put his bridle back on, instead of his halter, I thought you were preoccupied about Angie taking him away. Now I'm not so sure. What's up?"

I didn't have time to think while I was jumping Mac, but the minute I got off I started worrying about Rand. He must be so tired. And it's never been easy for him working with Jared, but after the ice cream thing last night – well, I wonder how he's doing.

I nod in the direction of the lean-to. "Just wondering how things are going over there."

"Hmm ..." Meg says. "Civilized, or at least they'd better be."

"What do you mean?"

"Let's just say, Jared and I did *not* go for ice cream last night. When I found out he hadn't invited Rand ... well, I was furious. I love Jared in a way I don't love anybody else, but that almost made it worse. The way he's been treating Rand ..." She shakes her head. "He's better than that. He's letting his fears and suspicion take over."

She unhooks the chain and opens the gate for me to lead Mac through. "I told him if he can't be nice, he has to at least be civil – for my sake, even if not for Rand's."

"Thanks," I say.

She shrugs. "It's just common decency. Rand deserves to be treated well."

I think of Rand wondering how many days he has left at this place where he's just starting to fit in. I imagine him sitting in that house, all alone, battling with his demons – staring at a bottle of booze. I picture the dark circles I noticed under his eyes when we left our bikes leaning against the tree this morning.

I think of my summer before I met him, and my summer now.

I let Mac loose and turn to Meg. "Yes, he does. He really, really does."

• RAND •

Chapter Thirty

"How was it?" Austen's weaving her bike across the gravel road, swooping close to me, then away again.

I'm tired, but in a relaxed, easy way. In a way that's happy to be coasting my bike on this slight downhill with someone who wants to know about my day. "Yeah, fine. Surprisingly good, actually. He was pretty polite to me. He told me I did a good mitre cut."

"Good," Austen says. Then she giggles.

"What's so funny?"

"Meg told him off."

"She what?"

"She was really angry when she found out he didn't invite you for ice cream. She let him have it. She told him to smarten up."

Her words hit me like a punch to the gut. I thought I was making headway with Jared. I thought he was starting to like me; to be impressed by my work. Now I find out his girlfriend told him to be nice to me.

"I don't know why you think it's so funny."

"I think it's funny in a divine justice kind of way. He was awful to you, and he paid for it. It shows there's balance – karma – in the world." She's grinning, looking at me, clearly waiting for me to smile too.

She's going to wait a long time.

"I can't believe you did that to me."

There: smile gone. "Did what?"

"I thought you were on my side. I thought you believed I could do good enough work to impress him on my own. But no – you go and tell Meg to get Jared to go easy on me."

"What are you talking about?" Austen's not swerving anymore; she's matching my pace, cycling right alongside me. She's so close I can see the flush spreading through her cheeks – the skin of her forehead furrowing.

"What did you do – pay him to hire me? You know what we were talking about before? Maybe you do help too much. Maybe you should back off."

Even as I'm saying the last few words, I know I'm delivering a low blow – using words designed to hurt her. Her tears from earlier today spring into my mind, and

I'm seized with instant remorse. Oh no. I've gone too far. I shouldn't have said that. I didn't mean it. I don't want her to cry again.

Turns out I don't have to worry. She's not going to cry or, if she is, I'm not going to see it.

She's quick and to the point. "If you used half your brains, you'd know I didn't tell Meg anything, because I didn't go for ice cream last night – I left, *with you*. So if you're going to be a complete asshole, at least get your facts straight first."

Then she stands on her pedals, and pulls away from me quickly and easily, flying right past the turn-off for my uncle's driveway, disappearing around the bend, leaving me all alone.

There's the only person who's liked me unconditionally for as long as I can remember.

Correction: there she *goes*. Sent by me.

Nice work.

• AUSTEN •

Chapter Thirty-One

He's such a shit.

And, since I think he's such a shit, it should be easy to stop caring about him, right?

Right.

Phew, well it's a good thing I got that figured out.

Alright. I'm just going to enjoy the evening breeze – one of the best things about being out of the city is that it always cools down for sleeping here – and look for deer, and notice the wash of the rising moon across the river, and ...

"Eliot?" I slew my bike to a gravel-spitting sideways stop. "Are you OK?"

She's at the side of the road, knees bent, head between them.

Not moving.

Oh shit. Oh crap. Oh hell.

Oh no. This is it. This is my punishment for every time I thought she was selfish, or should snap out of it, or I wished she'd just sit down, shut up, and have dinner with us.

She's dead, and it's my fault, and I've lost my sister.

I'm running to her as these thoughts bash around in my brain.

I felt fear like it once. When I turned away from Shaw swimming in the river for thirty seconds and turned back to see him floating, face down, limp limbs spread wide.

I froze for two seconds and, in the third second, he flicked his head up, grinning, saying, "There's somethin' crawlin' on the bottom here, Austen."

I had truly felt then, that time had gone backwards for me for just a tiny flutter. That I had lived in a world where I'd lost my brother, and now, miraculously, I was back living in a world where he was alive and well.

My whole day after that had felt different. Probably my whole life since then has been just a tiny bit different.

And now ... can I dare to hope it can happen again? Do I get two second chances? How can I?

I drop to my knees beside her, and grab her arm. "Eliot!"

Her skin's clammy, and her arm's bony, but there's body heat there; there's a pulse. "Oh, Eliot ... Eliot ..."

She doesn't look at me, though. Everything in this situation, except her beating pulse, is wrong.

In a moment of clarity I stand, and summon every huff of breath in me, every ounce of strength, harness all my fear, and scream, "RAND!"

And again – "RAND!" – and this time something in me tears, and I think that's it for my voice for today.

I drop back down in the grass by my sister, and haul her against me, and make fists in her hair, and murmur, "I am so, so sorry," and "I'll go without boyfriends, and a horse of my own, and I'll live with never having ice cream in the house," and "I should have told Mom more." That one makes me hesitate, though, and I continue, "But I'll be on your side, Eliot. I will. If you'll just finally get better. If you'll just try."

I gulp, and it's like somebody's stabbed me from the inside-out, "I thought you were dead, Eliot."

She swats at me and mumbles, "Not dead, stupid," and I give a giggle-sob and say, "That's the nicest thing you've ever said to me."

• RAND •

Chapter Thirty-Two

Wow. Great. Another good day's work, Rand. If I wasn't done with drinking I'd go home and dig out the bottle of Peppermint Schnapps again.

No, finish the swing. Much better idea. Because, likely, a large gift of old wood for a girl who doesn't even own a porch to hang it on will fix everything.

More great thinking on my part – couldn't just buy her flowers, could I?

"RAND!"

Nobody has ever screamed my name quite like that.

"Rand!"

There's no doubt it's Austen, and the horrible possibilities crowd my brain.

A coyote. A tractor. A stupid, stupid, drunk driver hitting her – bike crumpling under his wheels, her body ... *I could have killed someone. I could have killed a person like Austen.*

I'm pedaling, sweating, gasping, flying, standing on my pedals to ride out ruts.

I round the corner, sending gravel spraying out to the side, and she's right in front of me. Crouching, whole – thank God; in one piece – but not alone.

"Austen? What?"

She looks up at me – equal parts anguish and panic in her eyes – "My sister. She – I don't know – collapsed? She's barely conscious." Her eyes fix on mine. "I don't know what to do."

Oh, wow. As if I do.

Except, as it turns out, I do. At least in the immediate moment I do.

"Go," I say.

"What?"

"Get on your bike and go home. Call 9-1-1, or tell your mom to call 9-1-1. Come back with water. I'll try to get her home."

"But ..."

"Go!"

She looks at me, bike dropped by the side of the road now, standing as tall as I can – the strongest person here

– and she nods. "OK." She yanks her bike up from the gravel. "I'll be as fast as I can."

She goes, and I turn to her motionless sister. Eliot. The sick one. The anorexic one.

OK. Let's go.

I crouch down. "Hi Eliot. I'm Rand." I put her arm around my neck and grab it against my far shoulder. "This isn't exactly the way I wanted to meet you, but ..." I straighten my back, knees, keep my shoulders back, and she comes with me; heavier than she looks. Heavier than I'd like her to be.

Shit. I'm no weightlifter.

But I'm healthy and strong, and she's sick and weak, so this is on me.

"Come on," I say. "Help if you can. One foot in front of the other would be awesome."

She sort of does that. Enough to get us to the turn-off for their driveway.

Just as I'm looking along the drive – trying to figure out how far it stretches, and how long it will take to struggle down it, there's a sharp pain in my side.

"Ow!" I turn to Eliot. "What did you do that for? Your elbow is frigging sharp!"

"That's the idea," she mumbles. "Don't hurt my sister, or I'll get you."

"*Me,* hurt your sister? Jesus Christ, girl, who's the one hurting your sister? I should be the one bruising your ribs for turning her life inside-out."

That's it, though. Eliot appears to be done talking. Which, thankfully, seems to also mean she's done assaulting me.

She's leaning on me more heavily than ever, and this is a long driveway.

"OK," I say, more to myself than her. "Here goes."

I've only ever seen it done on TV – I've never actually tried a fireman's lift myself – but if it works for firefighters carrying full-grown adults out of burning buildings, I figure I might as well give it a shot.

"Alley-oop!" I say, and heave, and she doesn't even protest as I start to move forward with her bony body slung across my shoulders.

It's fine at first. This was a good decision. I'll get there in no time.

If the driveway is 300 metres, the first seventy-five go really well.

As I head into the next seventy-five, my shoulders are getting sore, and my breath's coming shorter.

I'm only halfway there, and I'm already stumbling. I don't know if I can carry her the rest of the way.

I'm mostly staring at the ground, but in one of my periodic upward glances, I see Austen, coming back toward me.

Austen, saying, "Oh, Rand, I can't believe you're carrying her like that."

Austen, carrying a water gun – it would make me laugh if this wasn't a medical emergency and I wasn't totally exhausted – saying, "It was the only thing I could find." She's behind me now, and the rogue spray hitting me tells me she's shooting water at her sister. "Mom's filling the tub with cool water."

"Tell me it's not upstairs." I can hardly put one foot in front of the other; forget stairs.

Austen giggles. "It's not." Then she says, "Sorry, it's not funny. None of this is funny."

The final part of the trip is a blur. *One foot in front of the other. One foot in front of the other.*

When I reach the five steps leading up to the front porch I think, No. I cannot do this. It's too much.

"Here, Rand. I'll take her." Austen taps my shoulder. "Come on; just kneel down and I can lift her off you."

"Mom!" She yells. "You have to come help!"

Austen and her mom peel Eliot off my back, and I sink back into the grass, and stare at the sky, and don't even try to move, reasoning whatever's going on inside with girls and bathtubs, I'm much better left out of.

I sit up when the paramedics arrive – I don't want them to cart me off – and Eliot's little brother ducks outside as they open the door to go in.

He sees me and walks over. "Hey."

"Hey, Shakespeare," I say.

"Shaw! My name is Shaw!"

"I knew that – I was just teasing." Which is a lie. I knew his name wasn't Shakespeare but I couldn't at all remember it was Shaw.

"You're Ayn Rand," he says. "*The Fountainhead.*"

"Sure. If you say so."

"That's funny 'cause she's a lady."

"Yeah? Well your sister's named after a lady, who was named after a guy."

"You mean my stupid, bloody, selfish, bugger of a sister?"

I straighten, quickly. "I did *not* say that. Don't you dare say I said that."

He shrugs. "No, my mom did."

They're bringing Eliot out now. I guess there are too many twists and turns inside the house to use a stretcher; the paramedics are carrying her between them in a two-handed lift. I'm glad – it's probably better for Shaw to see her this way, than completely prone.

Not that he seems like the most delicate child to begin with. Right now he's dived into the base of a shrub and is rustling the entire thing, telling me, "I'm diggin' for worms. I wanna' go fishin.'" He yanks his head back out. "Will you help me?"

Thank goodness for Austen. She ruffles Shaw's leaf-and-twig entwined hair. "Nobody's going fishing right now, Mr. Shaw. It's already your bedtime and we haven't even had dinner. We're going in to eat now and, if he wants to, Rand's coming with us."

She lifts her eyebrows at me. "You want?"

"That depends – is it going to be better than what you made me for breakfast?"

Too late I remember we're fighting. I wince for anger or tears, but the status quo seems to have returned. Instead of furious Austen, I face always helpful Austen, who holds out her hand to tug me to my feet.

"Come on," she says. "Let's eat."

***

She makes Kraft Dinner. Two boxes worth. With cut-up hot dogs in it.

I can't even tell you how good it tastes.

Or how disgusting Austen's looks, smothered in a close-drawn spiral of ketchup.

She catches me looking at it and opens her eyes wide. "What? I like ketchup."

"There's liking and there's addiction," I say. "I don't eat that much ketchup in a month."

She sticks out her tongue, and reaches for the Heinz bottle again. "I think I missed a spot."

"Austen's KD looks like a horrible movie," Shaw says, before spearing a chunk of hot dog and popping it in his mouth.

"Our dad always says that," Austen explains. "Except he says 'horror movie.'" She turns to Shaw. "Daddy's coming."

The boy nods. "That's 'cause Eliot's in the hospital."

"Well, and he wants to see us," Austen says.

Shaw's using his chubby fingers to chase an errant noodle around his plate. He doesn't even look up when he says, "But mostly 'cause Eliot might die."

I'll hand it to Austen; she doesn't even hesitate. "Nobody's dying." Her voice is loud and clear. It's less like an answer; more like a declaration.

The phone rings, and I'm happy for Austen's sake. It means she gets to end this conversation on her positive, "Nobody's dying," note instead of whatever raw, uncensored reply her little brother might come back with.

Austen carries her plate to the counter and scoops up the receiver. "Hello? Oh, hi Nanna. Dad called you? Well, I don't know much ..."

'Sorry,' she mouths to me as she backs out of view around the corner.

"My nanna can talk forever," Shaw says. "So, can you get me dessert?"

"I, uh, I don't know what you have."

Shaw turns in his booster seat to point at the fridge. "Neapolitan ice cream in the freezer. It's the only kind we're allowed to have 'cause Eliot doesn't like it. Choc'lit sauce in the fridge. Sprinkles in the cupboard."

So, I get the kid dessert and, while I'm at it, I get myself some, too.

Halfway through his bowl Shaw puts his finger over his lips and leans toward me. "This is the most ice cream I have *ever* had in my *life*."

OK, so I don't know much about looking after kids. I guess an extra-big bowl of ice cream won't kill him.

Austen drifts back into the room, snapping her hand open and closed by her face, and rolling her eyes. Shaw giggles and she pokes him in the ribs, then glances down at his ice cream bowl.

'Holy shit!' she mouths to me. Then says "Uh-huh, yes, I think that's right," into the phone, and continues to the counter where she starts stacking dishes.

"OK!" Shaw holds out his hands. "Wipe me! I'm sticky!"

It's the weirdest night I've ever had. The kid talks me through putting him to bed.

"This is when you watch me brush my teeth to make sure I do a good job," and "Make sure my pyjamas aren't inside-out," and, finally, "Put the blind mostly closed, and turn out the light, and turn on the fan."

Austen's gotten off the phone twice, and both times it's rung again immediately after. She walks into the bedroom, holding the phone, saying "Shaw-boy ..." and he dives under the covers. "Listen," she clicks the speaker button on the receiver, "Manda wants to talk to you."

"Shaw-meister!" a girl's voice powers into the room. "How are you my small dude?"

Shaw flings the covers away to take the phone. "I'm good! I had Kraft Dinner, and the biggest bowl of ice cream in the world, and Rand helped me get ready for bed."

"Who's Rand, dude?"

This is when I should probably leave. I learned a long time ago if I don't want to hear anything bad about myself, I shouldn't eavesdrop. But I want to know. Who am I? Who am I to this kid and his sister? What am I doing here?

Austen seems to know the same thing about being careful what you overhear. She's reaching for the phone but Shaw pops back under the covers and says, "He's a guy who came here for breakfast one day and he carried Eliot home today."

"Oh ... is he Eliot's boyfriend?"

Shaw snorts, and the girl on the other end of the phone snorts, too. "OK, stupid question, since Eliot only leaves her room to run. Is he Austen's boyfriend?" There's an upturn to her voice that suggests this question is really aimed wider – like at Austen, who begins grabbing at Shaw's wriggling body in earnest.

Shaw's giggling now, and squealing. "Silly Manda, Mom told Dad she's only *afraid* Rand's going to be Austen's boyfriend. Mom liked Tyler better."

"Whoa! Where'd you hear that Shaw?"

"Mom told Dad on the phone. I don't like Tyler, though."

"'Cause he dumped Austen?"

"No, 'cause he took my favourite basketball and didn't give it back."

Austen's finally managed to pull the quilt right off her brother, leaving him exposed on the mattress. "Time to say good-night to Manda," she says.

Just like that Shaw delivers a wide yawn and rolls over. "Night-night Manda."

Austen presses the phone back off speaker, tucks the receiver between her cheek and shoulder and says, "Nice work Silly Manda," as she settles the quilt back over her brother.

"Yes," she says. "Of course he heard."

She smooths the wrinkles out of the covers.

"The only person who didn't hear was Eliot, because she's in the hospital."

She walks to the door where I'm standing, staring, and reaches behind me to flick off the light. Her eyes lock with mine as she says, "He's not your type."

She's so close I can hear the other girl's laughter, and her reply, "But if he was my type?"

Austen's nostrils flare, and her breath warms my skin. "If he was your type, he'd probably be your type."

"That good, huh?"

Austen swallows, and I can hear the movement of her throat. "I can't talk about it right now. I'll let you know what happens with Eliot."

She clicks the phone off, and we're standing face-to-face in a semi-dark hallway. My body wants to wrap one hand around the back of her head and twine my fingers through her hair and pull her close so our lips are touching, our noses brushing, then put my other hand in the small of her back and press her body tight to mine ...

My brain jumps into, "So, you had a boyfriend ...?"

"Before," she says.

She smells like hay and horses. Dirty, I would have said before meeting her. Intoxicating, I think now. "Before what?"

"Before I came here."

I have a million questions. I think about our sex conversation that never quite ended. Where I said "I don't do it," and she never answered. I wonder how lucky her ex-boyfriend was. Then again, he's not with her anymore, so not that lucky. Where did she meet him? How long were they together? What was he like? Why did they break up?

She shrugs. "Ancient history. I'm sure you don't really care. Right?"

Who cares? It was my tagline. My mantra. For a long time before. Before I came here. It's not brave to stick to it, but it is easy. "Right."

"So? See?" Her teeth are so white they flash even in the dim light as she smiles. "You don't get to give me a hard time for something that doesn't even matter to you." She starts walking away, and says over her shoulder. "That's a move reserved for mothers."

I bark. "Ha!" Because she's nailed it. There's no way my mom can actually care about which way the toilet paper roll goes on, or the shape of the Snippit opening on the milk bag, or which spoons and forks we use at dinner – but riding me about all these things keeps her in good practice.

I follow Austen to the kitchen. "You can always make me laugh."

"I guess there's something to be said for not taking life too seriously." She opens the fridge. "I'm sorry I called you a complete asshole."

"I'm sorry for making you have to say it."

Is that enough? It doesn't feel like much, but something in the way she just looks at me for a few seconds – blinking, not speaking – makes me think I'm OK to leave it at that for now.

Finally she gives her head a little twitch. "Is that it? Are we apologized?"

"I am if you are."

"Well I can't stand up any longer, so if we're going to continue, I have to get off my feet." She hands me a root beer – "Sorry, no actual beer" – and winks. "I can still make fun of you, right? That's fair game?"

She can do anything if she winks at me that way.

She grabs a can herself, then heads into the unlit living room where a big couch faces an even bigger window, then pats the squishy cushion beside her. "Sit, if you want."

I lower myself to the couch, sitting straight and stiff. Not manspreading. Uncomfortable.

She yawns. "No doubt soon I'll tell you how amazing you've been, and how I couldn't have gotten through tonight without you, and how Shaw a-double-dores you but, for now, I'm just going to chill."

She leans her head against my shoulder and mumbles, "Just for a sec," and one second later, when I turn to look at her, she's eyes-closed, mouth open just a bit, face relaxed.

***

I, eventually, manspread. Which makes things way more comfortable. I stare at my root beer, on the coffee table just out of my reach, and decide I'm not thirsty anyway. I watch a ship slip by in the dark – strings of lights defining its length and height – and I scratch an itch on my thigh and, just for a minute, I lean my own head onto Austen's, and she sleeps through it all.

I could go anytime. I could stand up and leave and she'd probably wake up, but maybe not – I have no idea how deep a sleeper she is.

But there's this feeling I have that I don't think I've ever had before. Not that I remember, anyway. *Peace.* The day might have started badly, but I worked through it – worked hard. I walked into a crisis and helped make it better. I've done enough today, and now I don't have anything left to do, and this couch is really comfortable and the girl leaning on me is giving off just enough body heat to be comforting as the evening temperatures fall.

I'm happy.

It feels weird.

I want it to last, which won't happen if my mom swoops in here, and picks me up and plunks me into boarding school. And why shouldn't she? I've done precisely nothing – other than wishing it won't happen – to keep her from doing just that. And, judging by how well ignoring the boarding school questionnaire went, if avoidance is my strategy, I might as well start packing now.

I'm not the same person I was when I came here, but I guess there's no way she'd know that. I have to talk to my mom, talk to my dad. I have to finish the swing I'm making for Joe – to somehow make up for what I took away from him that day. Or maybe, to at least show I realize I took something away.

Soon. I'll do that soon. But right now I can't do anything except sit on this couch, so I might as well enjoy it while I'm here.

Austen's weight gets heavier against my side while I step through the things I still have to do to finish her swing and Joe's – small finishing touches to add, sanding, varnishing – then she shifts and sighs, and slips down so her head's in my lap, eyes still closed and a little smile on her face, and that's when it gets harder to keep thinking about what grit of sandpaper to use, and how many passes to make, and whether the work I'm doing will make any difference at all, anyway.

In fact, the only thing I can think is: *There's a beautiful girl in my lap.*

Which makes it awkward when light washes across us; beaming through the side window, picking the high points of Austen's prone body, and making me blink.

Someone's here – probably Austen's dad – and he's going to find me hanging out with his daughter in a dark house, and, unless I can think about something else, it's going to be really obvious just how much I've been thinking about Austen.

I re-direct my brain: *my mom's underwear hanging on the clothesline, the smell of my grandmother's perfume, clowns, the irreconcilable vastness of the universe.* Surely even Austen's hotness can't compete with those.

Clomp-clomp-clomp. Shoes on the wooden porch.

Fear should do it, right? I'm afraid to look at my crotch to see how bad it is, because then I'll see Austen's head resting there and we'll be back to square one.

The screen door opens with a jiggle-jiggle and a creak, and a man's voice says, "Austen?"

She's stirring, but not fast enough to answer.

"Austen?" he says again, and I wonder if it's worse for me to answer instead of her, or for me to say nothing and just let him walk in on us. I can't decide, so I say, "She's in here," and hope it's the lesser of two evils.

As Austen wakes up, she does this twisting rolling thing, and her face actually turns toward my groin, and I'm like, *Please, no, don't let him step in at this exact moment.* There's a flick, and light floods the room, and Austen's sitting up, blinking – not face-down in my lap, thank goodness – but her hair is super-mussed, and her shirt's twisted and I don't have to be a dad to know this is not what a father wants to see when he walks into his house late at night.

"Oh, hey Dad ..." She stretches, and yawns, and I might think the sleepiness in her voice was pretty sexy if I wasn't desperate not to think that. "Sorry, I was totally zonked," she says, and then adds. "Oh, have you met Rand?"

AUSTEN

Chapter Thirty-Three

"How much does he hate me?" Rand asks when I hand him the flashlight at the end of our driveway.

"Do you want me to walk farther with you?" I ask.

"No. I'm fine – especially with this ..." He waves the beam of light up along the trees then back again. "But how much does he hate me?"

"He doesn't hate you. He's worried about Eliot. He's always snappy when he's worried. If anything he'll love you when he finds out how much you helped us."

I love Rand for how much he helped us. I would have been on my own without him, and it would have been nerve-wracking, and tiring, and lonely.

I want him to kiss me but he's showing no signs of it.

I step toward him, grab him in a stiff hug, and he whispers in my ear, "I'm afraid he's watching us."

I laugh. "He'd have to have night-vision goggles."

"Are you sure he doesn't?"

"Ninety-nine per cent sure."

Rand shakes his head. "That final one per cent leaves room for a lot of bad things to happen." He trains the flashlight along the driveway, "Go. I'll hold the light until you get to the end of the beam."

"But ..."

"Go, Austen. I'll see you tomorrow."

I start walking, then stop, run back, stand on my tiptoes and smush my lips tight to his. "There! Sorry, had to do it. I'll take the heat if I get back and find him sitting on the front porch wearing night vision goggles."

Then I run away again.

"You're bad!" Rand calls after me.

"You ain't seen nothin' yet!" I call back, and keep going before I run out of willpower and go back for one more kiss.

***

My dad is not sitting on the porch wearing night vision gear.

When I push through the door he's inside, unloading the last of the groceries he brought into the fridge.

I want to be happy to see him. He couldn't come last weekend, so we all missed him, and Eliot's sick, so I feel like we should pull together, but I'm undeniably irritated at how few words he said to Rand, before grunting something about checking on Shaw, and disappearing down the hall.

"All good?" I ask him now, and it's a dare. I dare him to say no – to give me grief about me being asleep on the couch with Rand – and then I'm totally willing to get into it with him. I dare him to say yes, because then, fine, I'll take him at his word. All's good. Rand is accepted. My decisions are trusted. Perfect. Nothing to discuss.

Instead he drops his head into his hand and rubs his forehead. "She doesn't look good."

"Oh, Dad, I know." I step straight into his strong hug.

That's one thing about having Eliot for a sister – there's always a bigger problem to worry about.

***

Maybe my nap on the couch has made it too hard to sleep – I toss and turn.

I raise up on my elbows and look over to Eliot's bed.

Empty. Weird.

I go back to bed, and let my mind drift back over the evening. The horror of finding Eliot. The relief of seeing Rand. The embarrassment of Manda and Shaw discussing my love life at full volume. The release – *peace,* really –

of leaning against Rand and letting consciousness seep out of me.

Just thinking about it lulls me off to sleep again. His shoulder was strong. His body was warm.

He drove drunk, he has a police record, he has a foul mouth, he's often rude, he doesn't ride horses - when it comes right down to it, Rand's not my type.

But ... I have to admit ... if he was my type, he'd totally be my type. Manda called that one.

***

Partly because I'm wide-awake anyway, and mostly because I'm afraid I won't have him around for long, I tiptoe out of the house while my dad and Shaw are still sleeping and head up to Meg's early to lunge Mac before work.

I start him on a line – it helps establish the circle I like him to follow – then take the line away and free lunge him.

The lunge line is always an extra thing for me to worry about; don't let it drag on the ground, don't tangle it around my ankles, readjust it when I want Mac to change reins.

Without it, we're both free. Without it, I can focus completely on the long lines of his muscles, the cadence of his gaits, and the tiniest details of my body positioning in relation to him.

I use voice commands and body language alone to take him up, then down, through his paces on both reins.

He's good – we've practiced a lot – but near the end, as a fresh breeze licks in off the river, and a couple of swallows swoop low over his head, Mac doesn't want to come back to a trot from the canter he's in.

"Come on, Mac," I say. "Tuh-rot." My voice sounds soothing to me, but to him it's probably bossy and grating. Still, I keep at it. *Inhale.* Ask again. *Exhale.* Try another time.

Finally, finally, he steps forward into the two-beat trot and I call, "Good boy!" Then immediately reward him with what he's been waiting for. "Go!"

He takes my breath away. He makes me forget every single other thing in the world.

His head snakes down between his front legs and he flings his hind end up, energy uncoiling the length of his sleek body. After that long, stretching buck he runs, tail up, farting, to the far end of the ring, then slows for a series of crow hops, then bolts again.

I watch, until his ears swivel and lock onto me, and he drops to a walk and moseys up to me. "Fun?" I ask.

He presses his face against my shirt and exhales with a long, satisfied rattle.

I bury my face in his forelock. "Good boy," I say. "Nice boy. I love you."

***

Meg comes to the gate as I let Mac loose in the paddock again. Her hand's curled around a steaming mug of green tea; her eyes crinkled with concern. "I heard the ambulance was at your place last night."

Of course she did. Everybody who a) saw the ambulance b) was on the ferry, works on the ferry, or knows anybody who was on, or works on the ferry c) knows anybody in any way associated with the island's volunteer paramedic service, knows the ambulance was at our place last night. Which means ninety per cent of the island knows.

"Was it ...?" Her question trails off.

I pick it up. "Eliot," I confirm. Then add, "Those runs she's been doing in the full sun, and no food, hardly any water."

"Not good," Meg says. "I'm sorry. If you need to go ..."

"Thanks. I probably will, at some point." I run my hand through my hair, pause to twirl a strand. "It was a bit of a weird night – my dad got in late – I think he's going to stop by here on his way over to the hospital. Depending how things are going, I might go with him."

There's movement behind her. Boy on bike.

Rand.

"I ... uh ..."

She glances over her shoulder; turns back to me with a smile on her face. "Of course. Go. And go to the hospital, too. Whenever you need to."

***

I meet Rand under the tree where we always lean our bikes.

"Hey."

There are dark smudges in the creases alongside his nose. His face looks hollow. It makes his eyes stand out more.

"You look ..."

"Like shit?" he suggests.

I shake my head. "Not exactly."

"Worse?"

"Better."

"But not quite like your type?" There's a twist to his mouth – almost a smile.

I punch the tree trunk. "Oh, Manda. It's a good thing I love her."

"Manda sounds interesting. Are you sure I'm not *her* type?"

I gasp out a laugh. "Positive!" I hook my thumb under the strap of my tank top. "*I'm* her type."

"Oh." He glances away, then quickly back at me. "Is that why ... the weirdness talking about your ex-boyfriend? Have I been completely dense?"

"No!" *Whoa, take a breath Austen.* "I mean ..."

"You mean I'm just not your type anyway."

The mini-van is pulling into the driveway. Full of campers, and noise, and responsibilities, and distractions.

"Come on ..." I fix my eyes directly on his and wait.

He looks away, then back. Clears his throat. "Come on, what?"

"Who was the one going on about night vision goggles last night?"

He blushes.

"In fact," I continue, "If anything I'd say I should worry I'm not your type."

The van doors are opening. Little girls are jumping out.

I glance over at them, then back at him. "I've gotta go."

He reaches out and grabs my arm. "You are. You so, so are."

I raise my eyebrows. "Easy for you to say here, now. Let's see what you do next time you have a chance. It's over to you, buddy."

I start work with an unsettled feeling in my stomach and I can't figure out if I'm nervous, or excited at the challenge I just set for Rand. Probably both, in equal measures.

***

Angie comes in a compact hatchback. Not pulling a trailer. So, whatever happens, I guess I'm not losing Mac today.

She's complimentary left, right and centre. "He looks great," and "I've never seen his coat so shiny," and "His stable manners are excellent."

She also watches the video of Mac's exuberant buck, and my four-leaf-clover-lucky landing.

"Nice," Angie says, after Vanessa plays it back to her; producing her smart phone out of her back pocket despite Meg's eye-rolling. "Austen's landing, of course, but the buck, too. He looks more like the Mac I know." There's hope in her eyes, and as I lean on the fence watching her warm him up, I'm hoping he lives up to her expectations. Meeting Angie, seeing how she looks at Mac ... it's obvious how much she cares about him.

The girls gather around me and murmur, "Oooh, he's so pretty," and "Do you think he'll buck again?" and "I want to jump every day from now on."

A Google search for "healthy, happy horse" would bring up a picture of the way Mac looks right now. Fine thoroughbred lines, but more filled out than many horses off the track. Substantial, not just because of his seventeen plus hands, but the muscle and shape of him. Fine, gleaming coat sliding over all those muscles, catching the sun. Swinging, easy, strides. Neck carried with a pleasing arch – not high, not low – positioning his head well to let him see, hear, smell, breathe easily.

Angie looks like she's not moving at all, which really means she's moving well with him. Her legs are long and wrap nicely along his girth. The line from her elbows to his mouth is unbroken; contact steady, but light. Back straight, eyes forward.

"What do you think?" Meg nudges me.

"I think they're a great team."

"They weren't working so well together when she brought him here. You've made a big difference in him."

I watch them sweep over their first fence. Smooth, easy, forward.

"Is that how I looked jumping yesterday, Austen?" One of the campers asks. I look at the little girl with her shining eyes; remember her pudgy pony heaving himself over the same jump set to half its current height. I also remember his pricked ears and her forward, giving hands, and the huge smile on her face.

"You looked a lot like that," I say.

After Angie's taken Mac through a couple of variations of courses, she rides him forward into a square halt. "Wow!" She says. "He feels great. Is it possible to take him over a few cross-country jumps?"

"Of course!" Meg steps back from the fence. "Girls, come with me. We're going to do a quick check on the jumps in the near cross-country field." She points to each girl, and assigns them a jump – "You the tires," "You take the log," "You look at the coop."

"Run to the jump I gave you, look all around on both sides. Make sure there are no branches, rocks, or groundhog holes that could have appeared since the last time we were out there. Once we know all the jumps are clear, Angie will take Mac around and you can see how a real eventer takes those jumps."

***

The way he takes them is fast, big, and eager. As they go away from us there's a slight downhill slope to the field. I watch Angie give one, decisive, half-halt. Mac reacts; comes back to her; correction made, accepted, and moved past. She rides him forward again, this time with more of his attention, his respect re-established, and they head for the final three jumps. Straw bales – easy, brush – simple, and then they're aiming for the final – a log pile with a lower and a higher side.

Angie rides to the higher option, and as though saying, "I'll take your challenge and raise it," Mac rockets over the jump from an incredibly long spot and arches a good eighteen inches clear of it. He lands with a tail flourish, and the entire group of us watching, says, "Ohhhh ..."

He's going to buck again.

Sure enough, the energy whipcracks through him, starting in his head, traveling through his neck and body, and exploding through his flying heels.

Angie sits it like a bronc rider, appearing completely unfazed except for her helmet which she has to tip back into place after it skews across her forehead.

The girl and her horse canter back toward us, complete a beautiful, round circle, and sweep forward into a suspended trot, before walking toward us.

"He's amazing. He feels like his old self. No, wait, he feels better than his old self. He feels the best I've ever felt him. How on earth did you do it?"

***

Meg's set the girls up taking bridles apart and putting them back together in the shade of a big tree. "See if you can do it without looking," she challenged them.

I'm grooming Mac.

"You don't have to do that," Angie said. "I rode him – I can groom him."

"I'm happy to." Which is true. I fall into a rhythm. I curry him with steady, even, circles. Flick the resulting dust away with quick, swipes of the dandy brush. Smooth the body brush over his clean baby-soft coat.

While I work, Meg and Angie chat about how her other horses are going, a five-year-old Angie has on trial, her plans to upgrade her backyard barn so she can keep her horses at home – at least part of the year – then she says, "So, seriously, what did you do with him?" she asks Meg.

"Well, first of all, I didn't really do anything except assign him to Austen. I felt like they'd be a good fit, and I was right. She's been the main person working with him since he's been here."

"Awesome job, Austen," Angie says, and I smile before ducking out of sight to Mac's far side.

Meg continues. "Overall, philosophy-wise, it was just about letting him be *him*. Be a horse. He had lots of turnout. He had time on his own and with other horses. Austen hacked him, swam him, rode him with and without tack. We asked him to do lots, but mostly things that were new to him, or maybe that he hadn't done for a while. Anything else, Austen?"

I'm running my fingers through Mac's tail, now. I've never known a horse to be such a burr magnet. He somehow picked up a few just while Angie was riding him in the cross-country field. "Um ... well, just that he was great to work with. He's beautiful, of course, but he's really smart, too. He's patient, as well – which not all horses are. I'd ask him to do something different and he'd stay calm, and try it, and wait to see if that was right or if I wanted something else. It was cool – I could almost see him learning."

Meg nods. "I agree with Austen, I've seen him do that, too." She wrinkles her nose. "I'm not sure if I'll explain this properly but I kind of have this theory that our role is to give the horses the tools they need, then put them in a position where they want to do what we're asking them to. For some things, it's small, and quick – like it doesn't take long for them to figure out if they step sideways when we ask, they get praise, so they pretty quickly want to do it.

"For big things like Mac's entire attitude toward his work and jumping, it's a longer road – with some bends in it. But he got there eventually, and that's what's important; for him to decide himself."

Angie steps forward and Mac drops his nose into her cupped hands. "I've never had a horse go sour on me like he did."

Meg shrugs. "They're all different, right? I mean, that's what makes them so fun – and so frustrating – to work with."

"It's hard to tell you how much I appreciate what you've done," Angie says. "I wish there was something I could do to thank you properly."

I look at my watch, then over to Angie. "Well, if you were planning on leaving soon, there is one thing you could do."

"What's that?"

"If Meg's OK with me leaving now, it would be great if I could get a lift to the ferry."

Meg swats at me. "How many times today have I told you to leave any time?"

"I know," I say. "Too many to count." I look at Angie. "If we go in five or ten minutes we should be able to catch the next ferry."

• RAND •

Chapter Thirty-Four

Austen sticks her head around the corner, to where Jared and I are building partitions inside the lean-to, and says, "I just wanted to let you know I'm going over to Kingston now – Angie's giving me a lift to the ferry – so, uh, I thought ... I mean, I wondered, I mean ... is there anything you want over there? I can get anything you need; it's always good to have a reason to leave the hospital."

I'm holding a framed-up half wall in place while Jared hunts for the box of nails we've somehow misplaced since securing the last panel five minutes ago. Which means I can't let go. Can't accept her challenge and walk over and kiss her. Which sucks. "I'm good," I say. "I don't need anything. But ..." What do you say to somebody who's visiting their sister in the hospital? What's proper protocol? I don't really know. "… I hope it goes OK."

Lame, but likely not offensive. It'll have to do.

I guess it's OK, because she smiles a big, beaming, sweet, Austen smile and yells "Thanks! See you later!" over her shoulder as she disappears around the corner.

***

A couple of cars have come and gone; picking up the girls from camp, and I'm getting to the point where even the shade of the barn isn't giving me enough of a break from the temperature. The heat of the day has worked its way into me, and I'm going to need an icy drink and a cold shower – or maybe a swim; Austen would have a swim – to recover.

One more car pulls in, and it hasn't left yet, when I hear Meg calling, "I'll just check with the guys."

She trots over to us, and she also looks hot and tired as she pushes her hair away from her face. "I don't suppose you guys have seen a smart phone lying around anywhere?"

Jared says "No," at the same time as I say, "Nuh-uh," and Meg sighs.

"I didn't think so – I told Vanessa she shouldn't have brought it, but she got that video of Austen's crazy landing off Mac yesterday, and she's been showing it around all day and now, sure enough, the phone's missing. I don't think her mom's very happy – apparently it was brand new for her birthday last week."

"Yikes," Jared says.

"Yup. Tell me about it. Wanna trade? I'll build the shed, and you can tell the mother the five-hundred-dollar birthday gift is nowhere to be found."

It doesn't take long after that to finish securing all the framed-up panels into place and – voila – the inside has form, shape, stalls … well nearly. They're stalls you can walk right through, but it's cool to see the project coming together.

This work is hot, tiring, and blister-forming, but it's also satisfying. I'm glad Austen called me. Happy I came. Relieved Jared and I have worked together with almost no hostility today.

"Can you clean up here while I go phone in some of the supplies we're going to need for tomorrow?" Jared asks. "If I get the order in before they close, they'll put them on one of the morning ferries tomorrow and we can pick them up at the dock."

"My pleasure," I say. And it is. I like stacking the materials neatly against the barn walls. I like raking the area where we've been working – partly to pick up any stray nails, but mostly because it leaves neat criss-cross tracks in the dirt.

I'm done. At least I think I'm done. I wouldn't feel right leaving without checking in though, so I leave the rake propped next to my tidy pile of building stuff and head toward the house.

I'm walking along the side of the barn, trying to picture the food in my uncle's fridge; figuring out how I can combine it into a meal, when I hear my name. "Rand ..." It drifts out of the open door of the barn.

"Jared ..." It's Meg's voice, and something in her tone tells me the sentence she's replying to wasn't, 'I'm really enjoying working with Rand,' or 'I've never met such a hard worker as Rand.'

"I'm just saying ..." Jared says.

Meg interrupts. "He's working hard for you, isn't he? And Austen really likes him."

I don't have time to bask in the idea of Austen really liking me, because Jared's talking again. "I don't know, Meg. Yes, he's a good worker. And, yes, he must be doing something right for Austen to like him. But there's an expensive phone missing – remember Austen even told us he doesn't have a cell – and he's got a record."

"Everything you've heard is rumours."

"I know you don't want me to jump to conclusions, but I also don't want to keep my head in the sand ..."

My fists are clenched, and when that happens I know I should take a deep breath. My arms are shaking, and this is definitely the right time to count to ten.

I don't though – don't breathe, or count – just stride right through the door, then stand like an idiot for a second because in the sudden switch from bright sunlight to the dim interior, I can hardly see at all.

My fumble makes me ever angrier, and with my pupils adjusted I whirl to Jared. "You know, if you were smart, you'd make sure I can't overhear you when you talk about me behind my back."

"Rand ..." Meg steps forward.

I shake my head, without taking my eyes off Jared. "I don't need some little girl's stupid smart phone, and I don't need to work for somebody like you. And, you know what? Yes, I did some dumb things, but I'm still more honest than you – I wouldn't sneak around talking about you behind your back."

There are a lot of ways I'd like to finish that thought – most of them pretty profane – but Meg's there, and this isn't about Meg. And the tiny part of me that's still thinking, that's holding on to reason, knows a very good way to lose my edge – to pull myself off the high horse I'm riding on – would be to start spewing four-letter words.

So I leave it at that, spin on my heel and walk away.

I walk so fast, and the blood's rushing so loud in my ears, that I'm halfway back to my uncle's place before I realize my bike's still back at Jared's house, propped against the tree I leaned it against when I arrived this morning.

When I arrived, energized and happy to go to work.

There's no way I'm going back there now. I'll figure it out later.

***

If I ever deserved a beer, it's tonight.

I'm staring into the fridge, eyes closed, loving the feeling of the cold air on my front; kind of wishing I could crawl in and shut the door behind me; just live in a cool, sound-proofed box full of beer and bacon – when Dole starts whining and scratching at the screen door, pushing a choking smell ahead of him.

Skunk. Great.

This dog. This stupid, accident-prone, trouble-on-four-legs, ridiculous dog.

I kind of love him.

If Austen was the first person to listen to me, to ask me how I was after the accident, this dog was the first creature to make me feel like he needed me. Feeling needed – well, there's something about it that's hard to resist. "Come on dummy. Let's go de-skunk you."

I'm crouched on the lawn, sore-backed, hands pruning with tomato juice, and Dole turned from a yellow to a pink lab, when my uncle drives in.

Coal jumps out of the truck barking, tail wagging, and I take a tight hold of Dole's collar to keep him from taking off after his buddy.

"Ah, that's why I couldn't find him when I left earlier," my uncle says.

"Yup," I say. "This is my fourth can of tomato juice."

He grins. "Lucky for me you got home from work early. Skunks, dogs, and tomato juice are a combination I really hate."

Work.

I could just let it go. But this is a small island, with lots of talk. I wonder how long it'll take for my uncle to hear some version of what happened today. I could let that happen when he's at the general store, or at the dump, or on the ferry. Or, I could tell him now and make sure he hears my side of the story.

I don't want to. But if I have any hope of staying here I think I have to.

"About work," I say. "There's something I have to tell you ..."

***

A flush of red has spread across my uncle's face, and he's shaking his head – angry but, to my surprise, not at me. "That Strickland kid's always had a stubborn streak in him." He pulls off his baseball cap, runs his hands through his hair. "To be honest, I was surprised he let you work up there. I knew he was asking around about you and I was pretty sure he'd hear a bunch of half-truths. When he hired you, I figured that girl had something to do with it, and when he kept you on, I figured you were showing him you were a good worker."

He seems to be waiting for a reaction from me so I say, "I tried."

He nods. "I know. I've seen you help out around here. That Delaney girl you've been hanging out with – she's a nice kid – she wouldn't spend time with you if you weren't pulling your weight."

An ache spears through me; I miss Austen. I wish she was here.

My uncle continues. "That Jared, I reckon he was set against you from the beginning. Now he's just making stupid accusations without thinking. I should go up there and talk to him."

I absolutely didn't expect support like this from my uncle. I still wish Austen was here, but him having my back is pretty nice.

"I appreciate your support, but you don't have to fight my battles for me. I'll figure it out somehow."

"I won't say anything for now," my uncle says. "But if you need help, let me know. In the meantime, how hungry are you? I was thinking of going into the village for a burger."

"I'd love that."

My uncle settles his cap back on his head. "Strickland's loss can be my gain – why don't you come do some work for me at the lodge tomorrow?"

"Yeah. Sure. That would be great."

"If we're going out to eat you'd better change out of those clothes."

He picks up a stick and whips it into the bay and both dogs bound after it. He grins. "Easiest way to rinse him off."

As I get up to head inside he adds, "Put the clothes somewhere you can wear them again, though. That dog's about five more tomato juice cans away from being allowed in the house."

I clear my throat. "Gotcha."

My uncle laughs. "You might as well get good at tomato-juice baths if you're going to stick around here. This is the fourth time this year that dog's been skunked."

If you're going to stick around here.

Could I? Would he have me? I feel like he's opened the door for me to at least ask. There is one question I want to ask right away. "Could you help me with something?"

"Sure. What?"

"Those swings I'm working on. I want to customize them – you know engrave names on them – I don't know the best way."

"No problem. Eat first, then after dinner we'll look at them together. I'll give you a couple of options and you can figure out how you want to do it."

"Thanks."

He shrugs. "No big deal. You just need to ask."

• AUSTEN •

Chapter Thirty-Five

Eliot looks – I don't know – it depends which part of her you look at.

It's been that way for a while. Her knees, and wrists, and elbows are disgusting. Sharp and bony.

I love her, but I don't want to touch her. It's too repellent, too upsetting. I Googled once, to see if I could find a word that describes a phobia of touching bony people. I found a few specific ones – like carpophobia, the fear of wrists, or the fear of touching collarbones, clavicaphobia – but nothing that addresses the overall feeling I have that a good, strong squeeze from me could re-arrange all my sister's bones. So I avoid contact.

I still love Eliot's face – her eyes – they're still big, and dark, like my mom's. Now, with my parents gone to take

Shaw to the nearby park to run off some energy, Eliot makes fun of them, of the doctors, of the nurses. Not in a mean way – just eerily accurately. She says, "Oh, Steven!" in my mom's exact voice – even down to the little sigh on the end – drifting an image of my dad's shrugging shoulders into my mind.

"It wasn't me ..." I protest and Eliot's eyes fill with laughter at my imitation of my dad.

"For his birthday we should totally get him a shirt that says that."

If you're alive for his birthday.

Even though I don't say the words out loud, Eliot's smart enough to read into my hesitation. It sucks the sparkle from her eyes, opens me up to feel my first deep pang of sadness of the day.

My sister's not giving in, though. No true confessions, no deep discussions. "Speaking of Dad, I hear he's not exactly a fan of my rescuing hero ... or should I say, *your* rescuing hero, since what I heard him complaining about is that Rand was still at the cottage when he showed up last night."

I wave my hand. "Mom and Dad have themselves all worked up about him. They think ... I don't know what they think."

"Yes you do," Eliot says. "You know exactly what they think."

She crosses her arms, leans back in her bed and grins, while my cheeks begin to burn. She points at me, "And from the colour of your face I can see they're right."

I shake my head.

"Don't deny it, Austen. He is super-cute." Her skinny fingers encircle my lower arm. I look at them and breathe deeply – *don't flinch, don't pull away* – and force myself to meet her eyes instead. "What's making you blush?" Her face is animated, again – so pretty, and inviting. It's how I want her to be; what I miss. So I reward her.

"OK, I'll admit he's cute. And really smart. And funny."

She brushes her hand across her forehead. "Phew, well that's a relief. I can tell Mom and Dad not to worry because I can see how all those attributes make him really unattractive."

I shift in my seat, and the cracked vinyl of the chair pinches my skin. "Even though Rand's all those things I said, he's really not my type. And I'm almost positive I'm not his. And I don't even know how long he's here for ... so, yeah, nothing for them to worry about ..."

"But?" Eliot asks.

"But it makes me mad how they won't give him a chance. And, it seems like they don't trust me even though I've never done anything to make them not trust me. They give me these 'don't give us a hard time,' speeches ..." I trail off. This is getting close to the bone.

"... because I'm giving them enough of a hard time." Eliot finishes.

"Something like that," I say.

Eliot fiddles with the tubing leading from her drip into her body. I try not to look because anything going into human skin also freaks me out quite a bit. Trypanophobia, it's called. I looked it up once. These days, the entire physical presence of my sister flares my phobias.

"You know what I think?" she asks.

"What?"

"You should give them a hard time."

"You think, huh?" Now I'm sitting back, crossing my arms.

She holds up her palm. "I'm not saying do it on purpose to bug them. I'm saying do what makes you happy. Don't let them stop you. I know ..."

Her voice trails off. She looks away, bites her lip.

"You know what, Eliot?"

"He – Rand – he said to me yesterday, that I make your life hard." When she looks back, her eyes are shiny. "Look at me telling you not to let Mom and Dad stop you from doing what makes you happy, when it's actually me that does it. I know they sold your pony to pay for my first rehab. And then you could never get another horse, because ... well ... more rehab. And I know I screwed up the weekend you were supposed to spend with Tyler the last time I went to the hospital."

"Eliot!"

She blinks. "I'm not sorry about Tyler. He might have had Mom and Dad fooled – might have looked like the perfect boyfriend – but, in my opinion, he was just a perfect asshole. And, as for the money thing, I just won't go to rehab. It's not like I want to. And if I don't go, there won't be any bills, so you can afford a matched team of horses, no problem."

I just look at her. She sighs. "I know. As if."

I lean forward and pat her leg. I don't mind touching her when there are covers padding her out. "The you-having-any-choice-about-going-to-rehab ship has long sailed, my friend. You're going."

"What? I'm pretty sure I didn't pick the tall ships rehab. I wanted the rescue dog one."

She has saline dripping into her, the jut of her collarbone gives me the heebie-jeebies, she attracts mice to our bedroom, but she's still my sister and she can still make me laugh.

It starts as laughing, anyway, but then I think of a time when I can't laugh with her anymore, because she's dead, and a few sobs start creeping in.

"Austen? What is it, Austen?"

This time I'm going to be brave. This time I'm going to say it. Because what's the point of not saying it? "Right now I don't mind there not being money for a horse for me, and I don't mind having my entire summer – carefully planned, I might add ..." I raise one eyebrow at her when I say this "... yanked out from under me. But I will start to resent them – quite a bit – if you keep starving yourself."

Eliot freezes. Her eyes go huge and round. Her face goes white, except for irregular red splotches on her cheeks. "I. Am. Not. Starving. Myself."

I lift my hand. "I know, I know, Eliot. Believe me, I get it. It's complicated. And – OK – so you're not precisely, exactly, trying to starve yourself. But guess what? That's what's happening. Like if I jump out of an airplane without a parachute, I can tell you my main aim is to see what it feels like to fly, but in the end – guess what? – I'm going to die."

I stop, drop my hands into my lap, and look straight at my sister. "I'm sick of not saying it, and I'm sick of nobody else ever saying it either. You. Are. Going. To. Die."

I look down, then back up again. "And I have to live with that. And keep living. And if that's what happens, I'm at least going to know I said something to you."

I brace for her to tell me to shut up and get out of her room – except using a less-polite term than "shut up." I wait for her to pop earbuds in and turn away from me with her knobby spine and blaring music sending an even clearer message than any version of "shut up" ever could.

What I don't expect is the tear that runs down her left cheek, closely followed by one trickling down her right. What I'm not ready for, is her sobbing gulp, "What do you expect me to do, Austen?"

It's the question I've been waiting for as long as I can remember. It's one years of overhearing my parents' conversations, and listening in on doctors, and spending long hours on Google, and just my own common sense has equipped me to answer. No problem. I'm itching to give her a list of ten things to do.

Except. I flash back to Meg's answer to Angie's question about Mac – how did we get him to love jumping again? Meg said it was important for him to decide for himself. She explained we gave him the tools, then tried to put him in a position where he wanted to do what we were asking him to.

And I agreed with her. Wholeheartedly. She summed it up exactly.

So I bite my tongue. I hold back the deep instinct to tell my sister 'I know what you should do, and when and how you should do it, and I'll hold your hand the whole time.'

Instead I say, "You need to decide, Eliot. You need to decide what you really, really want to do. I think that's the hardest part of all. I think after that everything will be easier."

Then, because my sister looks, not angry, or defiant, and because – for these few seconds anyway – she's not up to her ears in denial telling me I'm crazy, I cave just the little, tiniest bit, and say, "And I will be here. Because I love you." And I lean forward and gather her scrawny bones against me and, actually, to my surprise, it feels quite nice.

• RAND •

Chapter Thirty-Six

I wait until my uncle's eaten his burger, and most of his fries. Until he's had a coffee, and chatted with the owner about catering for a big event the hunting group wants to have at the lodge.

As I contemplate asking him for what's probably the biggest favour I've ever asked of anybody, I realize I haven't been very good at asking for help in the past. In fact, I've been terrible. I never asked my dad if he could stay around more. I never asked if he could help me deal with my mom. I never told her the things she was doing that bothered me. I just figured she must know, and was choosing to keep doing them ... I wonder if it would have been different if I'd asked.

I clear my throat.

"What's up?" my uncle asks.

"I need to ask you a favour."

"Shoot."

"It's kind of a big favour. It's actually huge. You should just say no if it's too much. In fact, I probably shouldn't ask ..."

"Rand?"

"Yeah?"

"Shut up and ask the question."

I take a deep breath. "OK. Here goes. I like it here. On this island. At your place. A lot. I feel more at home here than I can remember ever feeling anywhere else. I don't want to go back to the city – not now, and not at the end of the summer. I'd like to stay. But to stay here, well, I'd have to stay with you."

"So, what exactly are you asking me, Rand?"

"Would you ever consider letting me stay with you? And going to school on the mainland? On a trial basis. To be kicked out at any time ..."

He cuts me off. "I was wondering if you'd ask."

"You were?"

"Yup. Ever since you started getting up before noon, and got a job, and started mowing the lawn, and buying groceries, and washing the dog, I wondered if you were starting to feel at home."

"Oh, so would you let me?"

He pops a fry in his mouth, leans back in his chair, and looks at me. "Well, I think the bigger question might be, would your parents let you? Don't you think?"

I nod. "Yes. That is a huge question. But I figure there's no point asking them if you want nothing to do with me."

He laughs. "Fair enough. OK, let's say, I do want something to do with you. Surprisingly, I like having you around. You're a lot more fun than the last time your mom visited with you."

"I was four."

"You whined a lot."

I open my mouth to defend my four-year-old self, then the penny drops. He's saying I can stay. *If* I can convince my parents.

Which is a huge if.

But his yes also feels like a massive yes.

I stop. Grin. "Really?"

"Yeah, really."

"Wow, OK. Dinner's on me."

"I already said yes Rand, you don't have to bribe me."

"Just making sure you don't change your mind before I can email my parents."

***

It's the first thing I do when we get back.

I coax the old laptop to life – if I'm going to stay here, I'll bring my laptop from home and it'll be much faster.

If I'm going to stay.

I login, and while it's tempting to email just my dad, I figure I've got to do this right. I select both my parents' addresses.

Mom and Dad,

There's something I need to discuss with you.

I'm doing really well here. I like it a lot.

I'd like to ask you to consider letting me stay here.

Uncle Kurt says he'd allow it, if you will. I'd go to high school in Kingston. There's a school bus that takes all the high school kids across on the ferry every day.

I know this is a big ask. I don't know what your reaction will be.

I'm prepared to do whatever I need to convince you.

Please let me know what you think.

Rand

P.S. A friend I've made here has made me see things I didn't see before. I understand how dangerous what I did was. I've been working on a kind of project to try to apologize to Joe and I'd like to talk to you about it.

I cross my fingers as I hit send. Cross them because I want this so badly. Cross them because I'm going to need luck. Cross them because of that line – "I'm doing really well here" – this thing with Jared could really mess things up for me.

It's great that my uncle believes me but I'm not sure that'll be enough to sway my mom.

If I'm going to be able to stay here, I need a spotless reputation, and I need it soon.

For what feels like the twentieth time today, I wish Austen was here.

Which is so selfish, because I'm the one who watched the paramedics carry her sister away, and I know she needs to be with her sister.

But, I need her too.

I go so far as to walk to the end of the dock and look across at her cottage. Her completely dark cottage.

Tomorrow will have to do. I have to find a time tomorrow to talk to her. Maybe by then I'll have a plan. Maybe I can run it by her.

As I'm walking back from the water, my uncle ducks out from under the propped-up hood of his truck. "Hey, you want to look at those swings now? Figure out the engraving?"

"Yeah," I say. "Definitely. Thanks."

***

It's great working with my uncle. He talks me through using hand-held tools or a power rotary. We discuss what type of lettering might look best, and where I want to place it.

At first I thought I'd put Austen's name right across the front, but I have an idea to make a kind of secret of the lettering – to place the letters of her name strategically so it's like a treasure hunt to find them. "Neat idea," Kurt says.

I think I'll do Joe's across the front – maybe with their family name, or the address – I'll ask him first, so it's customized to his taste, but working on Austen's it's fun to figure out how best to scatter her name.

My uncle seeks out particularly rough patches on the swing, and sands them smooth, while I use the router.

When I'm done he asks, "Do you want to hang it up now? It'll make varnishing it much easier."

"I ... yeah ... sure – won't that be a big job?"

"Nah." He points to the rafters. "There's already chain looped over them from when we did some work on a buddy's car in here – we lifted the whole transmission out. We can get that swing hung up in no time, and it hardly weighs anything compared to a car transmission."

He's right – it doesn't take long. We both stand back and look at it. I squint, and tilt my head, and pretend I'm making sure it's hanging level but really I'm just filled with immense satisfaction to see something I designed, and built, that's so, so close to being done.

He claps his hand on my shoulder. "Nice work."

I shrug. "I like it, but every now and then I wonder if it's the stupidest gift on earth. I mean a great big swing. It's not exactly a gift someone can tuck away in a cupboard."

"Now, come on Rand. For your neighbour – well, you and I both know he has a porch – right? And this is something really beautiful – you'd pay lots of money for it, if you could even find something similar."

"And for the girl, well ..." he shrugs. "I'm not a teenage girl, but I think she'll be amazed. And if she doesn't have room for it right now, no need to worry – I'll keep it for her, as long as you, or she, wants me to."

I don't know why, but something in his words hits a spot so deep and tender I have to blink back tears.

"Thanks Uncle Kurt," I say.

"My pleasure." He squeezes my shoulder. "Now, it's time to hit the hay. We have a lot to do tomorrow."

I can't remember the last time somebody gave even the slightest indication of caring when I went to bed. It feels nice. So, I push down my instinct to say, 'Don't worry about me. I'll be fine,' and instead I say, "Sure. OK. Thanks."

I'll go to bed on time every night if I get to stay here.

• AUSTEN •

Chapter Thirty-Seven

It's my second early wake up in a row. I eat yogurt mixed with granola while leaning against the kitchen counter, put most of the contents of the fruit bowl in my backpack and leave a note for my parents before I tiptoe out the door.

Going to work. Hope you guys have / had a nice sleep-in. I'll come over later to see Eliot again.

Then I cycle up to work.

The first thing I notice as I walk toward the barn, is Rand's bike propped against the tree where he usually leaves it.

Rand. I didn't expect him to be here so early. It's hard to talk to my parents about Eliot. They don't like to let me be too hopeful, but they also don't like me to despair. I guess I'm the same way with them. The result is, we don't tend to tell each other exactly how we're feeling about my sister.

I want to talk to someone about it, and Rand feels like the right person.

Maybe we'll have lunch together. Maybe I'll get brave and invite him to come to Kingston with me when I go to see Eliot. That would be cool. Maybe I'll even introduce him to my sister. When she's properly conscious, that is. We could get ice cream in Kingston. We could go out for dinner …

I meander over to peer around the corner of the barn where the lean-to's nearly done.

No Jared, no Rand, no building, no action. Just a framed-up shell and neatly piled materials.

Huh. Weird. Maybe they're working on something else Jared needs help with. Fencing, or something like that.

Before I can wonder about it too much, Meg comes out of the house, catches my eye and motions me over to the porch.

"Here," she says. "I'm having green tea. When I saw you cycle up I made you a mug, too. Sit down," she says.

As soon as I've taken a seat next to her on the top step, she says, "So, I have good news, and bad news. Which do you want first?"

Normally I'd take bad. I usually do – I like getting it over with and having something nice to look forward to, but for some reason I say, "Good, please."

She nods, picks up her phone, scrolls around, and hands it to me. I find myself reading an email from Angie. Or at least part of an email:

Meg, as you know I was very impressed with how Mac's looking, feeling, everything. You – or you and Austen – have worked wonders with him. I was wondering what you thought about Austen taking Mac in a short course event to ease him back into competing. I haven't seen her ride him, but from the way he's going, she must be capable. Do you think she'd be interested? There's an event coming up in a few weeks not far from you.

"Whoa! Am I interested? Wow! And does that mean Mac stays here until then? Oh Meg, I am so super-excited. Can I reply right now? To this email? Or do you want to answer her?"

Meg laughs and hands her phone over and I thumb a reply. **Angie – it's me – Austen! Yes, yes, yes. That's all I can say right now, other than "Thank you!" I'm really, really excited.**

Meg reads it over. "Perfect. We'll get you guys registered and figure out all the details."

I can't wait to tell Manda. I can't wait to tell Rand. This is so cool. This is amazing. This is ...

"... bad news," Meg's saying.

Oh yeah. I kind of conveniently forgot about that.

"What is it?" I ask.

"I'm guessing you haven't talked to Rand."

"Why? What? Is he OK? Did something happen?" My heart goes zero to sixty – hammering hard against my chest.

Meg puts her hand on my arm. "He's fine. But he won't be here today."

I'm confused. "But his bike's here."

She sighs. "Yes. He left so quickly yesterday he went without it." Then she starts telling me something about Vanessa's cell phone – the one she used to record my unplanned dismount from Mac – and it being missing, and my eyebrows are hurting because they're knitting together so tightly, and I say, "I'm sorry to cut you off, but what on earth does that have to do with Rand?"

Meg sighs, and says, "Well, Jared ..." and in a flash the pieces click together for me. Jared, and how he feels about Rand, and a missing cell phone.

"Rand didn't take it." I state it as flat fact. He didn't. I know as sure as I anything in this world he didn't. I know in the same way I know everything is not going to be fixed with Eliot just because we had a few frank words.

How can I explain to Meg how certain I am? It has nothing to do with me wearing blinkers, or being overly optimistic, or not facing reality. I don't think – not for one second do I think – that Rand has only ever done good things in his life. But what I do believe, more than anything, is there's a very good reason he'd never do such a stupid thing. I look Meg straight in the eye and say, "He likes me too much to do that."

Meg's gaze never wavers from mine. "I think that's true, Austen."

"Then, why send him away? Tell him you believe him. Bring him back."

"I wish it was that simple." She places two mugs on the counter, one handle angled toward me; the other facing her.

"Why isn't it?"

"Rand overheard Jared talking to me. Jared saying he was suspicious ..."

"Oh." Such an inadequate word for the pang of pain stabbing me as I imagine how that would feel. "And, I'm guessing Rand didn't take it very well."

Meg shrugs. "About how you'd expect. Hence going so fast he left his bike behind."

The bike that made me smile just a little while ago. Now I'm going to feel sick to my stomach every time I look at it.

"I'm sorry," I say. "I can't finish this drink. I'm going to go groom Mac. I need to think."

***

It's all I do the rest of the morning – think, and try to call Rand.

I only have a couple of chances – it's a personal rule of mine not to use my phone when I'm responsible for kids or animals – so I pull it out once in the bathroom, and another time when Meg sends me to the kitchen to fill up a pitcher of water for the girls to drink.

Both times Rand's uncle's phone rings and rings. Both times, I curse his uncle's voice asking me to leave a message. I don't want to leave a message. I want to talk to Rand.

Jared drives in around noon, and he and Meg eat lunch on the deck together, while I sit in the shade with the girls and let their light-hearted, horsey chatter wash around me while I think some more.

I force myself to eat slowly. Count to ten so many times I've probably counted to a thousand. Use the acronym I read somewhere on the internet – *THINK before you speak; is it True? Is it Helpful? Is it Inspiring? Is it Necessary? Is it Kind?*

What I have to say passes on some counts, maybe not on others. I don't feel like there's a lot of kindness in this whole transaction, however I'm going to tell the truth about how I feel and, yes, to me that seems necessary.

I feel like a marked man – *person,* I guess – on my way over to Jared and Meg. They watch me coming, I know they're watching me coming, and they know I know they're watching me coming.

Awkward.

I stop in front of them, take a deep breath, and say, "So, I have to tell you something."

As easy as it would be to imagine Jared as a big, mean, brute, he's not. He's just a normal guy in worn jeans and a t-shirt. He has tanned cheeks and chapped lips, and tiny smile creases at the corners of his eyes. He's been nice to me since the moment Meg introduced us. I think he'd say, when it comes to Rand, he's tried to protect me.

And now, he nods, and says, "Shoot."

See? A nice guy.

Which is why it's hard to say, "I can't work here anymore."

"Oh!" Meg says.

"I'm sorry." I look at Meg. "I don't want to leave you hanging. I'll finish today, but that's all I can do."

Jared puts his hand on Meg's knee and looks at me. "Austen, if this is about the phone – and I'm assuming it is about the phone – it's got nothing to do with you."

I shake my head. "It does, though. I called Rand to work here. I'm in the middle of it. I like you guys, and I like Rand. I don't want to choose between you, but *he didn't do it.*"

It was hard to start, but now that I'm talking, I'm on a roll. The trick is going to be not saying too much. *Wrap it up,* I tell myself.

"I'm really sorry Vanessa lost her phone. It must be upsetting. I don't want my paycheque tomorrow Meg." The cheque is for two weeks work, and it'll be more than enough to get Vanessa a new phone. "You can give the money to Vanessa's parents."

Meg's shaking her head. "I'm giving you the cheque."

I shrug. "Your choice. You can't force me to cash it."

"Why are we even talking about a cheque? You don't have to stop work here."

"Yes. I do. I'm sorry, but I do. I'm leaving at three to get on the three-thirty boat to see my sister. I'll come back tomorrow if there are things you need me to wrap up, but otherwise, that's it."

Jared stands, takes a step toward me. "Austen, really, we wish you'd stay."

"I wish you'd call Rand and tell him you made a mistake."

Jared doesn't move, speak, nothing.

I nod. "Yeah, well, you need to do what feels right to you, and I need to do what feels right to me."

I turn, walk a few steps, then hesitate. The polite girl in me – the girl who likes to do what's right, and play by the rules, and smooth things over – wants to say sorry. I'm not, though. Not at all.

Don't say it.

I've just walked myself out of a job I really, really like, surrounded by horses all day, and it feels like the right thing to do.

So, I'm glad I did it.

It still doesn't make any of this easy, though.

• RAND •

Chapter Thirty-Eight

After my uncle sends me off to bed, I do fall asleep – easily and quickly.

Until I snap awake, fast and fully alert.

I don't know if it was a branch rubbing against the house, or the wind gusting up and rattling the window, or just that I rolled over the wrong way and set off a muscle cramp – whatever happened, I wake up at two-seventeen and I cannot get back to sleep.

Toss. Turn. Think. Worry.

Long for Austen. For everything about her. Remember her pulled down beside me on this very mattress. Sprawled across me on her couch.

If it wouldn't make her parents hate me even more, I'd cycle, run, swim, row – whatever – over to her cottage now, and throw rocks at her bedroom window.

Maybe with some Peppermint Schnapps in me, I'd do that anyway. However, the sane, sober, sensible me decides to use my energy for something else.

I pad downstairs and put a mug of milk in the microwave while I bring up my email.

Bingo. My dad's name is bolded in my inbox.

Rand and Liv,

Travel details attached. I fly into Toronto tomorrow.

Liv, I'd like to pick you up and drive to see Rand. I'm hoping you'll clear your schedule to do this.

Rand, we'll arrive late afternoon. Aiming for the 4:00 or 5:00 boat.

We need to sort things out.

See you both soon.

Dan / Dad

I'm having a hard time remembering the last time I saw my dad. I can't remember the last time he called my mom "Liv."

I'm hoping both are good signs.

I guess I'll find out soon.

I send a quick reply. **OK. That sounds good. I'll try to meet the ferry if I can.**

The microwave dings that my milk is warm and I'm suddenly too tired to even drink it. I just put the mug back in the fridge and pad upstairs to bed.

***

I have to, want to, need to talk to Austen.

After yesterday, I'm not even sure how her day will go, but assuming she's going to work, she'll get there and I won't be there, and somebody else will tell her about yesterday's drama.

She should hear about it from me.

I'm going to have to call her.

I force myself to wait. To eat breakfast and put my dishes away. To kill time until it's a reasonable hour for phone calls.

I double-check the number scrawled on a yellowing list my uncle keeps under the phone; punch in the number written next to "Traherne."

I hold my breath the whole time the phone's ringing so, by the time, a man's voice says, "Hello?" I have to take a huge gasp of air.

For the first time in a long time I'm thankful for my mom – for her drilling phone manners into my head as a kid – so my response is automatic: “Oh, hi. This is Rand calling. May I please speak with Austen?”

There are a couple of seconds of silence I really don’t enjoy waiting through, then he says. “I’m afraid she’s already left for work.”

“Oh.” Is he lying? Is that what the pause was about? But even if he is, what am I supposed to do about it?

“Is there a message you’d like me to give her?”

“I, uh, no thank you. That’s fine. I’m sure I’ll speak to her later.”

Because, really, what kind of message am I supposed to leave with the-dad-who-already-doesn’t-like-me?

Crap. How am I going to talk to her now?

***

I’m in my uncle Kurt’s pick-up, heading to the lodge.

“My parents are coming,” I tell him.

“OK,” he says.

“Here,” I say. “Like, arriving on one of the late afternoon boats.”

“Alright,” he says.

“Probably to discuss ...” I lift my fingers to make air quotes, “My Future.”

“Well,” he says. “I guess we’d better make up another bedroom.”

“Or two,” I say.

He looks at me for the first time. “Really? It’s like that?”

"Last I knew."

He runs his hand through his hair. "Well, after we have our talk about your future, maybe I'd better have a talk with my little sister about hers."

***

My uncle's proud of the lodge, and with good reason. The entrance is tiled, with tonnes of space for boots and heavy outdoor gear, and it turns into a kind of corridor, also tiled, which is also a kitchen. Or, precisely, two kitchens in a row. Those open up into a massive living / eating room with a dining room table that starts seating twelve, and can pull out to add nearly twice as many places.

This is clearly a place where big, hungry men come to play, eat and, in between, sleep.

It's the sleeping part we're tackling today. Apart from one room holding a king-sized bed, the rest of the sleeping accommodations are bunks. This place is like sleepover camp for grown-ups.

My uncle shows me an awkward corner, currently unused – "Do you see where we could fit two bunks in there?"

I walk in, turn around. "Uh-huh, I think they'd just go. I mean, they might not be a standard bed size."

"No big deal," he says. "We build 'em in then take the inside measurements. There's a place in town that'll make us custom mattresses. I've got the materials, the question is; do you think you can do it?"

I think of the straight, sturdy walls of the almost-finished lean-to at Jared's. Think of the growing confidence I had in measuring, planning, and executing different parts of that project. Think of the mental and physical satisfaction I felt at the end of every day. Then, for some reason, I think of Austen and I know what she'd say.

"Yeah. I can do it."

"Great. I'll show you where I keep the tools."

***

"You OK, Rand?"

While I had a focus in front of me – wood, space, a project to make – I did alright, but now, while my uncle puts all his tools away with a precision I would never have expected having lived in his house for a few weeks, I'm pacing.

I know I do this. Walk, and fiddle. I pick things up and put them down, and sometimes I drop them, and they break, and my mom / teacher / the adult in charge of me, asks, "Do you have to touch *everything*?"

I'm aware that "You OK?" is a nice way of saying, 'You're driving me frickin' crazy with your incessant motion.'

"I just ..." I'm tempted to tell him about Austen. About not being able to talk to her. Wondering how she's reacting to the news of my quitting / firing. I take the easy way out, though. "I left my bike at Jared's place yesterday."

"You mean *my* bike, right?"

"I ... uh ..." Whoops. I never asked my uncle if I could use the bike. It seemed pretty neglected – I didn't think he'd mind.

He continues, "Since it's mine, we definitely have to get it back. I'll take you over there now."

"I feel really awkward about it."

"I know you do. That's why I'm going too."

• AUSTEN •

Chapter Thirty-Nine

Even though I believe it's the right thing to do, leaving Meg's for the last time feels weird.

It turns out I'm going to have no problem catching the three-thirty ferry since Vanessa's birthday celebration is tonight so all the girls are being picked up early to change and go over to Kingston for a dinner-and-a-movie night.

With their tack put away, and their ponies snug in their stalls, I'm left with an empty aisle to sweep; no stray halters, abandoned brushes, or dropped hoodies to work around.

When the barn is spotless – with only a lazy pattern of floating dust motes to adorn it – I hang up the broom and take hold of the wheelbarrow full of hay to go to the ponies in the sand ring. Double-check all their water buckets and I'll be done.

When I get to the final stall containing Vanessa's pony – the smallest, chunkiest of them – he reaches his nose out and I give it a rub. His velvety muzzle wrinkles back, exposing big, stained teeth. "Ew, you need some tooth whitener, don't you?"

I move my hand higher, to scratch his poll and my eye travels along his neck to his withers. "Oh boy – are the flies bugging you?"

Unlike the mare I used to ride at home, who was driven to distraction by the flies, and always had to wear a bonnet for turn-out, these guys are pretty nonchalant about insects. However, I've rarely seen this many swarming any of them at one time.

Just around his withers, though. Weird ...

... his withers. His withers. What is that making me think of?

"Meg!" I call.

The pony swivels his ear to me.

"Sorry, bud," I say. "But I have to talk to Meg. This could be important."

• RAND •

Chapter Forty

As we make the turn to head up to Jared's, I blurt out. "There's something else."

"What?"

"Austen. She doesn't know what happened. Well, I mean she does know by now, but it wasn't me who told her. I tried to call her this morning, and her dad said she'd already left for work ..."

"Will she be here now?"

I look at the dashboard clock. "She should be."

"Then talk to her. I'll wait."

"Yeah. OK. Thanks."

I climb out of the cab and look back at my uncle before heading over toward my bike. "I appreciate it."

He shakes his head. "Don't be stupid. I'll help you out anytime I can."

"Ditto," I say.

"Of course," he says. "Of course. Now go."

***

"Rand!"

I freeze. It's a girl's voice, but not the one I wanted to hear.

"Hi Meg," I say. "I was just picking up my bike."

"Oh good." She glances over at my uncle's truck, raises her hand in a wave to him. "I was going to throw it in the back of the truck and bring it down to you later."

I clear my throat. My eyes dodge hers. "That would have been nice of you, but no need now."

"Listen, Rand. I'm really sorry about what happened. We've been worried about you."

I snort. "We?" I find it hard to believe Jared's very worried about me.

"Austen was really upset when she heard about it."

Austen. Meg mentioned her. Now I can take the opening and follow up. "To be honest, I mostly came to see Austen. Can I talk to her?"

Meg's shaking her head. "I'm sorry – she's not here."

"Oh." I'm more inclined to believe Meg than I was to believe Austen's dad this morning, but Austen is starting to feel like a will-o'-the-wisp flitting just out of my reach.

"She quit, Rand."

"She what?" My eyes float to Mac – No Faults at All, she told me his show name was, and she said she thought it was perfect because, to her, he has no faults – it's hard to believe she left *him.*

"She said you didn't take that phone. She told us – Jared and me – that she knew you didn't do it and she couldn't work here under the circumstances. She told me not to pay her this week and to give the money to Vanessa's mom to buy her a new phone."

"I can't believe she did that."

"I can," Meg says. "She trusts you, and she believes in you, but mostly she likes you."

My brain is spinning. When am I going to talk to her? Movement catches my eye and I glance over to see Jared coming around the corner of the barn. I really, deeply, intensely, don't want to talk to him right now.

"I've got to go," I tell Meg, and start to wheel my bike away. "Thanks for telling me."

"Of course," Meg says. "If you need anything, you know where I am."

I lift the bike into the back of the truck, climb into the passenger seat, and tell my uncle. "Thanks. Great. Can we go?"

He's already got the truck moving.

I glance at the dashboard clock. "And, actually ..."

"I'm one step ahead of you," he says. "We're heading to the village to see if they're on the next boat."

• AUSTEN •

Chapter Forty-One

"What is *up* with you, Austen? That's the second time you've knocked the tablet over."

I'm crammed next to Eliot, watching North and South on her tablet and, oh, I love this story. I adore this adaptation. I want to have lunch with Richard Armitage.

But I can't sit still.

Eliot and I both actually adore Victorian literature. Jane Austen sucks me into her world and puts me into a trance. Eliot laughs out loud when she reads George Eliot. But we share a stubborn streak that keeps us from ever wanting to admit our yen for Jane and George to our mother.

It's not easy going through life with names like ours, and we don't want our mother to gloat and say "I told you so." So we read Austen and Eliot on the sly, and we openly satisfy our fetish for romantic Victorian literature with Gaskell.

But even Gaskell – and, yes, even Mr. Thornton – can't hold my attention right now. I keep wondering if the possibly foundering pony's going to be OK.

Meg said she was going to call the vet – when will she come? What will she say?

It's easier said than done to walk away from Meg and her horses and the girls and their ponies. A job with horses isn't just a job. It's a responsibility. And not one that just goes away at four or five o'clock or whenever you're done.

Am I being stubborn about Rand? What would he think if he knew I'd quit in solidarity? I might have some idea if someone would answer the stupid phone at his uncle's house.

I'm done calling for now. I've pretty much decided to drop in on my way home tonight, when he's bound to be there. I'm sure my parents will be cool with the idea – they'll probably offer to drive me over ... *not*. Oh well – I'll worry about it later.

That pony ... what happened? Maybe the wives tale was wrong – maybe the cluster of flies wasn't a laminitis warning. But I've never seen anything like it before – never seen such a concentrated grouping – it had to mean something, and that pony is certainly the type to be a founder risk.

My brain flips back and forth between Rand, and the pony, and the missing smart phone, and the flies on the pony, while the grim, grey surroundings of Milton fill the tablet screen.

Eliot nudges me, hard, between the ribs.

"Ow!"

"Bessy Higgins just died and you didn't even cry. What is *wrong* with you?" My sister pauses the movie, folds her arms, and makes a *humphing* noise. "Well? I'm waiting ..."

I might as well tell her – about the Rand thing; not the pony – Eliot doesn't have a horse-crazy bone in her body, but she does like complicated boy-girl problems ... we're watching North and South; I rest my case.

"It started when one of the camp girls' phones went missing ..." I stop, suck my breath in so hard there's a flutter behind my breastbone, then I cough and choke. "Oh!" I'm holding my hand up while I try to get air back into my lungs. "Wait! I" - *cough* - "know" - *wheeze* - "where" - *splutter* - "it is!"

"What are you talking about?" my sister asks.

"I know where the phone is!" I slide off the bed, taking half the sheets with me.

"What do you mean?"

I look at my watch. "I have to go! Now! I have to make the next boat!"

"Austen! You're just going to leave me?"

"Mom and Dad will be back with Shaw any minute. And you have Mr. Thornton."

I'm struggling to get the strap of my first flip-flop between my toes. *Damn*. Finally it goes, just in time for me to dance out of the way of Eliot's swiping hand, grabbing for my arm.

"It's not fair for you to just run out, while I'm stuck here."

I pause for one second. Shrug. "Sorry, sis. That's the way it is. You want out of here, you figure out a way to get better. Nobody ever said life was fair."

Now it's her turn to cough, and choke, and splutter. "I cannot believe you just said that to me! It's mean!"

Where is my other flip-flop? I have to go. "It's not mean, Eliot – it's true." *True, helpful, inspiring, necessary, kind* ... well, four out of five ain't bad. And if the first four work, then maybe in retrospect it'll turn out to have been a kind thing to say.

Suddenly I'm hit with a thump around my knees. My parents are back, with Shaw, who's thrown himself at me. He waves a Happy Meal bag in front of me: "Austen! I gots the last figure I need for the whole set!"

"Super-cool dude. Can you show them to me all together tomorrow? Right now I have to go."

My mom frowns. "Your dad and I were about to head out for dinner. We wanted you to watch Shaw."

"I'm sorry, but I can't. Something's come up that's really important."

My dad chips in. "Austen, we've hardly seen you lately."

"Well, if you're going out for dinner alone, you're not going to see me now either."

I'm careful to keep my voice even but Eliot snickers. *She's going to get me in trouble ...*

"Austen, your dad and I have things to discuss." My mom's eyes slide to Eliot. "We need to sit down alone ..." now her eyes go to Shaw "... for just a little while."

"Hello!" Eliot waves. "Yoo-hoo, I'm here! In the room. Shaw's other big sister. He can stay with me, and you can go out for dinner and talk about me, and Austen can have a life."

My mom shakes her head. "Don't be ridiculous."

"What's ridiculous about that?" Eliot asks. She holds up her tablet. "Hey, Shaw, you wanna show me your Happy Meal treat then watch *Daniel Tiger's Neighbourhood* with me?"

"Yes! Yes! Yes!" Shaw's already tossed his Happy Meal bag on Eliot's bed and is trying to climb up beside her.

"Do you know Rand ate dinner with us, Eliot? And he gave me the biggest bowl of ice cream ever in the world?"

Shaw's mention of Rand's name seems to give my mom permission to drop any pretense of politeness and just say what she's thinking. "That's who you're going to see, isn't it? Rand?"

I already resisted saying sorry to Jared today. Now I resist taking the easy way out. *Bring it,* I think. "And if I am?"

"If you are, then I'm disappointed. If you are, then I question your judgment. I don't know if you want to spend time with him as some kind of rebellion toward us, or as a slap in the face to Tyler for breaking up with you, but I expect better of you, Austen."

I've disagreed with Jared, and he's made me angry, but he's never been smug. He's never been condescending. I think Jared's wrong, but I don't hate him.

In this moment, I hate my mom with a fist-clenching, heart-pounding, temple-throbbing intensity that scares me.

Eliot saves me.

"Take that back," she tells my mother.

I look at Eliot, and she looks at me, and she flashes me a little OK sign with her thumb and index finger. *I've got your back,* she's telling me. *Leave this to me.*

For the first time in a long time she feels like my big sister.

I nod. I let her talk.

"Mom," she says. "You have no idea what you're talking about. You haven't been fair to Austen, and I know it's partly because of me, but I don't think you've taken the time to add up all the babysitting she does at the last minute. Everything she's given up when I've been sick. You and Dad just assume she'll do it, and she does it. I wish she'd stand up to you more, but I probably need to stand up for her too."

"And about Rand. Well, the only time I met the guy he had me slung across his shoulders and he was sweating like a racehorse and, guess what? He wasn't doing that because he likes me. Rand cares about Austen, and he's worth six, twelve, a hundred of Tyler. Do you know, nice Tyler, who you've known forever, and is Mr. Polite to your face, broke up with Austen because she wouldn't sleep with him?"

Eliot sits straighter, "So I'd stop questioning Austen's judgment because she was smart enough not to have sex with that slime bag."

'Shaw,' I mouth.

Eliot shrugs – "Tablet," she answers, and it's true; he's mouth open staring at the screen.

My mom is also mouth open. All the anger drains out of me when I see her that way; listening to one daughter tell her off about her other daughter's sex life – or lack thereof. It must be a shock.

Thank you, I want to tell Eliot.

It'll be OK, I want to tell my parents.

You are adorable, I want to tell Shaw.

I look at my watch. "I've got to go."

I look around the room. "I love you." I mean all of them.

"Go," my dad says.

I hesitate.

"Go. It's good. We're fine," he repeats.

"I'll see you at home," I say.

And I'm gone, out of the still, cold, hospital air and into the wash of summer heat radiating up from asphalt, and I'm weaving my way along gum-splattered sidewalks, in and out between girls wearing tank tops and guys with shorts waistbands four inches lower than their boxers, and *I-need-to-make-this-boat, I-need-to-make-this-boat,* and I smell my first whiff of breeze off the lake and I run to the dock, to the ramp, to my bike propped on the island side of the ferry dock, and to the stupid, ridiculous smart phone that started all of this.

At least I hope I'm running to that phone.

***

It's already August and it's already getting dark noticeably earlier than it did at the beginning of the summer.

Too noticeably for my liking, as I pedal out of the village.

It's been a long day, and I'm tired anyway. Now my leg muscles are straining. And the wind is blowing against me. Which is a bad sign because the wind only ever blows this direction when there's a storm coming. And the darkness which, right now, is gathering, will soon descend, just like that. It happens so fast around here – the sun dips below the horizon, and it's like somebody blew a candle out.

By the time I struggle up the final rise to Jared's house – a rise I don't even notice when I'm full of energy – we are very, very close to candle-snuffing time.

I don't even pause to catch my breath before I head over to the paddocks; start walking the fencelines.

One by one the turned-out horses lift their heads to look at me, before resuming their grazing. "Hey Salem, Hi Jessie," I call out to Meg and Lacey's BFF mares. Lacey, who by being on her extended vacation let me have the dream summer job that would normally be hers.

Until today.

Don't think about it.

I walk past the mares' field and continue to the next one, to where Mac spies me and wanders over, walking faster and faster until I'm positive he has to either trip over himself, or start trotting.

"Hey buddy," I whisper. I started my day inside-out with the excitement of being able to event him.

Does the offer still stand? I don't even know.

Don't think about it. I have a phone to find.

This is ridiculous.

It seemed so obvious when I was sitting in the bare, white hospital room with Eliot. It was like that moment when you finally see how the six jigsaw puzzle pieces you've been staring at all fit together. All of a sudden the things I knew added up – the pony was showing signs of founder + founder can be caused by eating fresh, lush grass + when I found Vanessa grazing him a few days ago she was more annoyed at being caught, than repentant = I'll bet anything she was grazing him again, only this time nobody caught her.

From there I could actually visualize how her phone could have fallen out of her pocket. How she'd never see it in the long grass. How we now had a birthday-girl with a missing phone. How Rand got blamed.

In Eliot's bright, stark room it was easy to picture a dark phone. But now, cloaked in near-dark myself, looking for a black phone in vegetation so deep I've already figured out it would have hidden the cell from Vanessa's notice, I realize I'm not just going to reach down into the thigh-high tangle of grass, and clover, and alfalfa and pluck it up with an easy, "Ah-ha!"

Crap.

I wish it would ring. Then I'd find it ... *maybe* ... at least I'd have a better chance of finding it.

I pull out my own phone, check that I have service – and smile when I see the still of me flying off Mac – the one I made into my new wallpaper.

Vanessa sent me that.

Which ... *holy crap* ... means I have her number somewhere in my phone.

My hands are shaking, and thumb's slipping, and I'm screwing up, and starting back at my home page but, finally, there it is in my history – Vanessa's number.

A whine zings past my ear and I slap at my arm. Great – the wind's died down enough to let the mosquitoes come out. Just what I need.

I hit dial.

The first mosquito has called his mosquito friends and they're feasting on me. I grip my phone. *Buzz.* Come on. *Buzz.*

Connecting.

I take a couple of steps – as quietly as I can – and wait.

Nothing. I dial again.

It takes three separate calls, ringing six or seven times, then going to voicemail before I find it, ringing in the long grass, screen beaming light up at me.

Oh. Yay. I *knew* I'd find it.

No I didn't. Not at all.

I *hoped* I'd find it.

I actually can't believe I found it.

But I did know – one-hundred per cent – that Rand didn't take it, and this proves it.

In fact, the culprit has left his print, quite literally, on the phone.

There's a curving line consisting of finely clustered, spider-webbing cracks, bisecting the screen in the shape of a pony's hoof.

I found the phone, and it's broken, but that's not anybody's fault other than the little girl who brought her pony out to graze where she shouldn't have.

I text Meg. **Are you in the house? Meet me at the kitchen door.**

And I run through the newly fallen night to where the door's opening; spilling light onto the porch, and for just this minute, I am utterly satisfied.

• RAND •

Chapter Forty-Two

As far as I can tell, it's going pretty well.

We're sitting at the round table in the kitchen that's come to feel like home to me.

It's funny that the uncle I barely knew a couple of months ago is now the face I feel most comfortable with.

Having said that, my dad, who normally feels really foreign to me – sweeping in from faraway places that are almost always warmer, looking sun-tanned and exotic – feels less different to me than he normally does. I'm sun-tanned and confident, too – about some things, anyway. It makes a difference.

And my mother - seeing her here, away from the house where we've had all our battles lately; without a briefcase or a smart phone in her hand, and without Dan by her side – she looks more like my *mom* than she has in a long time.

There are beers in front of my parents and Cokes in front of my uncle and me, and a couple of empty pizza boxes on the counter.

My mom's been quiet – stiff – toward me, but when we met them at the dock her smile for her brother seemed genuine, and my dad – who can be really funny – has cracked her up, along with the rest of us, with a couple of his traveling tall tales.

My dad doesn't know my uncle that well, but his journalistic training kicks in, and he asks him a bunch of questions about the lodge, which my uncle's happy to answer, and those lead to him telling my parents about the bunks I built today, and the shed he wants me to build next.

"Rand's got a knack for it," Kurt says. "He's got an eye for space, and he's careful. He does nice work."

My mom's eyebrows are climbing but my dad nods, slowly. "He always did, I guess. As a kid he used to help me with little jobs around the house. He was good at it."

My uncle nods. "With some training – one of my buddy's kids is taking a construction program at one of the high schools in town – with something like that, I think Rand could do as good work as anyone I know around here."

The room goes quiet. We're there. Up against the reason all four of us are sitting in this room together.

Will I stay or will I go? It's a big question – I get it. It touches on everything from the day-to-day logistics of where I actually eat and sleep, right up to the very big picture of my entire future. A construction program at an alternative high school in Kingston, is a different world from the ivy-league-track private school I've attended up until now.

Then again, we all know the status quo is no longer an option.

The possibility – or likelihood – of big changes silences us all.

Until my dad shifts in his chair, takes a sip of beer, places his bottle back down, and says, "OK. High school here. Let's talk about what that looks like ..."

***

After a fairly intense discussion addressing groceries, transportation, chores, part-time jobs, and quite a bit about expectations – what grades I'd need to have, how much money I still have to pay back to my parents, what I'd do around my uncle's house, what things I'd never do – no matter what, anywhere – my dad has a scribbled list with lots of arrows and boxes.

Both my uncle and I have contributed a fair bit to what's on that list.

My mom has mostly sat with her arms folded in front of her.

"What do you think, Liv?" my dad asks.

She leans back and re-adjusts her arms. "I don't know."

"Here, look at it." My dad slides the list over in front of her and she uncrosses her arms and leans forward. She instantly looks more receptive. I wonder if my dad's just used a Jedi-like veteran journalist interview trick on her. If so, I'm impressed.

She's working her way through, tracing my dad's scribbles with her fingers. "Remind me about this? I can't read it."

He leans over and laughs at himself. "With my handwriting I should have been a doctor," and my mom glances up at him and smiles, before he continues, "That was just that we need to double-check he doesn't lose out on his academic basics if he takes this alternative program ..."

This looks promising. My uncle taps his knee against mine under the table and I'm afraid to look at him. I'm afraid to hope too much, or to breathe, as long as my mom's furrowing her brow, studying the list, considering – at least considering – the option.

Then the dogs bark, sharply, jumping up from where they're flopped on the floor, and all eyes lift to the door.

It's so close to dark, and the headlights are so bright, that it's hard to make out the vehicle until it pulls up in front of the porch and the porch light illuminates a pick-up truck.

Not just any pick-up. I know that pick-up.

It's Jared's.

Oh. Shit. No.

Just precisely, exactly what I don't need, as my mom teeters on the edge of giving me a chance to stay here, is any suggestion at all that I've done anything even slightly wrong. I can't imagine my mom ruling in my favour if she finds out I no longer have the job I bragged about to her earlier, and that it's because I've been accused of stealing.

It's only as everything inside me – heart, stomach – feels like it's in freefall, that I realize how much I want this: to stay, to go to school here, to live here.

I should go to the door. I'm frozen, though. I don't want to look defensive, but I don't want to look confrontational. And I'm scared. It's just true – I am.

My uncle gets up, and opens the screen door as Jared climbs the stairs.

"Evening," Jared says, and extends his hand.

"Evening," My uncle says, and takes Jared's hand. The bugs are flinging themselves with frantic abandon at the porch light. "Come on in, away from the bugs."

It's only as the two of them step inside that I see the other person behind Jared.

Austen.

Everything that dropped in me lifts. Oh, wow. I love her. Love seeing her. I'm so glad she's here.

She slips in behind Jared, and sidesteps over against the counter and nods, wordlessly, toward Jared. She hesitates a second, then winks at me and I think, *OK. Whatever Jared's come here to say I'll handle it.*

I hope.

My uncle's introducing Jared to my parents. When he's done Jared grabs his forehead, rubs it hard a couple of times. "I don't know what the right thing is to do here. Whether I should ask to talk to you alone, Rand, or whether this is something I should say in front of everyone."

My mouth's dry, and my voice croaks a bit, but I say, "Just go ahead with whatever it is."

His shoulders rise, and fall and he clears his throat. "Just in case any of you don't know, Rand's been working for me this last little while."

My parents nod. My mom says, "Oh, that's the job he was telling us about."

Jared continues. "I had my doubts. I was hard on Rand. But he worked hard, and the work he did was good quality. I couldn't fault him for that."

Even though I knew I worked hard, and I knew the project turned out well, I still feel a balloon of pride expand a tiny bit in my chest hearing Jared say it.

I sneak a peek at Austen. She's nodding.

Jared turns to me now. "Meg and Austen both warned me not to judge you based on rumours. They told me to give you a chance. I'm stubborn, though – a few people will tell you that."

In the background my uncle coughs. I struggle not to smile.

"Anyway, what I'm trying to say, is I was wrong. I'm incredibly sorry. And embarrassed. And wrong." He's holding something out and I take a step closer and recognize it as a phone with its smooth, shiny surface marred by an intricate network of wider cracks diminishing to hairline fissures.

"Oh ..." I bite my lip. Even though I knew I didn't take the phone I never, in a million years, thought I'd be able to *prove* I hadn't. Seeing it there – hard evidence in Jared's hand – I have to blink hard to keep the tears back. I finally mutter, "How?"

"Austen," he says. "She came back and tramped through the field in the dark, and got mosquito-bitten, and found this thing in knee-high grass."

I turn and look at her, and she's blinking, too. Suddenly I don't care who else is looking, I step forward and grab her and she hugs me back, hard, and whispers in my ear. "I *knew* you didn't take it."

I want to say, 'You're amazing,' 'You blow me away,' 'I'm so lucky to know you.' I can't though – for some reason the only stupid thing I can think to say is, "What are you, a bloody phone-whisperer?"

She laughs, and her body shakes against me, and I have never wanted a girl this much – wanted all of a girl – her brain, and her personality, and, it's true, her body feels pretty nice stretched against mine.

"Rand?" It's my mom's voice. "Rand, what's going on?"

***

Jared tells a lot of it, with punctuations from Austen and a few added details from my uncle.

It's only after the story's told that I really remember – really get a chance – to introduce Austen. I can tell by the way my dad's eyes are crinkling at the corners that he already likes her.

I'm pretty sure my mom will like her just because, how could you not? Austen's eyes sparkle, and her hands fly through the air as she talks – and that voice; it's still as musical as ever – and she's so, so pretty, but not in a way any mother could object to. The skin she's showing is smooth, and tanned, with enough exposed to make me want to see more, without actually showing butt, or boobs. I have, in the past, occasionally brought home friends displaying both, and heard about it later from my mom.

"Austen," I finally say. "I'd like you to meet my mom, Olivia, and my dad Dan, and Mom and Dad, this is Austen. Her cottage is across the bay, and she's my ..." I choke. I know what I want to say, but I'm not sure if I have the guts to say it. It's just a word – when have I ever worried about shocking anybody with my words, or actions. The whole reason I'm here is because of not caring enough.

I've changed, though. I care now.

And I care because of Austen.

So, "... she's my girlfriend," I finish.

Austen inhales so sharply her gasp is audible, but she recovers in an instant to step forward, hand out, meeting my parents' eyes in turn, saying, "Nice to meet you."

Man, she is good. At everything.

***

I'm walking Austen home. That's the official version of what I'm doing, anyway.

After Jared asked me to please consider coming back to work to finish the lean-to, and my uncle told him he could only have me for one more day because I'm needed at the lodge, and then everybody ate at least one slice of the lemon loaf Meg sent over as a peace offering, and

Jared said, "Hey, I can give you a lift home if you like, Austen," I'd said. "Actually, I think I'll walk Austen home."

"Are you sure?" he asked. "'Cause ..." I'd shot Jared a look, and he'd shut up, fast. "Of course, that makes sense," he'd said, then right before driving away told me, "Sorry, I'll try to stop sabotaging your life."

"You killed me in there," Austen says now.

"You killed *me* in there," I counter.

She stops dead in her tracks and claps her hand across her breastbone. "Me? How did I kill you?"

I laugh. "Miss 'Nice-to-Meet-You' shaking my parents' hands, pretending I hadn't just dropped the biggest bombshell right in your lap." I grin. "I never know how you're going to react. It's super-hot."

She tosses her hair. "Yeah, well I knew better than to take it seriously."

"Oh, and why's that?"

"Because you haven't even kissed me. You can't possibly be ready to call me your girlfriend without kissing me first.

"We did kiss. That night that Eliot went to hospital."

Austen shakes her head again. "That was me kissing you – not you kissing me. And it wasn't even a kiss – it was a peck. And if you don't know the difference between a kiss and a peck then – whoa – we should be worried about chemistry. What if there's none there?"

"Ha!" I put my hand on her arm and steer her toward the big storage barn. "Why do you think I wouldn't let Jared drive you home?"

She grins, and her white teeth gleam in the dark. "Because you're going to kiss me? Properly?"

"I'm going to kiss you, and I'm going to do it with feeling, and chemistry, and all the pent-up frustration of wanting to kiss you since the first second you poured gasoline all over me."

"I didn't pour gas on you ...!"

"But I did want to kiss you, and I still do."

My lips catch hers while she's still giggling, and there's something extra sweet and soft about laughing lips.

With my mouth on hers, I spin her the final step into the shelter of the barn. Her shoulder bangs the door frame on the way in, and she mumbles, "Ouch!"

I pull back, "Are you OK?"

Her eyes land on mine, then slide past me and widen, and she breathes, "Oh ... what *is* that?"

I've wanted to show her. I've wanted her to see it – wanted her to love it – but now I am so, so nervous.

Hanging as it is from the barn rafters, with the grey of the weathered barn board taking on a dull lustre in the black of the unlit barn, the swing has a ghostly, ethereal look to it. There's nothing obvious holding it up, and it's swaying oh-so-gently in the light breeze snaking between the gaps in the barn walls.

Austen walks over to it – rolling her feet heel to toe so the rubber soles of her sneakers are silent on the barn's dirt floor. She reaches out, and gives it a tiny push, then turns to me and with her teeth and eyes gleaming in the moonlight washing through the open barn door, says, "I absolutely love this."

"It's yours," I say.

"It's what?"

I step up beside her, take her hand and guide it to the "A." I trace her fingertips over it, then move them to the "U."

"Oh!" she says. "Where's the 'S?'"

I help her find the "T," and "E," but "Wait!" she says. She's figured out the sequence – the pattern I've used to step the letters along the boards – and she finds the "N" all by herself.

"Is it really mine?"

"Yeah. I'm sorry, it's not that practical ..."

"What are you talking about? It's the most practical thing I can think of." She turns and her eyes never leave mine as she lowers herself to the seat. "Will it hold me?"

I laugh. "It had better, or I need to find a new hobby."

As though to test it, she tucks her feet up under herself. "See? It's a place to sit, and a place that makes me smile, and a place to ..." she pauses, pats the seat beside her.

"To what?" I ask.

"Sit down and I'll show you."

It's only as she says it I realize I haven't actually sat on the swing yet. I've created it from scratch, but I haven't tested it. I lower myself beside her and lift my feet, and the seat itself is surprisingly stable, even as we rock through the air. "Oh!"

She laughs. "Isn't it great? Now turn sideways, like this."

She's cross-legged, facing me, one hand on the back of the swing, one gesturing to me to turn around, do what she says.

I do. I turn. It's hard to get my legs pulled in like hers are but at least it's easier than when I used to wear my skin-tight city jeans. "There," I say. "What now?"

"Now, hold on!" She drops one foot down just long enough to give us a good shove off, and we're zooming into the dark of the barn, then swinging back toward the moon, and she's leaning forward, cupping my cheek with her free hand, pulling my face to hers, and this kissing is the best ever, because we're flying, too.

We're light, and free, and the series of mini-explosions that pop through my body confirm the chemistry is here, and it's strong, just like I knew it would be.

It's so ridiculously intimate to have her holding my face like this. I love it. I love that she wants me just as close as I want her.

I reach for her waist; my hand starting high then sliding down the smooth cotton of her t-shirt until it finds the spot where the curve of her hips starts, and there's a gap there, between her shirt and her shorts, of bare, warm skin pulled tight across muscle.

She inhales, short and sharp, and the tremble that runs through her travels into me, too.

We're kissing the whole time. She tastes faintly of lemon and it's delicious and I can't get enough of it. Can't get close enough to her. Never want to stop.

She straightens so her mouth slides to my ear, and whispers, "I could kiss you forever."

Game on. Let's try.

It does feel like forever. Or at least a really, really long time, that we kiss.

The full-on rocking of the swing dies back to a sway, and we're still kissing in this sweet, teasing, dizzying way.

She's the first girl I've ever been with who doesn't immediately pause to yank off her shirt; who doesn't slide her hand against the front of my pants within two minutes.

Every encounter I've ever had before has felt like following a check list. Kiss, *check*. Hands over shirt, *check*. Hands under shirt, *check*. Don't get me wrong; they were exciting, but they were fast and, after, there was kind of this feeling of *now what*? Which is probably why none of those girls ever ended up being my girlfriend.

I'm starting to think the amount I already like Austen is just a tiny opening; a teensy indication of how much I *could* like her. We have places to go but there's no rush to get there.

She's caught my earlobe between her teeth and is giggling in my ear, and I'm pushing into the delicious tickle tingling into my jaw and radiating down my neck like a warm current, and I'm starting to wonder if this is it; is this when a shirt gets pushed up, or a button gets undone …

Until something cold and wet nudges the part of my knee hanging over the edge of the swing.

"Oh my …!" I lift my knee and it nearly whacks Austen in the jaw, but she's already laughing because she's figured out it's Dole who's found us in the barn and is quivering with excitement at having someone to hang out with.

"Buddy," I say. "I think you're supposed to be having a pee."

Austen and I hop off the swing and the dog lowers his head and lifts it back up with a massive stick jammed in his jaws.

"No, no, no! Ain't gonna happen!"

How to get rid of him? Touching the stick would be the kiss of death – it would only confirm that, yes, one of his humans is accepting his invitation to play fetch.

"Dole! Dole!" Oh, great. Now the dumb dog's brought my uncle out looking for him.

His footsteps are coming closer and he's muttering. "Stupid dog, better not have found a stupid skunk again …"

"What are we going to do?" I whisper to Austen. Dole isn't showing any signs of wanting to leave, and anything I do to try to make him go will just draw attention to us.

Austen tugs at her hem, then says, "Smooth your shirt out."

I'm still staring at her, wondering what she means, when she reaches down, grabs hold of the end of Dole's stick, and leads him out into the yard. "He's right here, Kurt."

"Oh!" She's clearly caught my uncle by surprise. "Sorry, I didn't know you were out here."

"Yup. Just fending off this guy's attentions."

At which point I step out behind her.

"Hey," I say.

"Hey," my uncle replies, then reaches down to grip the other end of Dole's stick. "Well, I'll just get him in before he does get sprayed by a skunk."

He looks from me to Austen, then back again and calls, "You two have a good night!" over his shoulder as he heads back to the house.

"We are!" Austen says it with a sing-song in her voice.

I flick at her arm.

"Ouch! What was that for?"

"You don't have to advertise that we were making out."

She snorts. "No. You're right – I don't. He definitely already knew."

"Austen ..."

"It doesn't matter anyway, Rand. I'm your girlfriend, right? So it's all good."

I lace my fingers through hers. "Yeah, OK. It's all good."

Then I walk my girlfriend home.

***

I walk back home thinking about Austen, and everything that happened today – and tonight – and Austen, and the swing, and Austen ...

I think of how much she loved it – I really believe she did – and I think in the morning I'll show it to my parents; hers hanging up, so they can see how it looks – even sit on it – and the one I made for Joe, assembled, but just not suspended yet.

I hope they'll see the work I put into it. Hope they'll understand it's my form of an apology. Hope they'll help me figure out how best to get it to Joe.

I'm walking down the hall to my bedroom, when voices drift to me from behind the closed door of one of the spare bedrooms next to mine.

I pause, for a second, lean toward the door and listen.

Two voices, definitely. Light enough – not arguing, anyway.

Then there's a low laugh.

I didn't think I cared anymore about my parents and their relationship. I figured it was their issue – not mine.

Maybe Austen's made me soft, or maybe it's just normal for a kid to want his parents to be together, but I go to bed happy for me and happy for them.

• AUSTEN •

Chapter Forty-Three

It's one of those days – the days you look forward to so much, that seem impossibly far in the distance, until one day you wake up and they've arrived.

And not just arrive, but go whipping by, far too quickly.

We're already sitting on a dressage score of 31.

I had zero expectations, but Angie's delighted.

As soon as I long-reined Mac out of the ring she said, "That's going to be good," and when we got the score she immediately texted her coach.

"Really?" I asked.

"Really," she confirmed. "You two were calm but energized at the same time. Anytime you can do that you'll nail dressage." She winked at me. "I can almost never do that."

I'm still getting used to having Angie as my groom.

She met Meg and me at the grounds, and immediately started hefting water buckets, buffing tack, and fiddling with Mac's haynet.

"I can't believe you're doing this," I said. "You don't have to."

She shrugged. "When my mare got that kick yesterday it seemed like an omen – she should have this weekend off, and I should come watch you guys go. This is fun for me and I'll probably get reminded of a bunch of things that will make life easier for my groom."

We have a nice long break before our cross-country time. Mac's dozing on the shady side of the trailer, hind leg hitched, lower lip drooping. "He looks calm," I tell Angie. "I'm just not sure about the energized bit."

She laughs. "He'll be pulling you like a train when he sees the first jump. Enjoy the calm while it lasts."

My phone buzzes **I'm here! Where are you?**

Angie lifts her eyebrows. "Something important?"

"Oh, my friend I ride with in Ottawa drove down for the day. She just got here."

"Go see her. I think Meg and I can handle Sir Snores-a-Lot for a while."

I'll meet you at the food truck in three minutes.

I make it in two, and Manda's already there, waiting for me.

The sun behind her makes a fuzzy halo of her riotously curling caramel-brown hair and her toffee-coloured skin sets off our barn's white show team polo shirt she's wearing.

If I liked her less I'd be super-jealous. But it's impossible to be jealous of somebody who only ever wants the best for me.

She grabs me in a suffocating hug. "How much have I missed you?"

I laugh, reaching up for her shoulders, swaying with her. "You too. I can't believe you came."

"As if I'd miss this when you're so close. Besides, I have something big to tell you which can only be done in person."

"What?"

She waves her hand. "Nuh-uh. Not yet. Let's get a couple of drinks and find a shady spot to watch some dressage, and we'll talk."

As we walk across the grounds toward a spreading tree, she says, "So? Did your parents end up coming?"

"No, but it's all good. Eliot wasn't supposed to get visitors yet, but apparently she's doing so well they said she could have a short visit today. Obviously it took about five seconds for Mom and Dad to decide to go ..."

"So Eliot's some kind of miracle patient this time around?"

"I don't know about that, but the certifiable miracle is that my parents are staying overnight in Toronto. Which means they're trusting me to stay in the cottage alone while they're away. With Rand just on the other side of the bay ..."

"Ha!" Manda says. "So is that bay going to stay between you and Rand tonight?"

I laugh. "You know, probably not *all* night, but ultimately, in terms of *overnight,* yes. I'd really like my parents to keep cutting me slack, so I'm not planning to completely abuse their trust on the first go."

We've stepped from direct sunlight to the dappled shade of the tree, and the temperature immediately drops three or four degrees. I turn to Manda. "Now, that's it – no more talking about my parents, or my sister – what's your big news?"

"I fired her."

I know right away what she means – who she means. "You did? What happened this time?"

"What *didn't*?" Manda sighs. "I mean, you know, I've been this close –" she holds up her finger and thumb just millimetres apart "– for ages now, but this week I got to the barn and my saddle was sitting on the saddle stand in the middle of the tack room. I was trying not to freak out instantly. I thought 'she must have just forgotten to put it away after she cleaned it' – not that I've known her to ever clean the tack – but no ..."

"No, what? Why was it out there?"

"My locker was full – and I mean jam-packed, stuffed full – of boxes. From Victoria's Secret, Zara, lululemon, you name it. There was literally no room for my saddle."

"Your beautiful, expensive, best-Kijiji-score-ever, Stubben?" I shake my head. "What on earth was she doing?"

"She got a bonus at work, but she told her parents she can't afford to pay any of her tuition, so she went online shopping and had it all shipped to the barn, care of me, so her parents wouldn't know she spent the money."

"I really have no idea what to say about that."

"No. Because you're *normal,*" Manda says. "When I told her that was it – we were done – she told me I was the most selfish person she'd ever met."

I giggle. "Well, if anyone's a selfishness expert ... but what are you going to do? How can you pay tuition, *and* pay full board? And there's no way you can ride six times a week and still keep up with your university coursework."

"No," Manda says. "You're right. I can't."

"OK, so ..."

"So, I know this girl who's pretty much the best rider ever, and she's amazingly easy to get along with, and she doesn't have a selfish bone in her body, and she's gotten used to riding every day this summer, so I was thinking she might want to half-lease in the fall ..." Manda's eyes are steady on me. "Did I mention my horse loves her? Did I mention I do?"

"I ... wow ... you want *me*?"

"Well, it's mostly Bandit who wants you, but I guess I can tolerate you ..." Manda hooks her arm around my neck and puts me in the gentlest headlock possible, "... of course I want you, my totally crazy BFF. What do you think?"

I think ... I think ... I think I never even thought this would be a possibility. I think Bandit isn't my dream horse – she's not a lean-mean-17.1h-off-the-track muscle machine like Mac. But I do have a huge soft spot for her. And she's feisty. And fun. And always a challenge.

"I think it could be pretty great," I say.

Manda jumps in. "That's all you have to say right now. No details. No promises. I don't want you to feel pressured. Although ..." she plants a kiss on my head in the vicinity of my ear, then makes a spitting noise. "Oooh, mouthful of hair ... although, I really do want you to say yes. But only because you want to!"

I laugh. "I have a fairly good feeling I'm going to want to, but right now I need to get back to Mac and start thinking about our cross-country."

***

Angie was right, and wrong. Mac is revved for the cross-country, but he's not pulling – he's floating, dancing, playing.

The short course format means we start and end in the ring with stadium jumping, and ride a series of cross-country fences in between.

The initial round in the ring is fine. Mac's eager, but listening, and anyone seeing him for the first time would see a spring-loaded, but controllable horse – big, beautiful, and clearing everything easily.

It's when we canter into the cross-country field that he shifts into a new gear. I don't stop him. The wide-open spaces are made for his huge strides which, actually, feel just reasonable – normal – out here.

He takes every jump with ears forward, always going long, and me perched over his withers, trying not to interfere.

The last one is a bank which brings us up to the level ground of the show ring again. The ring we have to go back into. The ring that suddenly looks so cramped, and confined, and inadequate to contain this rolling, momentum-filled force I've created.

I can't jerk him in the mouth on the way up the bank – have to let my hands float and let him use his head and neck – but the minute he's up, I have work to do.

Oh wow.

Heels down, back straight.

We're flying.

Whoa!

We're going to scatter these fences like matchsticks.

Half-halt. Half-halt again. Half-halt again.

Get the job done.

Those were Angie's last words to me on the way into the ring. This ring. It doesn't matter how we look – it just matters that we do this.

So, all together now – heels, back, voice, hands – definite and quick.

That does it.

He's at least controlled enough to canter through the gate and for me to bend him toward the first jump.

Bounce, I think. *Spring,* I think. *Light,* I think.

It isn't really any of those things, but it, and the next three jumps, stay up.

Job done.

Except ... he's feeling good, he's getting ready, he's lowering his head ... and if I come off before we stop the timer, the job's not done.

I thrust my heels down, and look up, ahead, through the timer. I catch Rand's eye.

I can do this.

"Go!" I yell. I ride Mac forward, right through his buck, and we're flying as we trip the timer, and I only manage to turn him with inches to spare before the end of the ring, but I stayed on, and we were clear, and we were fast.

Amazing.

***

I won't know about placing, or ribbons, until everyone's gone, but it really was all about the round, and our round was the best I could make it.

Angie, when she took Mac from me to cool him out, was bubbling over. "He looked so fresh. So eager. I can't wait to get on him."

I can't wait for her to, either. I loved my time with Mac, but she loves him, too. And I'm already starting to look forward to working with Bandit.

Rand and I are sitting in the stands watching the beginning and ends of the remaining cross-country rounds. I take a sip of my lemonade and bump my hip against his. "I'm so glad you made it."

"As if I wouldn't."

"Well, it helped you got a ride with Jared."

Rand laughs. "Yeah, I think Meg pretty much laid down the law about what time he needed to be here."

"So," he asks. "Now that Meg's camps are over, and Mac's going home with Angie, what are you doing tomorrow?"

I stretch and give an elaborate yawn. "Oh, you know me; sleep 'till noon. Get up in time to sunbathe. That sort of thing."

He rubs his shoulder against mine. "Well, if you can tear yourself away from your day of leisure, I thought you could do something with me."

"Oh yeah? What's that?"

"Come over to Kingston and drop my registration papers off at the new school."

I stop mid-sip, lift my sunglasses. "Seriously?"

He nods. "My mom's faxing the signed documents to the post office tomorrow morning. I can pick them up and go register."

"I ..." *couldn't be happier / couldn't be prouder / couldn't be more excited*. I can't decide which one to say, so instead I place my hand on his thigh and twist to reach my lips to his.

He kisses me back and I don't want to be *that* couple – the ones who need to get a room – but the kiss is so nice, and it's saying everything I can't put into words. I'll just kiss him for a second ...

Suddenly I hear clapping, and cheering, and it's coming from the ground right beside our seats.

I turn to see Angie, and Meg, and Jared looking up at us with Mac tearing at the grass by their feet.

Before I can even blush, Angie says. "Come on, they're announcing the ribbons." She tugs Mac's head up and they walk away ahead.

Rand and I jump down to follow her and she says over her shoulder. "If you win, you can spend the rest of the day kissing him, for all I care."

I cross my fingers and grin at Rand. "It would be nice to win."

PLEASE LEAVE A REVIEW!

Reviews help me sell books. More sales let me write more books. A simple star rating and a few quick words are all that's needed to help other readers evaluate my books and, hopefully, buy them!

To review on **Amazon**, please follow this link – https://tinyurl.com/TudorAmazon – and select the book you want to review.

To review on **Goodreads**, this is the link – https://tinyurl.com/TudorGoodreads.

If you liked this book ...

... you might enjoy Tudor's other books. Read the first chapter of *Objects in Mirror,* the first book in the Stonegate Series, to find out.

Chapter One

Objects in Mirror • Stonegate Series Book One

The whipper-in calls my number – "Seventy-two, you're on deck!" – and, as though he understands that's us, Sprite dances sideways, nearly slamming the clipboard-wielding gentleman into the white fence boards.

This is the big class of the day. I'm as excited as Sprite, but one of us has to stay calm. Serenity doesn't come naturally to hepped-up off-the-track thoroughbreds like Sprite. Which leaves me to be the sensible one.

I sink my heels deeper in my stirrups, settle my seat more firmly into the saddle, and point my thumbs up.

Back straight, big smile, look cool, and send Sprite, in his beautiful sweeping trot, into the ring.

Where he promptly grabs the bit, yanks his head down, and lets his back heels fly.

Sprite wants to jump. Sprite sees no need to bend or flex; to circle or warm up. He enters the ring with his eyes and ears flicking from jump to jump.

In Sprite's mind, all I'm good for is pointing him at the first obstacle, after which I should back off and stop bugging him so he can finish the course.

I've ridden horses that can autopilot courses. Some of my competitors own horses like that. Sprite, however, is not one of those horses. Given his head, Sprite would jump everything twice, then get bored and jump the fence out of the ring, to keep on running and jumping everything in his path.

I know this because I've seen him do it.

So I give him a firm half-halt as I smile wider than ever, mutter "bugger" under my breath, and step him into the forward canter we need for our approach to the first fence.

He clears it by eighteen inches, and jump two, as well. He leaves at least two feet between his belly and the top rail of jump three and throws in a tail flourish on the landing. Here we go.

Sure enough, as he rounds the far corner, Sprite throws out a lightning-fast series of bucks. There are always three in quick succession, and those trademark three bucks will leave me only four or five precious strides to set him up for the diagonal combination.

"Excuse me!" I use my seat and my legs and my hands and my voice, too – a horse like Sprite requires every aid in the box – and we battle our way over the three increasingly wide jumps. By the end of the line, he's flying, reaching, digging, and the sturdy white ring fence is coming faster and faster, and we need to turn the corner in enough control to get over the tall vertical propped on the short end.

"Listen!" I tell him, but it's a tool for me too, reminding me first and foremost to get it done. Forget pretty, forget elegant; those can come later if we make the flat phase but for now, my priorities are (1) don't knock down any jumps, (2) don't die.

We dig in deep to the base of the vertical and, with a super-athletic effort, Sprite twists himself over it without bringing the rail down. To celebrate, he indulges in his biggest buck yet.

Despite all the noise and activity of the show grounds, all I can hear is my own voice ordering Sprite to "Smarten up!" then Drew's yelling, "Go, girl!"

"Go!" I tell Sprite. Go, go, go, and, with that, we're not fighting any more. We're four jumps from being home and we want the same thing – to get over them fast and clean – I lean forward, give Sprite a nudge, and soften my hands.

The new gear he clicks into is so fast it's almost scary. I hardly have time to breathe, as Sprite pins his ears against his neck, throws all his energy forward, and jumps the jumps.

When he's not in mid-air, he's running flat-out, and when he clears the last jump, I have to keep him galloping around the ring because there's no way I can stop him in time for a polite exit from the gate.

Fantastic, amazing, exhilarating, unbelievable. I'm hooked, hooked, hooked. Want to go right back in and do it again. Want to jump like that all summer long.

"Pinch me!" I tell Drew as I ride out of the ring, because I can't believe Sprite's mine for the season and I do get to do this all summer long.

"Don't relax yet," Drew tells me. "You're through to the flat. Now you've got to make him behave."

***

Four days later, my Sprite-induced jumping high hasn't worn off. It doesn't hurt that we placed third; an amazing showing, considering Sprite had to suffer through the flat portion of the class.

It's not like school's been distracting me. With the temperature hitting twenty-eight by fourth period, even the teachers are more focused on beaches and cottages than learning objectives and curriculum.

When I get on the school bus for my final ride of the year, and settle my butt onto the ripped vinyl of my usual seat, I have nothing left to think about – nothing to plan for, study for, or worry about – other than riding, and showing, and Sprite. I drift into a play-by-play rerun of our weekend jumping round so vivid that half my brain's still back at the show grounds as I step off the bus at the end of our gravel country driveway.

Only to be rugby-tackled around the knees.

"Ooof!" I yell. My arms flail for something, anything, to break my fall. Finding nothing, I go down hard, hitting the ground with a thump, swiftly followed by the second thump of my backpack full of books, bouncing off the gravel to hit me on the head.

"I'm Sowwy, Gwacie!" It's Jamie, my three-year-old brother, straddling my waist.

"I might believe you if you didn't look so happy," I tell him.

"Come on, you; give Grace some peace." Annabelle says, hauling him off, then holding out her hand to help me up. "He's so excited to see you. He can't stop talking about how you're going to be around all summer long."

Jamie runs off ahead of us, weaving from side to side across the driveway, stopping every now and then to make a wild jump in the air or kick out at his shadow. He reminds me of Sprite but without the bad nature.

"He insisted we make lemonade for you." Annabelle's trying, just that little bit too hard, to keep her voice light and easy. How can one simple sentence be so loaded, mean so much more than the sum of its words?

"Good," I say. "I'm hot." And Annabelle smiles. I've said the right thing: I'll have some, just not in so many words.

She takes my hand and, even though I'm nearly sixteen and, even though she's my stepmom, I let her. Even squeeze back a bit and, actually, it feels quite nice.

If you liked the beginning of Objects in Mirror, why not read the rest of the book? Objects in Mirror is available as an eBook or paperback on Amazon.

ABOUT THE AUTHOR

Tudor Robins is the author of books that move – she wants to move your heart, mind, and pulse with her writing. Tudor lives in Ottawa, Canada, and when she's not writing she loves horseback riding, running, being outdoors, and spending time with her family.

Tudor would love to hear from you at
tudor@tudorrobins.ca.

Made in the USA
Columbia, SC
22 December 2019

85549474R00252